A Flower for Angus

Heaven's Gate, Volume 2

Brandy Golden

Published by Brandy Golden Books, 2024.

This is a work of fiction. Similarities to real people, places, or events are entirely coincidental.

A FLOWER FOR ANGUS

First edition. March 22, 2024.

Copyright © 2024 Brandy Golden.

Written by Brandy Golden.

Also by Brandy Golden

Brocton Chronicles
The Maddie Stories
A Shotgun Wedding

East Coast Spitfires
Taming His Irish Spitfire
Taming His Feisty Kitten
Taming His Whirlwind
Taming His Honeydoll

Heaven's Gate
Christmas Housekeeper Wanted
A Flower for Angus

Standalone
Marlie's Christmas Keeper

Catching His Snow Bunny
Hot Little Firecrackers
Protecting Vidalia
Back Off, Love
A Lass Worth Fighting For

Watch for more at https://brandygolden.com/.

Starting over is never easy in life. But a loving relationship is something everyone deserves to have.

Chapter 1

Angus Sangster studied the dinner plate before him with a judicious eye. His son watched him with a warning gaze while his daughter-in-law held her breath. He finally picked up his fork and speared a piece of the suspicious looking meat wallowing amid carrots and potatoes in a greasy looking gravy. He hesitated.

Angus tried to avoid dinner with Ben and Dorothy at all costs, but he hadn't been able to plead that his boss was slave driving him this time. Staunchly he took the bite of roast lamb off his fork and began the lengthy process of chewing it down enough that he could swallow it. That had been his experience thus far with Dorothy's cooking. After some time under Lucerne's tutelage, you would think Dorothy would have learned a bit more about the fine art of tenderizing meat, but alas, he hoped in vain.

When the fire hit the back of his throat, Angus started choking and reached for his tea. "Cripes! What in the name of Hades did ye put in the meat?" He finally choked out after drinking half his glass in one shot.

Dorothy beamed at him, her rounded, angelic face with her halo of blonde curls defying the demon he was sure lurked beneath her fair hide.

"I took yer advice, Dad," she replied with enthusiasm. "Ye said I needed some spice in my cooking, so I added a few things to my stew this time. Do ye like it?"

"It's certainly spicy," he admitted reluctantly. "Is that red pepper ye put in it?"

She shook her head. "Nay, it's habanera peppers. The recipe called for one pepper finely chopped, but I figured I might as well add a handful with them being so small."

Angus groaned silently. The lass was so pleased with herself he couldn't bring himself to disappoint her. "Where did ye get the recipe?"

"I got it from Lucerne," Dorothy gushed. "Roasted habanera lamb stew she called it. I had never heard of it so I just had to try it."

When Angus's cell phone went off, he sent a thank you heavenward and grabbed it from his shirt pocket. "I got to take this; it might be Darro needin' somethin.'"

Ben smirked as Angus shot up from the table like an explosive had been lit under him. He threw his son a killing glare as he virtually ran to the living room to take the call. It was Darro MacCandish, lord of Heaven's Gate, or Neamh in the Scottish translation, and his boss.

As prearranged.

"How are ye enjoying yer dinner tonight?" Darro's deep voice tinged with amusement, flowed across the air waves and into his ear.

"Ye need me back at Neamh?" Angus grunted, raising his voice slightly so Ben and Dorothy could hear from the kitchen. He ignored the humor in Darro's voice.

"Aye, Lucerne has extra lasagna and some peach cobbler she wants to have eaten before it goes to waste," Darro replied, chuckling.

What was left of Angus's burnt mouth watered. His boss's wife could make the angels sing with her cooking. Dorothy was supposed to be taking lessons from her, but so far, Angus hadn't seen any evidence that it was working. Ben visited him on a regular basis and he would share Lucerne's leftovers with him when he was lucky enough to get some.

"I'm surprised she has any left considering yer appetite," he growled low into the phone. He looked up when Ben came into the room.

"Everything all right, Dad?" Ben smirked again, a knowing gleam in his eye. "I'm guessing ye are wanted back at Neamh?"

"Ye guessed right." Then he lowered his voice. "Don't ye be dumpin' those leftovers into the chicken yard or ye may ruin yer laying hens fer the rest of the season."

Dorothy caroled from the kitchen. "Ben, darling, aren't ye going to eat?"

Ben cleared his throat. "Aye, honey, I'll be right there. I'm just going to see Dad out."

Dorothy appeared in the doorway, wiping her hands on her apron. "Would ye like me to pack ye some to have later tonight, Dad?"

Angus nodded. "Aye, that would be nice, honey. I have to get goin' though, sorry I can't stay. Ye'd best hurry."

Dorothy really was a beautiful lass with her nicely rounded curves and cherubic face, but his son was going to starve to death if he didn't do something. The lass was death on steroids in the kitchen. He shook his head as she hurried back to her task.

"Be sure to give Dad the lion's share, darling," Ben called back to the kitchen. "He doesn't have anyone to cook for him like I do."

"Lucky for ye I'm so understandin', lad," Angus growled.

Ben scoffed. "Understanding my arse," he replied cheerfully. "Ye can't bring yerself to hurt her feelings any more than I can."

"Why don't ye just hire a housekeeper to cook for ye? After all, Dorothy is doing full time work on her computer from home. It's not like she has a lot of time to be cookin' and washin' yer drawers fer ye."

"We can't afford that, Dad. Better yet, why don't ye just hire a housekeeper and we'll take our meals here with ye every night? After all, I'm working our spread while ye are working Darro's."

Ben had a point, but Angus wasn't going to acknowledge it. "Thistlewind will be yer place one day, so quit yer complainin'."

"I know, I know." Ben rolled his eyes. "I only have one more year at Uni and I'll have my business degree in accounting and a minor in animal management. Then I can take over yer books here and manage our place."

At that moment, Dorothy popped into the living room with a plastic storage dish full of the lamb roast meal for Angus. "Here ye go, Dad."

Angus took the dish gingerly from her, hoping the spice from inside didn't burn through the plastic. "Thank ye kindly, Dorothy. I'm sorry I don't have more time to eat with ye."

Ben snorted and then coughed into his hand. Angus shot him a dirty look.

"Oh, it's quite all right. I'm used to it by this time." Dorothy gave him a gleaming smile and Angus could have sworn there was devilment lurking behind those China blue orbs. It wasn't the first time he'd seen it either, but he was perplexed as to the cause of it.

The couple's marriage had been a quick one. Angus would have laid money on the lass expecting a child in eight and a half months, but it hadn't happened. Therefore, he had to reluctantly conclude that it really was love that pulled them together. He didn't know Dorothy very well, but he'd learned from painful experience that she couldn't cook. He couldn't fault Ben for his choice though, the lass was a real looker.

"I'll be on my way then," he hastily replied as he made a beeline for the door. He snickered when he heard Ben making excuses for not eating his dinner as he closed the front door of their cottage behind him. They lived on the property and he knew Ben would come sniffing around later this evening to see if he'd brought home any leftovers from Lucerne's cooking. Of course, not every woman was blessed with the skills of Lucerne MacCandish, nor of Ben's mother, Rosie.

Angus sighed. He sure missed his Rosie pie, as he used to call her. Losing her to Covid had been a huge blow for him and his boys. And to his grandchildren. Ben didn't have any yet, but Ross's bairns were young and might not remember their grandmother as the memories faded with age. And at times, Angus was just plain lonely for some feminine company.

Oh, he had women sniffing around him, there were no shortages in that department. He might not be a highland lord but he had property connected to Heaven's Gate and had done well for himself. He supposed it might be time to entertain the idea of marrying again. After all, 50 years old was nodding in his direction this year. The problem was, none of the lassies he knew in the highlands could compare to Rosie, or Rose, as she had been named. His mother's name had been Aster, and his grandmother in the same line had been named Heather. According to his dad, that made flower names a tradition. Cripes, even his oldest son had married a girl named after a beautiful flower. He'd already married and lost his flower though. What were the chances of him meeting another one?

Not very likely.

As he stepped outside, the smell of heather and gorse drifted on the summer's evening breeze. Sage and other wildflowers were mixed in with the unique scents—the scent of Scotland. It was bred into him, body and soul. He inhaled deeply, the feeling of being a part of the land itself deeply ingrained.

Generations of Sangster's had been born in these highlands, and his family background was finely intertwined with that of the lords of Neamh. Crofters from earlier centuries all the way down to today had worked raising sheep for the MacCandish family.

When so many crofters had been run off or been shipped away from their homeland by their lords who didn't need them anymore, Lord MacCandish had kept the Sangster family close. Eventually, Angus's ancestor had even been deeded the very property he was standing on right now. Loyalty ran deep in his blood and bones. His feet kicked up the smell of the heather even stronger as he walked to his lifted black pickup truck. Once inside, he started the rumbling engine and turned his truck toward Neamh.

"WHO WAS THAT, HONEY?" Lucerne asked, already knowing the answer as Darro hung up his cell phone and returned it to his jeans pocket. "Did Angus need another rescue?" Her foot tapped slightly as she eyed her husband and sipped her hot chocolate.

"Aye, it was Angus. Don't put all the lasagna away, he'll be needing his belly filled again." Darro put his long arms around her and tasted her lips with his tongue. Mm...chocolate with marshmallow."

"Would ye like me to make ye a cup?"

"Not right now, I've got some work to do in the barn. As long as Angus is coming over, I might as well make him work for his supper."

Lucerne wasn't quite sure what to do about this situation with Angus. It wasn't that she minded feeding him, she didn't. She also knew that Angus regularly avoided his daughter-in-law's meals if he could find a way to get out of it. When he couldn't, Darro rescued him with a phone call.

"Honestly, is Dorothy's cooking really that bad, or is Angus just spoiled?"

"Since I've no eaten the lass's cooking, I can't say, but Angus says she can't boil water. How have the lessons been going?" He lifted the lid on the biscuit jar and helped himself to a sugar biccie.

"I hate to say it," she admitted, "but Dorothy doesn't seem to have a knack for it. I rather suspect that she doesn't even like cooking, but she's too sweet to say so."

"I hope ye won't mind fixing him a plate?" He kissed her on the nose and grinned. "After all, I have the best little chef in the highlands. I'm a lucky man."

Lucerne turned pink. Although they had been married for almost five months, he still had the ability to make her blush. And to take her breath away. Just having him close to her made her girlie parts ache. "I'm the one who's lucky," she replied softly, reaching up and fisting the front of his shirt so she could pull him down to kiss him.

It wasn't long before the rumble of Angus's truck engine sounded at the back of the house. When the back door opened and Angus appeared in the doorway, they were still kissing.

"Is that all ye two ever do?" he complained. "Every time ye get near each other yer lips lock like magnets." He sniffed the air appreciatively. "What's that I smell?"

Darro grunted. "I already told ye she made lasagna, ye old coot."

"Help yerself, Angus," Lucerne offered with a smile. "I waited to put it away until ye got here." She passed him a plate she had put out on the counter for his arrival.

"Bless ye, Lucerne," he replied fervently. He gave Darro an evil side eye. "I never know with ye, lad. Things can change at a moment's notice."

"What did Dorothy make that was so bad this time?" Lucerne asked.

Angus pointed his fork at Lucerne as he helped himself to a heaping plate of the tantalizing lasagna and garlic toast. "I blame ye for that disaster, lassie," he scolded.

"Me?" Lucerne was aghast. "What did I have to do with it?"

"Ye told her about some hellfire recipe called habanero roast lamb. She decided to make it," he growled. "I'm lucky to have any gizzard left, it was so hot. My throat still hasna recovered either."

Lucerne couldn't help but giggle. "Well, ye told her she needed to spice it up a bit, so it's a good recipe for that. But it's not that hot, unless ye have a weak palate," she teased.

Angus glared at Darro. "Don't ye need to be takin' yer wee lassie in hand? She's insultin' my educated palate."

Darro hooted. "Is that what ye call that bottomless pit of a stomach?"

"Now, ye are showin' yer ignorance lad. Palate is yer tastebuds and mine are very well educated. If the lass hadn't thrown in a handful of them habanero things, it might not have created meat hot enough to take the paint off the barn door. She figured to cook by the *in for penny, in for a pound rule* and overdone it. Like I keep sayin', the lass can't cook." He sat down at the table with his prize and dug in.

Lucerne dissolved into helpless laughter. "Oh no—tell me she didn't!"

"Oh aye, she did," Angus reassured her between a mouthful of lasagna and a bite of garlic toast. "I swear, if it wasn't for ye, lass, I'd never get a decent meal."

"Well, that may change soon," Darro told him, taking a seat across from his second in command.

Angus actually stopped chewing. "What? Why? What have ye done to Lucerne?" he finally asked suspiciously.

Lucerne sat down by Darro with her hot chocolate. "He hasn't done anything to me," she replied, her eyes twinkling. "Darro just wants me to have some help now that we are expecting our own baby by Christmas. With Delilah and Corey to look after, and keeping an eye on Dad running my housekeeper's business, I'm picking up more responsibilities all the time."

Darro chimed in. "So, I'm hiring a housekeeper to help her."

Angus stared at Lucerne. "But—ye are going to keep cookin', right?"

"Probably not as much as I have been, but aye, I'll still be doing some cooking. There will be evening's when I won't be, but that's what the housekeeper is for. And of course, I love baking and such, so I'll still be doing plenty of that."

Angus nodded and then surprised Lucerne with his sensitivity. "Aye, it's a good thing for ye then. I keep tellin' Ben he needs to hire someone, but he says he can't afford it. Dorothy is very busy too and adds to the household income with her computer work. Ben is like me, can't cook but can always find somethin' to eat if we get tired of beans on toast."

"Dad is sending her up for her first trial day tomorrow," Lucerne replied. "I'll be in the city most of the day after getting breakfast and sending the kids off to school, and Macy will be fixing lunch and supper. I should be home in time to eat so we can all see how well she cooks. Just don't be expecting a first-class chef," she scolded, shaking her finger at Angus. "As long as her food is eatable and healthy, the chores I leave for her are done, and the kids like her, that's all I'm asking for."

Darro snorted. "That's all I was asking for too, but I couldn't even get that."

Angus pointed his fork at him. "That's cause the other lasses weren't here to keep house, they were here to play house," he cackled.

Lucerne wrinkled her nose at Darro. "Well...I don't think Macy will have any designs on ye, she's closer to Angus's age than ours. According to Dad, she is very nice and is eager to work. And, if we like her, she would agree to move in with us if we want her full-time. She said she doesn't mind living in remote places."

"What's her name?" Angus asked curiously.

"Macy Kennedy."

Darro stared thoughtfully. "That's not a Scottish name. Sounds more American than anything else. Did he say where she was from?"

"She told Dad she'd just moved here from Canada. He doesn't know any more than that."

"Canada huh?" Angus picked up his plate and headed to the counter for seconds. "I knew a lass from Ontario once. Swore she was going to run a dogsled in one of them Adirondack races. Of course, I don't know if she ever did."

"Ye mean the Iditarod? The race that's a thousand miles long?" Lucerne asked in disbelief.

"Don't pay any attention to Angus," Darro scoffed. "He used to know more women than ye can shake a stick at. How he ever met all of them when he never leaves the highlands is still a mystery."

Angus shot Darro an evil eye. "I was a man of the world when ye were still a twinkle in yer daddy's eye, so don't go tellin' me who I knew or didn't know."

Lucerne spluttered with laughter. The two men were always going at each other, but she knew they had a deep bond between them. "Well, now ye will meet one from Canada," she teased.

"She must be used to snow then, I reckon. Mayhap yer mysterious housekeeper will fit right in." He polished off the last of his lasagna by cleaning his plate with the last bite of his garlic toast, then rubbed his stomach. "Did I hear something about peach cobbler?" he asked hopefully.

Darro rolled his eyes. "Again, I don't know where ye put it all."

"I already told ye. I need the calories because ye're such a slavedriver," Angus replied with a wide grin.

Lucerne got up to fix Angus a big heaping bowl of the peach cobbler. "Would ye like it heated with ice cream or just cream?" she asked with a giggle.

"If it's no trouble, some cream would be nice," he replied with relish. "Darro doesn't deserve ye if I have to say so myself."

Darro snorted. "After ye've finished stuffing yerself, I have some work in the barn I could use some help with. One of the snowmobiles sounds like a sparkplug is misfiring."

Angus sent his gaze heavenward and stretched out his arms. "See what I mean, Lord? Always making me work after hours. And he wonders why I need to eat so much."

"Ye need to do something to make up for all the food ye scavenge, ye old fart."

Lucerne was used to their squabbling by this time and actually enjoyed it. She knew how close they were and that they would each do anything for the other.

Her thoughts drifted to the new housekeeper, wondering what she would be like. With things getting so busy for her now, it would be heaven sent to find someone who fit in with their household.

She automatically packed the rest of the lasagna in a takeout container for Angus. And most likely for Ben to, although Angus would probably never admit it.

She wondered if Angus would ever marry again? Rosie had been gone for over a year now and he seemed lonely at times. But like Darro had pointed out, Angus rarely left the highlands except to visit family. How in the world would he meet someone?

MACY KENNEDY TOOK THE written directions to the Highland Estate called Neamh from Jamie MacNamara, her new employer at Happy Housekeepers. This job was a godsend. Especially since she'd only been in Inverness just a little over 24 hours. "How long will it take for me to get there?" she asked.

"Usually about an hour depending on how many sheep herds are crossing the road on yer way," Jamie replied with a chuckle. "Ye never know what can cause a delay in the highlands, whether it be sheep, rockslides, or even water across the road. Especially with the run off from the mountains. Being from Canada, I'm sure ye must be used to some of the same road conditions we have here after the winter is over?"

Macy nodded, the question in his words not lost on her. "Potholes are certainly a huge factor too." She knew he was hoping for more information, but Macy was being reticent for a reason.

"Aye, the roads can be quite dangerous in places," he agreed suavely.

Macy was quite aware of the admiration in Jamie's gaze, but she wasn't looking for a male in her life. He was quite a handsome man with a tall, lean figure and white peppering his fine dark hair. You could easily call him a silver fox. His dark expressive eyes and cultured tones made him seem a real gentleman, but looks could be deceiving.

In another time and another place, she might have been interested in getting to know Jamie MacNamara as other than an employer. Today, she just wanted to get as far away from people as she could. The more remote the better.

"One more thing, Mr. MacNamara," she added quietly. "If anyone should call asking about me, tell them you don't know me. Please? Especially if it's a call from out of the country."

Jamie hesitated a moment, then nodded affirmatively. "Of course, Macy. Your privacy as an employee of Happy Housekeeper's will be protected. No one will give out any information about ye."

Macy bobbed her head gratefully. "Thank you so much. If your daughter and her family like me, I may not be coming back tonight. I'll let you know of course, if that's the case."

He frowned and seemed to want to say more, but he didn't. She didn't blame him; she was lucky he was taking a chance on her without references and being a stranger in the city.

"Be careful on yer way up to Neamh. The Highlands can be as unpredictable as they are beautiful."

"Thanks for the warning," Macy replied as she headed out the door. She quickly returned to her rented four-wheel drive SUV behind the office building and slid her slim figure into the driver's seat. Looking at the map Mr. MacNamara had given her, she studied it thoroughly.

She'd been to Inverness once before, years ago with her cousin, Molly O'Hara whose family lived in Dublin, Ireland. Molly was dead now, so no one could trace her through that line of questioning. Her memories of Scotland were hers alone, and there would be no earthly reason to look for her here.

Scotland, especially Inverness, was an enchanting place, and steeped in mystery and legend. A country with a proud, rich history. She'd always wanted to return one day, but never had the chance until now.

After her second husband, Julian Condoloro, had died in unusual circumstances, her stepson had blamed her for his father's death. Especially since the lawyer had informed them at the reading of the will that Julian had changed some things. He'd unexpectedly left her with some of his fortune and investments. The will stated that Adrian was to have their ancestral home and would inherit Condoloro Enterprises, but Julian wanted to make sure Macy had enough money to support herself where ever she might choose to live. Adrian had been furious and vigorously contested the will. She shivered at the memories. This last year had been a living nightmare.

After the brakes had gone out on her car, Macy began to fear for her safety. So, she moved to Canada six months ago to get away from Adrian and the endless subpoenas to appear in court. She hadn't been in Toronto long before she began to feel like someone was following her. Perhaps it was too close to Chicago, or perhaps she'd just been paranoid, but after she'd come home one day and realized someone had been in her home, she finally decided to move to Scotland and make a complete break. Traveling had always been on her agenda anyway.

After her arrival in Inverness, she'd perused the local paper for a rental home and had seen the ad for a housekeeper in a rural area. The idea occurred to her it might be a good place to hide until she knew for sure that Adrian had given up looking for her. It would save her money too. On the run and only using cash, her funds were limited. If no one were to call about her, or show up looking for her, then perhaps she was finally safe.

It had been so long since she'd felt safe.

Chapter 2

With a sigh, Macy turned over the engine of her sporty white vehicle and started navigating her way through the streets of Inverness and towards the tall mountain peaks she could see hovering over the city. She would dearly love to play tourist and revisit some of the places she and Molly had visited all those years ago, but she didn't dare. At least in the highland country, perhaps she would see her enemy coming.

Her reservation in the hotel could be cancelled with a phone call. She'd left them with enough money to cover tonight's fee if she didn't return, and instructions not to divulge her renting of the room to anyone asking for her. Budget Car Rentals had been given the same strict instructions.

For all intents and purposes, Mrs. Julian Condoloro had dropped out of sight after arriving at Heathrow airport in London. She'd created a totally fake name from restaurants and billboards that sounded English and got on a bus. She'd also worn a blonde wig and sunglasses to disguise herself. She'd changed her name a couple of more times when she'd changed buses along the route, satisfied that her trail wouldn't be followed. It was easy when you paid cash—no one asked questions.

She'd gone back to Macy once she was in Inverness, using the fake ID she'd had made in Chicago before she moved to Toronto. Aside from that, she was now completely off the grid.

Her son-in-law, Morgan Kincaid, had given her a booklet on how to stay under the radar and not attract attention to herself. She'd made good use of all his tips when she'd left Chicago, but she knew Adrian hadn't given up. Her daughter, Andrea, kept her informed as much as she could when Adrian would harass her for Macy's whereabouts. If Andrea hadn't been married to a competent FBI agent who didn't like Adrian Condoloro, and wasn't a man to be intimidated, Macy would never have left her daughter and her family.

How she missed Andrea and her two grandbabies.

Shaking herself out of her sudden bout of melancholy, Macy put the SUV in park while a local shepherd and his dogs coaxed a herd of sheep across the road. She was in no hurry. The sun was warm on her face, she was in no immediate danger, and the beauty of the rugged highland country was a balm to her soul. From the quaint walls of rocks along some of the roads to the waving wildflowers along the spreading grasslands, the vista was breathtaking.

Taking the map out while she waited, she realized she was already on Heaven's Gate land. It shouldn't be too long now before the turnoff to the main house. From Mr. Mac-Namara's description it was an impressive place, and she was looking forward to seeing it. Mr. MacCandish was an actual lord, but didn't go by Lord MacCandish, he'd told her. And the man highly valued a good cook.

A FLOWER FOR ANGUS

Macy had reasonable skills in the kitchen. Maybe she wasn't a grade A chef, but she could cook a satisfying pot roast and her angel food cake never fell in the pan. The hang of making good pie crust had eluded her, but she loved making hot yeast rolls. Italian food she adored, but had no idea how to cook traditional Scottish dishes. Lamb hadn't been something she'd ever cooked or eaten much, so she was looking forward to trying out some new recipes. After all, she had plenty of time to learn what the men around here liked to eat. Haggis she couldn't wrap her mind around and hadn't even been able to make herself sample that, but Mr. MacNamara had told her that his daughter, Lucerne, could teach her to cook it.

She would if she had too, she needed this job.

While shuddering at the thought of haggis, she drove past the turnoff to Neamh and stopped suddenly when she realized what she'd done. "I'm such an airhead," she muttered to herself. Backing up several yards, she finally got onto the road that would lead her to the long drive towards the main house.

Then her rental died—right in the middle of the road.

"No, no, no, no...NO!" She yelled her frustration into the windshield, slammed the shift into park, and rammed the gas pedal to the floor while she tried to get the key to magically restart the engine. When it wouldn't start after several tries, she dropped her forehead against the uncompromising steering wheel and groaned loudly. A wisp of smoke from the hood wafted up into the breeze and the smell of petrol and something burning hit her nose.

Just great.

Macy popped the hood latch and got out of the car. Making her way around to the front, she fished beneath the front of the hood for the latch that would allow her to open it and look inside. That's what men did, right?

Knowing what was wrong with a car engine was built into the male genders brain. It would forever remain a mystery to the female sex as to just how they had achieved that particular skill, but they had. Just like they were the species with all the muscle groups, their brains were hardwired to mechanical things while she on the other hand, knew nothing about engines.

Finally, flipping the hood up, she glared helplessly at the mechanical mass of metal connected to tubes and wires running in all directions and sighed deeply. There was a hissing noise coming from what she thought was called a radiator but she didn't dare touch it. She'd heard horror stories about people being scalded when trying to open a hot radiator lid.

Feeling helpless, she turned and scanned the horizon, wondering how far it was to Neamh from where she was? Could she walk in and then have someone come back for her bags?

Uneasily her gaze darted here and there. Did wolves live in the highlands? Did they run cattle with bulls that she couldn't see? What about snakes? Macy was deathly afraid of snakes. She was a pretty good sprinter but she knew she couldn't outrun bulls or wolves if it came to that.

Maybe she should just wait in the car and hope someone would come looking for her. Then she slapped herself on the forehead. Duh! She had a cell phone. She could call Mr. MacNamara and explain what had happened.

Hurrying back into the car, she opened her bag and pulled out the cheap cell phone she'd bought in town and added minutes to, but was dismayed to see she had no signal. Frustrated, she shook it as if it just needed some diodes or something rearranged to make it work, then finally gave up.

Huffing in exasperation, she laid her head back trying to decide what to do. After 15 minutes of putting off the inevitable, she got out of the car, retrieved her jacket and bag, and started walking along the road.

Macy kept glancing at her watch and after about 30 minutes, she decided to rest for a minute on a rock wall. She picked her way over to the picturesque stones stacked neatly and sat down gratefully for a breather. With her face to the sun and her eyes closed to bask in its warmth, she didn't realize she had company until she felt something touch her hand. It only took a fraction of a second for her to realize that a small snaky-looking creature was sitting on her hand. It was a greenish gray color with a darker striping down the sides...and it had legs?

Screaming in panic, Macy jumped up and flipped her hand as she started running to get away. When her foot landed in an indentation in the unlevel grasses, she went down, moaning in agony as her ankle twisted beneath her. Glancing back to see if the snake was following her, she realized it was gone. Only what appeared to be the tail was left in sight and it was wiggling on the wall. What kind of weird snake did that?

Not waiting around to find out, she forced herself back up and tried to hop on one foot as far away as she could get. That's when she saw the jacked up black pickup truck coming up the road from the direction of Neamh. Biting her lip, she tried to put her foot down and gasped in agony when her toes touched the ground.

Glancing from the wall to the truck, panic threatened to overwhelm her. Mr. MacNamara's additional warning leapt to the front of her mind. Was this someone who would help her? Or someone who might take advantage of her situation?

Barely able to breathe, Macy forced herself to calm down. Maybe she'd get lucky and it would be another woman.

When the big pickup accelerated, she knew she'd been spotted. And there was certainly a man behind the wheel. So much for hoping desperately that it might be a woman.

The truck stopped, the door opened, and a big man hopped out and started walking towards her. He certainly had plenty of muscle groups in the forearms where his long-sleeved thermal shirt was pushed up. The hat on his head blocked his eyes but his face looked strong with a grizzled lower jaw. It looked like he'd missed a few morning shaves.

"Would ye happen to be Macy Kennedy?" He called out to her as he moved forward.

She slumped slightly in relief at his words, tears threatening to spurt into her eyes. "Yes, I'm Macy Kennedy," she returned his call. "Are you from Heaven's Gate?"

"Aye," he replied, hurrying his pace. "Are ye all right?"

Macy watched his confidant stride eat up the grassland as he closed the gap between her and the road. "Yes...no...I'm afraid I've hurt my ankle," she stuttered as he reached her and glanced down at her foot barely touching the ground for balance.

His piercing gaze was disconcerting as he took her hand and placed it immediately on his own muscled arm for support. She snatched it away as if he'd burnt her and started to spin and fall, but he caught her by both her arms.

"Easy now, lassie, I'm no goin' to hurt ye."

Taking a deep breath and trying to calm her racing pulse, Macy nodded. "I-I'm sorry, you just startled me. I'm actually *so* glad you came by. My car died…and there was this snake…and then I fell…and it left its tail behind. What sort of snake does that?" She muttered helplessly, trying not to appear like a complete loony. She glanced back at the wall where the tail of the snake was still lying on the stone.

He chuckled rich and deep. "That was no a snake, lassie, it was just a common lizard. It's their way of gettin' away from an enemy. The tail piece wigglin' distracts the predator long enough for the lizard to escape and then it grows back. Ye see them all over Scotland and they are harmless," he assured her gently.

The soft burr of his highland accent was soothing and Macy found herself relaxing with a nod and a sigh. "I didn't know that."

"No reason ye should," he replied. "My name is Angus Sangster and I work at Neamh. Can ye walk, Macy? If not, I'll just carry ye to the truck."

Her face flamed. "Oh no, I can walk." When she bravely put her foot down, hoping desperately that the earlier pain was only temporary, she gasped and started spinning again. Pain jolted through her ankle as she tried to regain balance on one foot and the tears spurted into her eyes for sure this time. "Ow!"

"I've got ye, lass." Angus swept her up in his arms as if she was nothing but thistle in the wind and strode confidently towards his monstrous truck. "We may have to call a doctor for that ankle. It could be broken."

Macy held herself stiffly in his arms, not trusting herself to speak. She hadn't been this close to a male body for a long time, especially not one as fit and strong as Angus's body. It was causing her to feel things she hadn't felt in forever.

She peeped up at the uncompromising male jawline. His hair was laced with strands of white in the rich hazelnut color she could see beneath his cap. Tanned skin with sun wrinkles spreading from the corners of his eyes judged him to be in his late forties or early fifties. His hair was too long to be called neat...more like grizzled. As if he didn't have a reason to be neatly trimmed anymore. Was he married? She castigated herself for even wondering. Hadn't she had enough of men to last her a lifetime already?

"Open the door, lass," he instructed when he came to stand in front of the passenger's door. She reached out and did just that, wincing when he sat her in the seat and then picked up her foot to inspect it more closely. The sturdy leather loafers she was wearing couldn't disguise the fact that her ankle was swelling. She hissed when he gently moved it back and forth. "I no think it's broken, but ye are going to have to ice it down and stay off it for a few days."

"I can't do that, I'm going to a job," she protested.

"Housekeeper at Neamh?" He eyed her shrewdly.

"Yes," she replied with an anxious nod. "I want to make a good impression because I was hoping to stay on. Do you think Mr. MacCandish and his wife will be understanding?"

Angus's eyes twinkled. "Can ye cook?"

"Of course I can cook!" She scowled at him. "Maybe not haggis because I've never tried it before, but Mr. MacNamara said his daughter, Lucerne, could teach me. I'm always willing to try new recipes, even if they sound disgusting. Why? Is haggis a favorite of his?"

"Mr. MacCandish is no a picky eater as long as the food tastes good. He's like me," Angus replied, a small grin quirking around his lips. "And if he doesn't want ye, I might hire ye as long as ye can cook."

He closed the door before she could reply and she glared at him as he went around the front of the truck. When he opened his own door, she piped up, "I thought you worked for Neamh?"

"Aye, I do. But I'm always in the market for a good cook at my place."

"You mean you're not married?" Her eyebrow shot up in a skeptical arch.

"Does that mean ye are interested?"

Macy stiffened. "Certainly not!"

He grinned wickedly. "Let me know if ye change yer mind. I could be available for a good cook."

She huffed, caught off guard. She wasn't used to men flirting with her at this stage of her life. "Then why don't you ask Happy Housekeepers to send one up to you?"

"Because it's more fun to hire one away from Darro," he replied, his rich chuckle filling the cab while his eyes laughed at her. "Let's go get yer bags from the car and I'll send a couple of the boys out to bring it into Neamh. We'll figure out what happened to it."

"Thank you," she replied primly, not sure what to say after that. She supposed she'd learn all the undercurrents and how people related to one another at Neamh once she was in residence. In the meantime, she needed to be careful not to give away any of her own secrets. This garrulous Angus was easy to talk to, but that didn't mean she should trust him. She could only hope that the MacCandish's were willing to let her stay a few days until she could get into her duties. She was really vested in living out of sight and out of mind for a good while. At least until Adrian had finally given up on finding her.

If ever.

WHEN ANGUS FINALLY came out of the beautiful fir trees and into the gravel circle drive that ran around to the front of the definitely impressive home, Macy gasped in delight. He was used to the view, but to her he was sure it was like something out of a travel magazine, or a landscape photograph of Scotland's highlands. He slowed even more so she could appreciate every aspect. There were many outlying buildings but the main house was two stories of massive stonework. There was even a turret similar to what you'd see in a castle.

"Ye like it? Neamh has Gaelic origins and means Heaven's Gate in the English translation," he related proudly. "For folks around here, the two names are interchangeable."

"It is amazing," she replied in awe. "Such a beautiful place. Was it built like this all at once? Or has it been added onto through the years?"

"Good question," Angus replied, pulling up in front of the flagstones to the front deck. "It's been added onto twice now. Darro has done some more modern updates as far as conveniences, but back when families used to be larger, they added on bedrooms to accommodate family and visitors. The area is so widespread it used to be difficult to have guests for an evenin' and have them return home in the same evenin', so they were often invited to stay for a weekend or more," he added proudly.

"Do you live here as well as work here?"

"Nay, I have my own place, Thistlewind. Not near as grand as this, but it it's been in the Sangster family for generations. My family has always been closely intertwined with the MacCandish family. Kind of a symbiotic relationship of sorts." He grinned over at her and was delighted to see her smile tentatively back.

Macy Kennedy was a reserved little thing. After her initial outburst from the pain in her ankle and her scare from the lizard, she'd been pretty quiet. He'd asked her several questions about her background but all he'd gotten was that she had a married daughter with two children, and that her husband had passed away about a year ago. He wondered if Jamie had any more information on her than she'd given him? He made a mental note to go into town soon and have some tea with the man.

Bo and Misty were hanging out at the end of the flagstones, curiously staring at his truck as if they sensed something was up. The blue healers were usually in front of the house if Darro was inside. Sure enough, the front door opened and his boss stepped out of the house with Lucerne right behind him. "Looks like the boss has been waitin' fer ye."

Macy opened the door and tried to swing her legs out but Angus caught her arm. "Don't try to get down on yer own, ye'll only damage that ankle more if ye land on it again," he warned.

For a moment, defiance flared in her brown eyes and then she bit her lip and nodded. "Right. I don't want to be out of commission any longer than necessary," she replied stiffly.

Angus shook his head. It looked like she had a hidden fire that hadn't shown up yet. That was fine with him, he didn't much care for meek little lambs anyway. Of course, he had no interest in Macy one way or the other. She didn't even have a flower name. She was just a pretty lass with a creamy complexion, chocolate brown hair that shone like silk, and eyes to match. Nope…not interesting at all.

He got out of the truck and met Darro and Lucerne at the end of the flagstone path. "I found her, as ye can see. Her car broke down and she was on foot. She's injured her ankle so I'll have to carry her into the house. Where do ye want her, Lucerne?"

"Ye will have to carry her?" Darro teased, falling in step with Angus.

"She can't walk, her ankle is swollen," Angus replied testily.

"Oh dear, is she badly hurt?" Lucerne asked, following the men. "Does she want to go back to town? What about her position?"

"I'll let ye ask her those questions," Angus replied, opening the truck door. "Macy, this is Darro MacCandish and his wife, Lucerne."

"It's a pleasure to meet ye, Macy," Lucerne added warmly, taking Macy's hand in hers. "But do ye want to put off the trial period until yer ankle is better? Do ye need to go back to town and see a doctor?"

Macy shook her head frantically. "Oh no, please. I-I'd rather stay if you don't mind. Is that okay? I'm sure I'll be right as rain tomorrow. Or even if I could get it wrapped? I can probably fix dinner tonight if it's wrapped."

"Nonsense," Darro replied firmly, taking Macy's ankle in his own large hands and probing lightly with his fingers. "I don't believe anything is broken but ye will still stay off of it for a day or two. We don't mind having ye here, we have plenty of room. And we don't want any further injury. Besides, ye can't drive with yer right ankle in that condition."

Macy looked so relieved that it made Angus slightly suspicious. Was the girl hiding from something? Or someone? Or was she just broke, and needed a place to stay? What exactly was her story?

"I-I didn't think of that," she confessed. "Driving would be difficult, I agree."

Darro took over with his usual commanding style. "Angus, bring Macy inside and we'll take a good look at that injury. Have Dal come in to look at it as well. Lucerne, if ye still need to go to town today, then go ahead. The kids can look after Macy for a few hours until ye get back once we get that ankle wrapped." He looked up at Macy. "Do ye like children, Macy?"

Macy nodded. "Yes, I love kids. I-I was never blessed with more than one though. I do have two grandchildren I dearly love." She seemed to brighten at that thought.

Angus leaned in and plucked Macy from the seat. She couldn't weigh much; she was such a light little thing. The girl needed to eat more.

"Do ye want her on the sofa in the living room, Darro?"

Darro nodded. "Aye, that would be best for now."

Chapter 3

Macy gritted her teeth as Angus carried her tucked up against his strong body once more. She seemed to fit him perfectly as if they were two parts of a whole. No one had ever carried her like this before and it was very disconcerting. When he went up the steps to the porch, he hefted her a bit on the first step and she automatically put her arm around his broad neck to hold on. "I'm too heavy for you to be carrying around like this," she said stiffly, trying to shrink into as small a ball as possible.

"Nay, lass," he objected, his teeth gleaming down at her as he smiled his way across the deck to where Darro was opening the door for him. "Ye're just a bit of fluff in my arms."

"It felt like you needed to get a better grip or were going to drop me," she accused suspiciously.

He chuckled. "It got yer arm around me, didn't it?"

She glared up at him, not knowing quite what to say. On one hand she was flattered, but on the other hand, an alarm equivalent to a six-alarm fire bell was sounding off in her head, warning her of impending danger. This man was going to be hazardous to her piece of mind. Maybe she should reconsider her employment at Neamh. Her lips tightened in disapproval. Her breasts tightened in anticipation.

The next few minutes were a madhouse while Angus carried Macy in and placed her on the sofa. Shocked and embarrassed at her reaction to Angus's blatant flirting, Macy tried to ignore him after he put her down. She was greatly relieved when he set off on Darro's instructions to find Dal, whoever he was.

ANGUS HURRIED OFF IN search of Dal MacIntosh, his arms feeling empty after carrying his *uninteresting-turned-captivating* bundle into the house. He grimaced to himself, feeling like a fool over a pretty woman. He needed to get it together or she'd have him eating out of her hand before he could whistle the bonnie banks of Loch Lomond. In the barn, he found the man he was looking for.

Dal, short for Dallas, was new to Neamh this year, but his veterinarian studies were already coming in handy. He found him examining one of the pregnant cats with his stethoscope, although the cat didn't appear to be enjoying his services. Dal was the son of one of Angus's second cousins and a friend of his son Ben. He already had a soft spot for the bright young lad.

"I got another patient for ye, lad. The new housekeeper's car broke down on the way out here so she started walkin' and ended up sprainin' her ankle. Darro wants ye to have a look at it."

Dals eyes lit up. "Is she as pretty as the last housekeeper?" He joked, knowing Lucerne had been the last housekeeper.

Angus eyed him sourly. "Macy could be yer mother, laddie, and ye'll do well to remember yer manners around her."

A FLOWER FOR ANGUS

"I could fall in love with an older woman," Dal teased, his blue eyes tormenting Angus while he put his stethoscope back in his bag. "Is she married?"

"I just met her, I no have her life history yet," Angus snapped, uncertain why Dal's teasing was making him feel out of sorts. He already knew Macy was a widow but the nosey lad didn't need to know that.

Dal fell in step alongside Angus as they hurried to the house. "They say older women make beautiful lovers," he tormented. "Haven't ye heard the song?"

"Don't ye have a wee lassie?" Angus asked in exasperation. "Or have ye traded her in for another one already?"

Dal laughed. "I'm between love interests at the moment. I've got time to give an older lass a whirl."

Angus snorted. "More likely no self-respectin' lass wants to stay with ye once they find out yer *short*—comin's."

"Ha ha," chortled Dal. "Most men should be so blessed as me."

"Watch it," Angus growled. "Ye may be a friend of Ben's but I'll still box yer ears if ye get disrespectful in front of the womenfolk."

Dal held up his hands as he followed Angus into the house, his blue eyes twinkling. "No disrespect intended, sir." He wisely didn't point out that Angus had started it.

Darro motioned the men over to where Macy was seated. "Dal, I need ye to wrap Mrs. Kennedy's right ankle if ye please."

"Aye, sir," Dal replied respectfully, taking the ace bandage from Darro. He bent down to take off Macy's shoe and sock and then probed the ankle gently. "It's no broken, sir."

Angus grunted. The lad was smart enough to know not to mess with the boss. Darro didn't tolerate nonsense among his employees. Well...except for him. Angus was second in command and he and Darro had a very close relationship, just like he'd had with Darro's father, Old Whipcord, before he'd passed on. Their bonds were rooted deeply in friendship, honor, and family.

Darro nodded back at Dal. "I suspected as much, but I wanted ye to double check it."

"Aye, sir. With an icepack and some staying off it for at least 48 hours, ye should be well on the way to recovery," Dal said to Macy with an appreciative gaze.

"That's very kind of you both," Macy replied with a small smile.

The sudden rush of feet pounding in the hallway told Angus that Delilah and Corey were coming. Darro's brother and sister-in-law had died tragically in a car accident a few years ago, leaving their two children in Darro's custody.

Darro caught them up in his arms as they came running towards Macy sitting on the sofa. "Whoa, slow down. What have I said about running in the house?" He scolded them affectionately then set them down in front of him to face the new housekeeper.

"Mrs. Kennedy, this is Delilah and Corey, my niece and nephew."

"Hello," the children chorused, staring curiously at her.

Her smile to the children was certainly much warmer, Angus noted.

"Hello to you too," she replied softly. "Please, call me Macy. Mrs. Kennedy is far too formal."

"Ye talk different," Corey noted solemnly, his round blue eyes wide.

"It's because she isn't from Scotland, Corey," Delilah loftily informed her brother. "Remember? Uncle Darro said she's from a place called Canada."

"That's right, Delilah," Macy assured her. "Canada is above the United States on a world map."

"Is that a long way from here?" Corey asked.

Macy nodded. "It is quite a long way, that's for sure."

"Why did ye come to Scotland?"

"Corey," Darro scolded gently. "We don't ask personal questions. Remember?"

Angus would have liked to hear Macy's answer to that question himself.

Macy hesitated. "I was in Dublin once, many years ago, Corey. My cousin and I visited Scotland and I fell in love with it. I always vowed if I ever got the chance to return, I would. And so, here I am."

When Darro tweaked an eyebrow at Angus and shot him a wicked grin, Angus snorted and rolled his eyes. So, he'd known a woman from Dublin, who hadn't? It was a popular hotspot.

"You don't believe me?" Macy's tone was suddenly frigid, causing the two men to look away from each other and directly at her. Her face was red with embarrassment and something else, as if she were holding in boiling lava.

Lucerne hastily intervened. "Oh nay…it isn't that, Macy. It's a private torment between Darro and Angus. Those two are always pestering each other as ye shall see once ye've been here for a bit. Pay them no attention, please."

In his innocence, Corey had to ask. "Did ye meet Macy in Dublin, Angus?"

Angus gawped like a fish out of water and a flush started creeping up his throat. Darro couldn't help laughing like a recalcitrant schoolboy. Dal hooted, and Lucerne glared at all three of them in embarrassment.

A flash of understanding burst into Macy's eyes and a sudden wicked grin began creeping into the corners of her mouth. Her eyes started sparkling with pure mischief as she replied sweetly, "It must have been another woman, Corey. I can guarantee if Angus had met me in Dublin, he would never have forgotten me."

And that's when Angus fell in love.

"I-I got chores to get to," he muttered, practically falling backwards over himself as he hastily turned and left the room. As he rounded the corner, a caroling laugh followed him as Darro apologized on his and Angus's behalf. He stopped, entranced for a moment at the lovely sound, and then grinned as he continued on his way. His Macy had a wicked sense of humor. Maybe he'd rename her Violet in his mind. As he closed the door behind him, he decided Violet didn't really fit her nature. She was quiet and reserved like a beautiful violet, but with a hidden fire beneath that could reach up and burn you when you least expected it. Nay, she was no shrinking Violet. He'd have to come up with a different flower.

"That Macy is something else. A right wicked sense of humor, that one. I like a woman with some fire in her."

Angus turned to face Dal. "She's more woman than ye can handle, lad. Ye had best set yer sights elsewhere."

A FLOWER FOR ANGUS

"She sure is pretty," Dal teased. "For an older woman of course. Over in the states she'd be what ye call a cougar." He growled low in his throat and raked his hand at Angus like a paw. "She can lay her claws into me anytime."

Angus stopped and did some growling himself. "Ye are bordering on complete disrespect, Dallas MacIntosh. Don't make me have to set the seat of yer britches on fire with old Whipcord's horsewhip. Not another word about the new housekeeper. Do ye ken me?"

Dal backed down and held his hands up in surrender. "Aye, aye, sir. She's all yers." The cheekiness twinkled in his eyes. When Angus started advancing with his hands on his belt, Dal turned and ran like a highland chicken, laughing all the way.

Angus grinned and lowered his invisible hackles. Dal really was a good lad, but another one with a wicked sense of humor. The trouble with the young ones was that they didn't know when to quit pushing.

"WHAT DO YOU MEAN YOU can't find her?"

Vince Gallo winced as Adrian Condoloro roared his displeasure from across the desk in his Chicago office.

Condoloro had hired him to keep an eye on his stepmother's rental home in Toronto, Canada. His thick black mustache wiggled over his lip like a gaunt-faced version of Inspector Jacques Clouseau in the Pink Panther detective series, except there was nothing humorous about him. He was an intense young man with a weak chin from where a small bit of spittle slowly crawled down from his bottom lip. Desperate was a good word too if Vince had to give a description of his behavior.

"I send someone to check on my stepmother, he comes back reporting that no one appears to be living there, and you tell me you can't find her? What have I been paying you for all this time?" he asked with a menacing glare.

Vince shifted uneasily in his chair, his lean, muscled figure tense as he watched the mustache with distracted fascination. The man's obsession with his stepmother made him appear unhinged, but he paid well, and the job seemed easy enough. It hadn't taken him long at all to track Mrs. Condoloro, under the fake name of Macy Kennedy, to a rental home in Toronto. In retrospect, he hoped he hadn't made a dumb mistake by taking the additional pay to stay in the area and keep an eye on her movements. When he'd realized she'd somehow slipped away from him, he'd returned to his Chicago office.

He pulled the limp, damp collar of the faded orange and black Chicago Bears t-shirt away from his sweaty neck. It was already hot in his mid-town office even though his ratty window air conditioner was barreling away. The gray sprinkled in his dirty blond short cut felt like they were sending sweat beads trickling down in front of his ears.

The pointed ends of the paper mess on his desk were flipping up from the steady stream of air that barely felt cool. He made a mental note to have the air conditioner unit checked out, he might need to spring for a new one this year. After spending a good part of the last six months in Toronto, his office was a mess of dust and unwashed coffee cups, thanks to his business partner. Bald-pated, round-bellied Ernie Sanchez was crap at housekeeping, but he paid his share of the rent on the office. And he was a whiz on computers.

The vibes Vince was getting from his current client weren't good ones. He was beginning to appear more like a homicidal maniac.

"What I mean is that I'm working on it. I know she booked a flight out of Toronto to Heathrow in London under her real name, but after that, she just disappeared. There are no reservations anywhere out of Heathrow under her real name or her fake name. I'll find her, it will just take a little more time."

The silence was deafening, then Condoloro finally grated out a reply. "Do you have any idea where she might have gone? Any idea at all?"

"I do have an idea, but I don't know for sure," Vince replied slowly, thinking of the things he'd seen while going through the woman's belongings in her Toronto home. She only had a few scrapbooks, but from a couple of photos in those, he knew she had relatives in Dublin, Ireland. Research told him the cousin in the pictures was dead now, but what about the rest of the family? It was a place to start anyway.

Sharp words spewed in his ear like spitballs and just as nasty. "Well, out with it. I don't like to be kept waiting."

"She has distant relatives in Ireland," Vince hastily informed his client. "I found a picture of her in a scrapbook with a deceased cousin in front of Inverness Castle in Scotland. At least that's what the back of the picture says, I haven't been there myself."

Adrian swore a blue streak and grabbed the back of the hardwood chair in front of the desk. "*Find. Her.*"

The order was given through clenched teeth, as if the man was striving not to leap forward and tear Vince's throat out. His fingers were flexing like claws and his gaunt figure leaned forward over the chairback to drive his point home.

Vince instinctively rolled backward in his office chair as if warding off a demon from hell. He would dearly like to tell Condoloro he was done and to hire someone else, but the butt of the gun beneath his suit jacket held him back. He suddenly felt sorry for the stepmother.

"I'll find her for you," he shot back with a defensive scowl, "but I won't be a party to doing anything to harm her. I want to be perfectly clear about that."

"I never told you to harm her, I just want to know where she is so I can serve her with subpoenas when I have to. Now that you've let her get out of the country, it's going to make that a lot harder to do. *Isn't it?*"

The emphasis of his point was not lost on Vince as Condoloro went on, the mustache wiggling frantically again. "I'll pay your expenses, just make sure you don't come back until you can tell me exactly where she is."

Vince nodded warily, not liking it, but the things he'd heard about Condoloro made him hesitate to tell him where he could put his demands. "I'll find her."

"*You'd better.*"

After Condoloro left the office, the breath Vince had been holding left his chest like a balloon deflating. Subpoenas? Who did the man think he was fooling? You can't serve subpoenas when the subject is out of the country. Vince didn't know who Condoloro had sent to Toronto but he'd be willing to bet it wasn't his lawyer. And he'd also lay money it wasn't a subpoena he was going to serve. More like threats, or even a bullet. What had he gotten himself mixed up in?

Uneasy to the bone, he decided he'd find out where she was, and then take an extended vacation somewhere as far away from Chicago as he could until things settled down.

Sometimes being a PI really sucked. Especially when you got drawn into the sordid feuds between family members wrapped up in avarice and deceit.

On the surface, Adrian's stepmother looked to be your typical second wife trying to cash in on her rich husband's life insurance policies, but there was more to it than that. She'd actually made off with a fortune when her husband died, according to the scandal rags that is. How much of the stories were true was always anybody's guess, but they were based in truth, even it the rest was usually highly exaggerated. At the time he'd felt some sympathy for Adrian, which had resulted in him taking the case.

Now he wasn't so sure anymore.

It was funny how things were never what they appeared to be in this business. Shrugging, he bellied up to the desk and started tapping keys on his laptop. He'd finish the job he started, and then steer clear of the whole mess.

WHEN THE ALARM CLOCK on her Fitbit buzzed into her wrist, Macy stretched and yawned, then swung her slim legs off the bed to do a few bedside stretches before getting all the way up. It was 5:30 a.m. and she had 30 minutes to shower and prepare for her day. This would be her first official breakfast preparation at Neamh and Lucerne was teaching her how to make Scottish porridge. Spraining her ankle had been a small setback in her employment here at Neamh, but it was finally behind her if her employer and Angus would just leave it alone. Were all men in Scotland as protective and arrogant as those two? Or were they just a throwback to the clans of old where men ruled everything, the women included?

Grumbling to herself she finished her stretches and headed for the shower. Angus Sangster was like a nagging toothache that came and went. First, he would be totally solicitous while teasing and joking with Mr. MacCandish, and the next time they met he'd be scowling at her and running off like his tail was on fire. Trying to put the aggravating male out of her mind, she turned on the shower and slipped in while it was hot.

The time at Neamh so far had been surprisingly pleasant. It was good exercise and now that her ankle was fully recovered, she was planning to up her routine to walks outside. At the age of 46 she felt like she was reasonably healthy, but she was adamant about staying physically active and strong. She also wanted to explore Inverness again, in more depth this time. So many things she wanted to see and do.

If she could just feel safe again.

In the kitchen, Macy poured herself a cup of tea and filled a thermos with hot coffee for Mr. MacCandish to take with him. Having been on light duty, she'd spent time getting to know the children and prepared a few meals here and there, but today was her first official full day on the job doing all three meals and she was looking forward to it.

"Good morning, Macy."

The deep voice sounded behind her and Macy turned. "Good morning, Mr. MacCandish." He was a big man, bigger than Angus, with broad shoulders and a commanding air that set well on his handsome features. With long wavy hair and beautiful sea-green eyes, his wife Lucerne was a beautiful girl. They were both attractive young people, and had been very kind to her.

"Darro."

Macy felt the pink stealing into her cheeks. "It seems so informal," she protested, trying not to shrink under his sudden stern gaze. "After all, you are my employer."

He studied her. "If it makes ye more comfortable, then call me Mr. MacCandish. We are fairly informal here in the house though, so I hope ye will soon feel comfortable enough to do so. Would ye prefer me to address ye as Mrs. Kennedy?"

She shook her head. "No, no of course not. Macy is fine."

"Still arguing over who to call what?" The teasing voice came from Lucerne as she breezed into the kitchen with a grin.

"Angus and I will be in for breakfast this morning, Macy," Darro replied, dropping a kiss on Lucerne's lips. "Not arguing, Lucerne," he threw over his broad shoulder as he strode towards the back door hallway. "Macy will see things my way soon enough."

Lucerne just shook her head. "That man…always gets in the last word."

"Are all Scottish men so...so self-assured?" Macy fumbled for the right word without being offensive.

Lucerne laughed. "You mean arrogant, dominant, and bossy?"

"Well...since you put it that way..."

"Aye, most of them are." Lucerne's eyes twinkled at her. "Angus seems a bit taken with ye. He's even cut his hair and shaves since ye've been here. Is that what's worrying ye?"

Macy's mouth opened to a horrified O. "Uh...no...I mean...h-he can't be. Surely, he has a lady friend?" She stammered the words, trying to collect her thoughts without turning five shades of red. She had no intention of getting involved with another man.

Lucerne shook her head gently. "He lost his wife over a year ago from Covid. Sometimes I suspect he is a bit lonely, but he never lets on. At least not to me. He and Darro are very close, so he might confide in him. Darro isn't one to gossip or share a confidante's secrets though."

"I can certainly understand that, but I'm afraid I'm not in the market for a husband again," Macy stated firmly. For a moment, Julian crossed her thoughts, then they flew from him to his son, Adrian. Was her stepson still looking for her? She was sure by now that he knew she was gone. Why was he being so greedy anyway? He had the majority of Julian's fortune, his company, and the beautiful ancestral home. What more did he need?

"Macy? Are ye all right?"

Macy started and caught Lucerne staring curiously at her. "What? Oh...yes...I'm sorry. I just got distracted for a moment. We were going to make porridge, right?" She smiled at her employer, hoping to get off the subject of the garrulous station manager. "Where do we start?"

By the time the porridge was ready, Lucerne was giggling at Macy's efforts to memorize everything there was to know about porridge.

In the MacCandish household, they used Bob's Red Mill Steel Cut Oats used in the 2009 World Porridge Championship for the winning porridge. The porridge must be stirred often to prevent lumpiness. Don't add the salt too early, or it can make the oats tough. The longer you cook it, the thicker and creamier it will be unless you cook it too long, and then it becomes *'stodgy'*. If you don't cook it long enough, it will be thin and soupy.

Oh, and you must stir it with a spurtle, a wooden rod shaped like a chicken leg. Or you can substitute a wooden spoon and it will still turn out properly.

"For something that only contains three ingredients, this recipe is very complicated," Macy decided, suddenly giggling hysterically. "Oats, water and salt. How hard can it be? You Scots must take your oatmeal, as we call it, very seriously. In Chicago, we throw instant Quaker oats in a bowl with water, nuke them for one minute, add milk and sugar, and it's done. Blueberries or nuts are optional."

Lucerne nodded and then dissolved into giggles too. "I know, I lived in New Orleans off and on during my growing up years, so I'm well aware of the American tradition of taking shortcuts with everything in the interest of time."

"I bet they've never heard of bologna here," Macy chortled. "I was raised on bologna sandwiches."

"Nay, we have something similar called Mortadella, but it's not widely used around here."

"I loved fried bologna with a tomato slice and some mayo," Macy added fervently.

"Then how do ye have an aversion to haggis? Bologna is leftover meat fats and all sorts of awful meat byproducts packed into a round casing that you slice and eat cold. Same with the American Hot Dog, although people do cook that first."

Macy stared at Lucerne and they both burst out laughing again. "You might have a point. Okay, I'll try making haggis just to be fair."

"Sounds like you two lassies are having a grand old time. Did I hear someone mention haggis?"

Macy turned and spotted Darro and Angus leaning against the doorjamb from the back door hallway. Her breath caught in her throat and she choked on a giggle.

"Aye," replied Lucerne. "We were just discussing the differences and similarities of foods of different cultures. Macy has an aversion to haggis but loves American hot dogs and bologna."

"So ye grew up in Chicago," Angus commented. "I knew a lass from Chicago once."

Everyone groaned.

"I know I'm going to regret this, but what was her special skill?" Darro asked with a chuckle, coming over to give Lucerne a kiss.

"Let's just say she took after the *windy* city in great style," Angus replied, grinning unrepentantly at the responding groans and giggles. "That and the onions she ate on her hot dogs made it hard to have a decent conversation with a clothespin on yer nose."

"What were you doing in Chicago?" Macy had to ask.

"Ye're going to be sorry ye asked," Darro replied, shaking his head.

Angus shot a look at Darro. "I was with Whipcord on a business trip, and that's all I'll say about that."

Darro just grinned.

Apparently, this was another inside joke between Darro and Angus, but Macy wished she hadn't let it slip to Lucerne that she'd grown up in Chicago. It was just so difficult to stay closed when everyone around her was so open and friendly.

Talk of Chicago suddenly had her feeling homesick. She wondered how her daughter and grandchildren were doing? Was Adrian hassling them over her whereabouts? She wished she could get a decent phone and call them. The cheap phone she'd bought with minutes on it was very limited, but she couldn't afford to buy one and use her credit cards. She also didn't want to call them and maybe put them in danger. Her son-in-law, Morgan, had warned her not to call the house in case Adrian was monitoring their phones as well. Maybe she should just tell her lawyer to turn everything Julian had left her in the will over to Adrian and leave her out of it. Maybe she could finally get her life back then.

"Macy?" Lucerne asked. "Are ye all right?"

Startled, Macy realized she hadn't been listening. "Umm...yes...I'm sorry. I was just thinking."

"Thinkin' about makin' haggis, right, Macy?" Angus added helpfully.

Macy smiled at the garrulous teasing. "Not really, no."

Angus feigned shock. "Ye actually don't like haggis, Macy?"

"Do you like bologna and hot dogs?" Macy fired back defensively.

He winked at her and sauntered towards the breakfast table. "I'll eat just about anything that doesn't eat me first, lass. But a woman who can cook good haggis with neeps and tatties has the key to my heart."

Macy instinctively stepped back slightly as Angus patted her hand on his way to the table. The skin tingled where he touched her. Her lips tightened and she turned away to get the porridge from the stove. Did Angus always take breakfast with the boss's family as well as dinner and lunch now and then? She'd never actually been to the breakfast table yet because of her light duty.

In Chicago with Julian, she hadn't been required to cook anything, and she never ate breakfast anyway except for a slice of toast with some tea or coffee. He and the cook hadn't allowed her in the kitchen to prepare meals. Occasionally when the cook was off, she'd do some baking or fix simple snacks. It was only since she'd been on her own for the last year that she'd taken up cooking again. When she didn't order takeout that is.

Here in the highlands, Macy had expected an atmosphere more like Julian's home when she'd found out Darro MacCandish was a Scottish lord, but nothing was further from the truth. These people were kind and kept trying to draw her into their family atmosphere. Trying to stay reticent was getting harder to do. Finding herself attracted to the station manager with his dancing eyes and muscled forearms was the last thing she would have seen coming. Was Lucerne, right? Was Angus interested in her? Or was he just a natural flirt?

Confused at her feelings, she bit her lip and was grateful to hear the kids coming down the hallway at a dead run. Sighing with relief, she set the porridge pot on the table and the ensuing chaos from the children coming in prevented her from having to reply to Angus's comment.

Chapter 4

Once breakfast was over, Angus slipped his plate into the sink at Macy's elbow. He'd been working up the nerve to ask her to spend some time with him. He'd seen her frowning at her small cell phone a few times as if it wouldn't do what she wanted it to.

"Since Lucerne is staying home today, how would ye like to run into Inverness with me and I'll help ye pick out a decent phone? I've seen ye ready to heave the one ye have into the nearest loch and shaking it to get a better reception," he teased.

Macy shot him a panicked glance and stammered. "Well...uh...no, I can't leave. I'm on duty. The kids..." She looked around. The kids had already gone off to get ready for school. "And...and...I haven't gotten my first paycheck yet to buy a new phone."

Angus stared. The lass was making up excuses, no doubt about that.

Lucerne came up on the other side of Macy with a frown. "Macy, if ye need money, we can give ye an advance on yer salary. And I could use a few things from the grocer's if Angus can drop ye off there for a little shopping?" She glanced over at Angus with a questioning look.

Darro added to the conversation. "That's a great idea. Angus, we need a few more salt licks and some additional vitamin E for the south pasture flock. Pick that up while ye are in town."

Angus rolled his eyes. "See what ye did now, lass? Ye've no choice but to go with me, we've both been hijacked."

"Since Lucerne needs some things, I'll go with you then, but I don't need a phone," Macy denied, her eyes flashing.

Macy didn't seem at all interested in going with him and Angus narrowed his eyes in disappointment. He could have sworn she'd liked him a little when he'd picked her up on the side of the road. Mayhap he'd been mistaken.

Darro took some bills out of his wallet and handed them to Macy. "Here's an advance on yer salary, which ye'll have the rest of next week. Get a proper phone."

Macy's eyes flashed again. "I just told you I don't need a phone, there's no one I want to call," she sassed back.

Darro's eyes narrowed and he started to say something, but Lucerne hastily intervened. "It's all right, Macy, ye don't have to buy a phone if ye don't want one, but it's there if ye need it."

Darro's brows hit ground zero and he took his wife by the arm. "In my study, please."

Angus watched in amusement as Darro practically frog-marched Lucerne out of the kitchen. "Now see what ye've done with yer sassy tongue?"

Macy looked bewildered. "What? What have I done?"

"The boss doesn't like to be disrespected either by his employees or his wife," he replied with a chuckle.

"I wasn't being disrespectful, I was just being honest," she protested.

Angus's eyes narrowed. "Were ye now? I thought ye had a daughter and a couple of grandbabies. Did I get that wrong? Or are ye estranged?"

"That's none of your business," she snapped.

With a dismissive shrug, Angus replied. "I suppose not. I'll pick ye up out front in fifteen minutes." He tried not to be offended at her sigh of relief when he turned and went out through the front door. When his cell rang, he plucked it from his pocket. It was Dorothy, his son's wife calling.

"How do ye fend, lassie?"

"Fine, Dad, we are fine. I tried to call Lucerne to catch a ride into Inverness with her today and she's not answering her phone. Is she already gone?"

"Nay, she and Darro are having a discussion."

There was silence for a moment. "Oh...well...I don't want to disturb her."

"Don't worry, ye won't be," he replied with a chuckle. "Besides, Lucerne isn't going into town today, so Macy and I are running the errands. Ye're welcome to ride with us or we can pick somethin' up for ye."

"I really need to shop for myself," she replied. "I'll be right over."

The phone clicked in his ear and he shook his head and dropped it into his pocket. Bo and Misty stuck their noses into his palms as he started off the deck. Chuckling, he fussed with them for a minute. "Misty, it's too bad human females aren't as easy to understand as ye are. All ye require is food, a warm place to sleep, and cuddling now and then." He gave them both one last pat and then pointed at the front door. "Ye both stay now, the master will be out shortly and ye know he likes ye to be waitin' fer him."

Both dogs dropped to a sitting position and stayed there as he headed down the steps and onto the flagstone path.

He could have dropped by and picked Dorothy up, but apparently that hadn't occurred to his daughter-in-law. After all, they were only 10 minutes away. "The vagaries of the lassies," he muttered to himself as he went behind the barn to get his pickup. "Either yappin' yer leg off or silent as a tombstone in a graveyard when ye try to talk to it. This might be a good time to stop by Happy Housekeepers and have that talk with Jamie."

"Talking to yerself is a bad sign, ye know. It means the lass has ye in shreds."

Angus spun around to see Dal coming out of the other end of the barn, his eyes dancing and teasing. "Ye just be minding yer own business, lad," he growled. "Get yer arse back to work, ye aren't getting' paid to pester the adults."

"Aye, aye, sir," Dal replied with a laugh and ducked back inside the barn before Angus could retort.

Angus shook his head with a grin and got into his pickup. If two women together didn't take at least two hours in the grocery store, he'd be very surprised. Should give him plenty of time to pick up Darro's requests and have a cup of tea with Jamie before they went phone shopping. If they went phone shopping.

He would have liked to have some time alone with Macy, but at the rate things were going, it would be a long silent drive. Mayhap Dorothy could break up the tension and the ride would at least be pleasant.

Starting his truck, he backed out and came around front. When he pulled up to the flagstone walkway, Macy was just coming out of the house and Dorothy was just pulling in. He got out and went around to help the women into his truck. It was pretty high and neither of them had much height on them. They'd be lucky if they were 5 feet tall with a few more inches. "Yer chariot awaits, lass." He grinned at Macy and opened the door, then picked her up by the waist and set her on the seat before she could lift a foot.

"Oh," Macy gasped. "T-thank you, but I could have climbed in...I think."

"It's a tall step fer a wee mite like yerself," he replied with a teasing grin, enjoying the blush that was stealing up her throat. He decided he liked throwing her off kilter.

"Hey, Dad," Dorothy greeted as she rushed up. Her blonde locks were slightly out of order and her face was pink.

"Ye didna have to get in such a hurry, lass, I would have picked ye up," he scolded gently.

"I didn't want to be a bother," Dorothy replied.

"Can ye scootch on over, Macy? Dorothy needs a lift into town today and mayhap ye lassies can discuss haggis lessons from Lucerne and do yer market shoppin' together whilst I get Darro's supplies."

At first, Macy looked like she was going to object, but then she moved over and Angus picked Dorothy up and set her on the seat beside Macy.

"Hey there, Macy," Dorothy greeted cheerfully. "Have ye tried to make the haggis on yer own yet? I tried the other night and I thought it was awful. Ben was sweet to say it wasn't bad, but even I didn't like it. I just don't understand how Lucerne cooks like a champion. I do the same thing she does but mine never turns out the same."

Dorothy chattered on and Angus rolled his eyes as he went around the truck to get in. His daughter-in-law was right, her cooking never tasted anything like Lucerne's. He wasn't a cook and never claimed to be, but some of the flavors that ended up in Dorothy's food had yet to be defined.

Two weeks ago, he'd warned Ben about throwing out the leftover habanero roast lamb to the chickens, but Ben hadn't caught Dorothy in time to prevent it. Since Angus could scramble eggs quite easily, and often did for a supper with his beans on toast if he didn't eat with Darro, they supplied him with fresh eggs.

Two days after the spicy lamb meal, the fresh eggs he'd received had the weirdest color of yolks he'd ever seen. Instead of the nice orangish yellow color he was used to, they looked to have a deep pinkish hue. He'd shown them to Darro who promptly said it was probably the hot peppers tainting them to a salmon color. Needless to say, he'd elected to throw them out instead of eating them.

Apparently, Ben wouldn't eat them either. He'd told Angus he could have sworn the cake Dorothy baked around that time had a hot spice in it. One bite and he hadn't eaten any more of that cake.

Idly, Angus wondered how long before the rose-colored glasses wore off and Ben was finally ready to take his little wife to task?

SITTING SO CLOSE TO Angus was messing with Macy's breathing ability. Occasionally his elbow would brush her arm when they hit a bump in the road or went through a dip. They weren't more than two inches apart but she could feel him next to her as if she were a teenager in the thrall of a date with the football quarterback once again. One thing it did do for her was make her realize how lonely her life had actually been with Julian.

Julian, Andrea's father Sam, and Macy, had all met in college. Sam and Julian had immediately been in competition for Macy's interest, but it was Sam she'd fallen in love with. Although Sam didn't have the money and family that Julian had, he'd graduated in financial investments and stock analysis and had done well for their little family. Andrea had been their only child, much to the despair of both of them. And then tragedy had struck.

"What do ye think, Macy?"

Macy was brought back to the present with a start. "What? Oh, I'm sorry, Dorothy, my mind wandered. What was the question?"

"That's easy to do with country like this around ye, Macy," Angus inserted, patting her left knee. "It's a beauty that takes yer breath away."

"Yes, it does," Macy hastily agreed. It wasn't the countryside that was taking her breath away at the moment, the touch of Angus's hand on her leg was more than enough to do that. She regretted wearing shorts now. With every hair on the left side of her body seeming to be begging his attention, she was very uncomfortable. Were her hormones just out of whack? Was she going through menopause already? What the heck was making her feel like a dopey meme with hearts for eyes every time she got near the man?

"Aye," agreed Dorothy with a chuckle. "I asked ye if ye've tried haggis yet?"

Macy shuddered. "That's on the agenda for tonight. Lucerne is going to make some and show me how she does it. Then the next time we have it, I'll make it. Are you coming for the lesson tonight?"

"Nay, I've already had that lesson...three times," she replied with a deep sigh. "I just can't seem to get it right."

The peep Dorothy shot her from the corner of her eye made Macy slightly suspicious. Was there something more going on than Dorothy failing to learn from her cooking lessons? Lucerne told her she'd been giving the girl classes for the last year. Cooking simply wasn't that hard. The art of making simple, hearty, stick-to-the ribs foods were just basics every woman should know just from watching their mothers cook through the years.

"Did you do much cooking as a teenager at home, Dorothy?"

A sudden pink flush crept up Dorothy's throat. "I-I didn't do much. My mum preferred to cook for the family."

Macy took pity on her. "Do you have a big family?"

"Uh...nay...not really. Just two sisters and a brother, plus me, Dad and Mum."

"Does your Mum work," Macy asked, now even more curious.

"Nay...nay she doesn't work. Dad always said a woman's work is in the home," she added with a touch of sarcasm.

Angus jumped in with a comment. "I'd say a lasses *best* work is in the home," he replied gently. "But if she wants to add to the household income or develop other skills outside of that, there's no reason not to."

"Now that's surprising," Macy remarked, staring at Angus. "I would have sworn you were the male chauvinist type. Barefoot and pregnant and all that nonsense."

Angus's brown eyes suddenly danced. "I hadn't heard that expression but I used to like that too, in my day. Are ye the *stay-at-home* type mum or a worker?"

Flustered, Macy responded without thinking. "A combination of both. Since Sam and I were only blessed with one child, I put my college education to good use as well."

"Good for ye. What did ye do?"

"I worked with investments, like my husband."

"Were ye good at it?"

"Very good."

"Then I need to grab ye up and marry ye so ye can double my investments," he teased. "I could use a good cook too, of course."

Macy stared, not sure what to say but realized she'd already said too much. How did the man do it? "I-I'm not in the market for a husband," she stuttered, shrinking emotionally away and closing mental doors.

"That's all right," Angus replied cheerfully. "I can take both without marriage if ye just want to move in with me."

"Dad!" Dorothy stared at Angus with her mouth open, trying not to giggle. "Ye are embarrassing Macy."

Angus waggled his eyebrows and winked. "I was just hopin' to steal her away from Darro as my housekeeper. What did ye think I meant?"

Dorothy shook her head and patted Macy's other leg. "Ignore him, Macy, everyone else does."

"Now that's disrespectful, lass," scolded Angus. "I can see I need to have Ben take ye in hand."

"Hah! That's never going to happen."

"I wouldna be too sure, lass. Ye sound like ye need a good bottom warmin'."

"You surely wouldn't encourage your son to beat his wife, would you?" Macy's heart hammered as a shot of adrenaline hit her. Sam had threatened to spank her a few times but had never followed through. She hadn't known whether to be relieved or disappointed at the time. Julian was too sophisticated and cultured to ever make threats. His silent frown of disapproval had been all it took to make her feel like a bug under a microscope.

"A spankin' is no a beatin'," Angus assured her. "Sometimes a lass can benefit from it."

"That's one opinion," Macy replied with a frown.

Dorothy just shook her head and giggled. "Like I said, Macy. Just ignore Dad, he loves to tease and get folks riled up."

From the raised eyebrow Angus shot his daughter-in-law, Macy wasn't so sure Angus was just teasing. For some reason, that made her pulse trip even faster.

"I WONDERED HOW LONG it would take before ye came sniffing around to talk about Macy, Angus. It's been two weeks already."

Jamie MacNamara chuckled as he poured two cups of hot tea and placed them on the table in the kitchenette of The Happy Housekeeper's office.

Angus snorted. "Ye know I always drop by when I'm in town, so don't pretend it's me that wants to talk about the lassie. Ye're the one bringing her up."

Jamie huffed. "I hired her, so naturally I wonder how she's doing."

"What? Ye don't talk to yer own daughter every day?" Angus eyed him skeptically.

"Well...aye," he admitted. "Lucerne says Macy's doing well after the setback with her ankle. She just needs to brush up on her housekeeping and cooking skills. The kids like her and that's the most important thing, so it looks like she's working out for the household. That's my only interest. What's yers?"

"A bonnie lass like that and ye have no interest? Verra hard to believe," Angus scoffed.

"She can no hold a candle to my Rhonda," Jamie assured him suavely.

Angus studied the retired traveling businessman now running his daughter's housekeeping business. Surprisingly enough, they'd hit it off pretty well when Lucerne had become engaged to Darro. He and Jamie actually had quite a bit in common, both being raised around sheep. Neither of them was one for gossip, but something felt off about Macy, so Angus plowed on in the conversation.

"Did ye know that she's actually American and not Canadian? And that she's from *Chicago*?"

"Nay, I didn't know that, but what does that have to do with anything?"

Angus drummed his fingers on the table. "That city doesn't have the best reputation in the world, ye know. And I get a definite feelin' that the lass is afraid of somethin'."

Jamie's head shot up. "Beyond the fact that Chicago has been voted the number one best US big city as a world class travel destination six times in a row, why would ye think she was afraid?"

"So what?" Angus argued with a worried frown. "Chicago also has the reputation for bein' one of the most dangerous cities in America. Mayhap she got involved in somethin' she shouldna been involved in. I know ye aren't supposed to talk about yer clients, but that lass is hidin' somethin'. I can read people a lot better than most, if ye ken my meanin'. Somethin's up with her."

Jamie rolled his eyes, and then nodded with a sigh. "All I'll say is that she asked for complete privacy, and that if anyone should come around asking about her, that we don't know her."

"So, she is runnin' from somethin'...or someone." Angus leaned forward eagerly. "And has anyone come around asking fer her?"

"Nay, no one."

Angus huffed and sat back in his chair. "Bugger."

Jamie sat back and folded his hands behind his head, his blue eyes gleaming. "Ye're the one with the highland gossip network, do some digging."

Angus eyed the chair Jamie was leaning back in with the two front legs off the floor and wondered if he'd be quick enough to push it on backwards. "I don't gossip. I have family and friend connections in places that provide all sorts of interestin' information should it be needed," he retorted. "And fer yer information, we call it the Sinh, short for Sangster's information network hub."

Jamie chortled. "Sounds more like the telephone tree for the Ladies Aid Society."

"Make fun if ye want, but it works."

"So, show me."

Angus huffed and started typing in something on his phone, his fingers flying, then set his phone down, a grin playing on his lips. "I put the word out."

Jamie rolled his eyes and got up to grab some biscuits to go with their tea. While he was up, Angus's phone began dinging.

Angus studied his phone for a minute, then looked up. "Macy Kennedy checked into the Travel Lodge and rented a car at Budget Rentals on the same day, both with cash. Her name isn't to be given to anyone per strict instructions. She only spent one night at the hotel, the car hasn't been returned yet, no one has been askin' about her, and no one knows where she is."

Jamie's mouth dropped open and he flopped down into his chair, spilling the biscuits as he did so. "Cripes," he swore softly, impressed. "I have to hand it to ye, Angus, it does work."

Angus grabbed a few biscuits from the pile lying on the table and smirked. "It also tells me the wee lass is on the run."

A FLOWER FOR ANGUS

Jamie nodded. "It does sound that way. No cards, just cash, the first job she could find in a remote location…it all adds up."

"And barely in town for 24 hours," Angus added with pride. "She's a smart one. The question bein'…is she on the lam?"

"On the lam?"

"Don't ye know anythin'?" Angus scoffed. "It means is she runnin' from the law?"

Jamie frowned. "I can't see a wee thing like her being a criminal. She doesn't fit the profile."

"How many criminals have ye known?"

"None personally."

Angus nodded. "Exactly. Now that ye know the basics, what did she tell ye about herself?"

"I already told ye what she said," Jamie replied testily.

Angus stared. "That's all ye got? Ye didn't find out anythin' personal about her or ask for references? As an employer, ye're either daft or besotted to have hired her," he accused.

Just then Angus's cell phone rang.

"Dad? It's Dorothy. Macy and I are finished shopping and we're hungry. Can we get some lunch?"

"I'll be right there to pick ye up," Angus replied. "I've got to go," he told Jamie, slipping the cell phone in his pocket.

Jamie stood up, an irritated flush on his face. "For yer information, I'm neither daft nor besotted. Macy just seemed like she needed help so I did what I felt was right. If ye are that worried, check her purchases to make sure she didn't buy a knife to slip between yer ribs on the way home," he added sarcastically.

Angus grinned. "No need to get yer back up, I would of done the same thing. I get the feelin' she's in some sort of trouble and I intend to find out what it is."

"I tried to get more information out of her, but she wouldn't say anything."

"That's cause ye are lackin' the Angus charm. I'll have her talkin in no time."

Jamie rolled his eyes. "Lord, preserve us from criminals and bampots."

Angus smirked over his shoulder as he went out the back door. "Ye're just jealous."

Chapter 5

"Where do ye lasses want to eat?" Angus asked as they left the market.

Dorothy's eyes lit up and she bounced on her seat. "The Waterfront! Can we please go to The Waterfront Pub for fish and chips?"

"Unless you have a McDonalds, I don't know anything about the diners you have here," Macy added with a laugh. "McDonalds I know."

Angus glanced sideways at her. "Would ye prefer McDonalds?"

Macy could see that he wouldn't prefer it but then she didn't either. This was her chance to eat the local food. "Not necessarily. I'd prefer to try local cuisine while I'm here, especially from one of the infamous pubs that seem to dot the UK."

"Then The Waterfront it is. They have Haggis bon bons ye can sample," he added with a teasing grin.

Macy wrinkled her nose. "I hope they have something strong enough to wash them down with."

"Oh, aye, they have a great selection of whiskey flights. We export some of the best whiskey in the world from the Inverness distilleries. One of the oldest, The Singleton Distillery sits on land that the Mackenzie clan has owned for

700 years. It has a long history of famous single malts. We should take a distillery tour sometime."

"I'm afraid I don't know anything about how liquor is produced. When I drink, it's usually white wine," Macy replied, ignoring the hint of a possible date.

Angus grinned. "Noted. The bon bons come in a whiskey sauce, so mayhap that will help."

"I love the fish and chips," Dorothy enthused. "All their food is really good though."

Angus found a place to park and they walked to the pub. The cheerful blue wood signs on the stone background of the pub front, and the hanging pots of flowers were inviting and appealing as they approached the building.

Before they entered, Angus stopped them both. "Before we go in and get to the end of this meal and start arguin' about who's goin' to pay, this is my treat."

"I'm good with that," piped up Dorothy. "Thanks, Dad." She beamed at him.

"I can pay for my meal," Macy insisted with a frown. She didn't want to be beholden to Angus or encourage him.

"Do ye want to embarrass me in front of my friends?" Angus asked with a horrified scowl, his tone no longer jovial as he glared at Macy.

Macy's breath caught. "What do you mean?"

"I have a friend who works here and if Jonny sees ye payin' for yer own meal, he'll ban me from the pub. That just isn't done here in Scotland, lass."

Dorothy was giggling behind her hand and Macy didn't know what to think. Was Angus serious? Then again, when was Angus ever serious?

A FLOWER FOR ANGUS

"I've never heard of such a tradition," she finally scoffed, a grin hovering around her lips. "But if the future of your membership and palate is at stake, I'll do my part to see that it isn't destroyed."

"Ye are verra kind, lass," Angus replied with a satisfied grin as he opened the door and waved her and Dorothy through.

Inside the light, airy pub, the waiter led them to a table where they could see the view from the windows. "I always think of pubs as having low lighting, with high-backed private booths, and heavy wood floors that creek when you walk across them," Macy remarked as they were seated.

"What would ye like to drink?" the pretty young waitress asked politely.

"White wine for the ladies and I'll take yer best Whiskey Flight. We'll also have the haggis bon bons appetizer, and then fish and chips all around," Angus ordered.

"Dad, ye should bring Macy back here for dinner sometime," Dorothy chirped. "The seafood here is fabulous, Macy."

"She's right about that, the seafood is really great," Angus added, his eyes gleaming at her from across the table.

Macy was relieved when Angus started looking through the dessert menu. She shot Dorothy a disapproving side eye but the young girl was oblivious. From Dorothy's enthusiasm it was obvious that she loved food, but after discussing the upcoming haggis lesson for tonight at the market, she got the feeling that Dorothy didn't really want to cook. Her real interest, besides spending time with her husband, was her work. She positively glowed when she talked about it.

Her choices for her recipe ingredients that she had written down from Lucerne were just the first brand she came to. There was no careful selection of spices, cut of meats, or the vegetables. It was as if she had absolutely no interest in fixing food at all and didn't care what they ate. Her most careful selections were the junk food she picked up and her brand of tea.

And she had to admit, the lessons she had joined with Dorothy and Lucerne showed a decided lack of interest on Dorothy's part. She couldn't help but wonder when the penny would drop for Ben?

Oh well, it wasn't any of her business, they were all family and she was just the housekeeper. She smiled warmly at the waitress bringing their drinks and appetizer.

Macy didn't know what to expect when Angus spooned one of the haggis bon bons on a saucer for her and covered it with the whiskey cream sauce. It looked like there was no way out of her tasting it.

"There ye are lass, give that a go."

With a sigh, she speared the dark round blob with her fork and then delicately nipped off the tiniest piece she could get between her two front teeth. The whiskey sauce was delicious and smooth, which was a pleasant surprise. The tiny bit of haggis had a good taste as well. She took a bigger bite and gave this one a fair chew.

"It's actually quite good," she exclaimed. "It's not at all what I thought it would be. The casing reminds me of our smoked sausages but our sausages don't have oat fillers. At least I don't think they do." She popped the rest of it in her mouth.

"Atta lass," Angus praised. "Haggis is a dish born of tradition. It's a party favorite for Burns night."

"What's Burns night?" Macy asked curiously.

"It's when we celebrate the birth of the poet Robert Burns," Angus explained. "He was Scottish ye know, and even wrote a poem with a tribute to haggis in it."

"It's celebrated on January 25th every year. Burns was born in 1759, so Scotland has been celebrating the man for a long time," Dorothy added with a dry chuckle. "It's tradition."

The waiter delivered steaming fish and chips to their table and Macy and her two companions dug in. "Mm...this is really good," Macy mumbled through biting into a fat chip. "I'll have to remember this place."

"We'll make a Scot out ye if ye're here very long," Angus boasted. They all laughed and no one realized that someone was watching them intently.

VINCE GALLO HAD ALL but given up finding Mrs. Condoloro, and now, here she was, eating fish and chips with some locals right out in plain view. Since asking questions of the locals might get back to her if she was here, he'd been hacking into the airline's records for verification with no results. He couldn't find any credit card purchases with the local motels or car rentals and they didn't have a Macy Kennedy in their records. He'd also been acting like a tourist and taking tours, hoping to catch a glimpse of her somewhere along the way. In short, doing everything he could to blend in.

All that crap you see on TV isn't near as easy in real life. Answers don't just pop up at your fingertips when you start looking for somebody in an unknown location.

Like he'd told Adrian, she'd used a credit card for the flight to Heathrow under her real name, but then she'd dropped off the face of the earth. He hadn't been able to find Macy Kennedy anywhere. It looked like he'd caught a break now though.

He'd been working on his own fish and chips when they'd suddenly appeared. Since he was seated discretely at a small table in a back corner, per his request given his line of work, he'd ducked his head into his newspaper and her glance had swept by him without recognition.

As careful as you try to be, when someone is in hiding, they are doubly suspicious of everyone and everything, and she was no exception. Her uneasy glances about the restaurant finally seemed to relax once they were seated and ordering. She must have run from Toronto because she'd made him or his car at some point. Here, when he wasn't playing tourist, he'd tried to fit in more with the locals and had adopted a plain brown beret with a plaid band on the cap and given up his Chicago Bears T-shirt. He'd also cut off the beard he'd had while in Canada.

After hitting nothing but dead ends in Dublin, he'd headed to Inverness on the off chance she'd been drawn back here. It was almost as if she'd wanted her stepson to know she was leaving the country. He might try to follow, but the UK was a big place to get lost in. Without any leads after she got off in London, he wouldn't have known where to go if not for the photographs.

He had to give her credit, staying off the grid wasn't easy to do. She hadn't even phoned her daughter back in Chicago once that he could tell. Surreptitiously, he snapped a few photos of her and her companions, proof to Condoloro of where she was. His job would be finished once he found out where she was staying. He couldn't help studying her though, because she didn't fit the profile that he'd been led to believe.

Before he'd left Chicago, he'd had Ernie do a deep dive on Adrian Condoloro and hadn't liked what he'd found. His father had cousins tied into a local mob in south Chicago, and Adrian had been involved in some shady deals and borrowing money for gambling debts. Condoloro stocks had been slipping under Adrian's leadership and there were rumors that his company was bleeding cash. Vince figured that's why the man was so obsessed with breaking his father's will.

That had led to a lot of other speculation that was worrisome. Such as why Condoloro had even hired him knowing he was old-school? Did it make him more expendable? Now there was a gruesome thought.

Through a stroke of good fortune for Vince, here she was, living off the grid and acting nothing like the reported money-grubbing socialite who'd managed to off her rich husband and not get charged for it. He grimaced and took another sip of his beer. Damned good beer they had here in Inverness, he had to admit. A fellow could get used to living in a place like this if you could find the work. And the best golden battered fish and plump French fries he'd ever eaten. Or chips as they were called here. Once he'd found this place, McDonalds had hit the bottom on his food list.

Seeing that the subject of his troublesome thoughts and her companions were finishing up their food, he shoved the last chip in his mouth, swallowed the last drop of his beer, and shoved his chair back. He needed to find a vantage point where he could observe when they left the pub. Passing their table to leave was unavoidable, but he brushed on by without making eye contact, his phone pressed to his ear as if he were having a conversation and couldn't be bothered by his surroundings. His skin prickled though, and he knew she'd looked at him. He had a sixth sense about things like that and it had saved his life on a few occasions.

Had she made him though?

"WE NEED TO GET MOVIN' if we're goin' to get ye a cell phone and get back to Neamh," Angus remarked, glancing at his watch. "Are ye lasses about finished? We might even get a look around the Victorian Market."

Macy took the last drink of her wine, her fingers trembling on the stem of the glass. "I-I just want to get back to Neamh," she insisted. "I really don't need a phone right now, Angus."

Angus had noted her face pale slightly when the last pub patron had left. His sharp gaze latched onto the tall, older man's back as he went out the door. The man didn't stop to pay at the counter, so he must have left payment on his table. In fact, Macy hadn't been very relaxed since they'd arrived in town. Her furtive glances around her everywhere they went had convinced him even more that she was in hiding.

"I'm headed to the loo, Dad, I'll be right back," Dorothy announced, pushing her chair back.

"Don't fall in," Angus teased.

"Och, Dad."

As soon as Dorothy left the table, Angus leaned forward and placed his hand over Macy's. It was cold and trembling. "If ye admit to me that yer hidin' from somethin', Macy, I'll no take ye to get that phone because it would explain a lot of yer behavior since ye've come to Neamh."

She looked straight down her little nose with a glare that would have frozen him on the spot if he'd been a lesser man. "I just don't want a phone, is that so hard to believe?"

"Don't lie to me, lass. I'll get the truth, one way or another," he growled sternly, all teasing and banter done. "No judgements, Macy, we'll talk about it later, but I want the truth about that phone right now. I *mean* it." He used his commanding voice that made the men under him jump to do his bidding and she responded, albeit reluctantly. He had to admit she was a plucky wee thing.

With a stubborn grunt, she finally nodded, and then pulled her hand from beneath his. "Yes, but it's still none of your business."

Angus leaned back, satisfied for the moment. "Since we have a little time then, would ye like to take a tour of Inverness? I can drive ye around and show ye a few things if ye like."

Sudden panic flared in her eyes. "N-No, let's just go home."

Interesting that she'd used the word home after only two weeks on the job. It made Angus want to curl his arm around her, tuck her into his side, and take her to Thistlewind where he could protect her from whatever was haunting her. And put her over his knee if she refused to talk to him.

His eyes narrowed as he studied the flush beginning to replace the color in her face. "If we drive around a bit, we might see if we pick up a tail," he replied evenly. "The man who just passed us caught yer attention. Is he stalkin' ye?"

"Yes…no…maybe. I'm not sure," she grudgingly admitted.

"But there *is* someone stalkin' ye," he insisted.

Macy scowled at him. "All right…yes. I believe there is someone stalking me, but I don't want to talk about it."

Angus persisted. "If he *was* someone ye recognize, he left early enough to get into place to follow us after we leave."

Her eyes lit up with worry as she suddenly chewed on her lip. "H-He did seem familiar. His size and body shape, the way he moved, little things like that. But if he's the same man from Toronto, then he's cut off his beard and isn't dressed like he normally would be."

"That's normal, if he's following ye. He would want to blend in with the area," Angus agreed, feeling like he was finally getting somewhere. His tone softened and he reached for her hand again. "I've known somethin' was bothering ye ever since ye arrived at Neamh. Let me help ye, Macy."

The sudden confusion and doubt on her face told him that whatever had happened, she felt helpless to do anything about it but run. He was going to reassure her, but then he saw Dorothy coming back so he stood up instead. "Looks like the lass didna fall in after all, so let's get on out of here," he teased his daughter-in-law as she rushed up to the table.

"I'm ready," Dorothy gushed.

They drove around for about an hour, Angus and Dorothy pointing out local sights such as the joining of the River Ness and the Moray Firth. The river Ness flowed from Loch Ness, the legendary lake of the monster the locals called Nessie. The fresh water was a boon to the city of Inverness and sported some of the best fishing in the area. Then it fed into the Moray Firth, which flowed on to the sea. Angus kept a sharp eye for a tail in the mirror.

"I'd love to do some hiking along the Ness River," Macy said wistfully. "It's so beautiful, and I love the walkways going into the islands in the middle. Inverness has really grown, hasn't it?"

"Ye sound like ye've been here before," Dorothy replied curiously.

Angus side eyed Macy, noting her sudden confusion. "Well...a-actually I was...but it was a long time ago," she confessed. "So much has changed since I was here. And it was only for a few days, so I didn't get to see much."

At last, another crumb of information.

He turned right at the next corner near the clock tower. Angus was betting the stranger had rented a car, and that was what he'd been looking for. Unfortunately, there were many car rental places in the popular tourist destination of Inverness, and dozens of rented cars floating around. Even Macy had one.

"Have ye been to Culloden?" he asked her.

Her eyes lit up. "No, but I've seen Outlander, so I'm familiar with some of the Jacobite history. I know a lot of men died there."

"Aye, they did," Angus replied soberly. "It was a total massacre, not only of men, but of a way of religion, and the beginnin' death throes of the clan's way of life."

"I know Jamie is hot in that movie," gushed Dorothy.

Angus rolled his eyes and grinned, the solemn moment behind them. "I'll tell Ben ye said that."

"Don't be a jobbie, Dad, Ben doesn't need to know everything," Dorothy scoffed, her blue eyes twinkling.

Angus narrowed his eyes in warning. "But he does need to take ye in hand, lass. Ye need to watch yer tongue with yer elders."

Macy snickered. "What's a jobbie?"

"It's a turd, Macy," Dorothy explained with an unrepentant grin.

Macy shook her head and laughed, and to Angus it was good to hear, even if he was the butt of the joke. Having him sitting next to her felt good too. He liked brushing her arm with his bare elbow, or patting the warm skin of her knee and lower thigh. Since they had been back in the truck, she'd even moved a little closer to his shoulder as if seeking his protection. It made him feel like beating his chest like a caveman and showing her that he could.

And he would.

Dorothy's cell phone dinged and she pulled it from her pocket. "It's Ben, speak of the devil."

A FLOWER FOR ANGUS

"Best let me talk to him," Angus growled and suddenly grabbed across Macy for the phone, brushing her soft breasts with his arm.

Macy gasped.

"Keep yer eyes on the road, Dad," Dorothy squealed with a giggle when they swerved slightly. She held the phone out of his reach and put it up to her ear by the window. "Oh...it's just yer dad being his usual self," she sang into the phone while giving them both a mischievous side eye.

Angus raised his voice. "Ye and I need to have a talk, lad!" He grinned down at Macy's pink face with a knowing glance, his own pulse picking up a pace.

"Ignore him, Ben. Where do ye want to meet?" Dorothy talked into the phone, holding her hand up as if shutting out something annoying.

Macy giggled at Dorothy's antics.

Dorothy put her hand over the phone. "Dad, can ye drop me off at the Victorian Market to meet Ben? He decided he wanted a break and came to town. I'll ride home with him."

Jumping at the chance to be alone with Macy, Angus nodded. "Be there in five minutes."

There weren't very many women in his life who had made his pulse race. The lass from Dublin, his Rosie, and now Macy. Without a doubt, he was attracted to Macy, even if she didn't have a flower name, and had been like a prickly pear since she'd arrived. It appeared she might just have a good reason. He couldn't help but wonder what that was? He was sure it wasn't criminal, but if it was, where did that leave him? If it was criminal, he was still sure there was a very good reason.

Instinctively, he caught her hand and squeezed it. He was delighted when she didn't jerk away from him. Criminal or not, he was very interested in the bonnie wee lass.

Chapter 6

Macy tried to pull her hand discreetly from Angus's big warm palm, but he refused to let her go. In just minutes they pulled up at an entrance to the Victorian Market. A handsome young man in jeans and a light blue polo moved eagerly towards the truck. The family resemblance was obvious.

"Ben," Dorothy squealed, opening the door and dropping into strong arms that hugged her close.

"We need to talk, Ben," Angus shot his son a knowing grin, his hand finally releasing Macy's to waggle a finger at his precocious daughter-in-law.

"Hasn't she been behaving herself?" Ben asked with a stern look at his wife.

"Of course, I have," Dorothy replied gaily. "Ben, this is Macy. I don't think ye've met her yet, have ye?"

"It's a pleasure to meet ye, Macy," Ben replied with an easy charm like his father.

"It's a pleasure to meet you as well, and your wife is lovely, Ben. Don't believe anything your dad says about her," Macy replied, throwing Dorothy a conspiratorial wink.

"The lassies are gangin' up on me, lad," Angus complained.

Ben chuckled. "Aye, I can see that."

"Ben, grab my bags out of the back, please, yer dad's blocking traffic," Dorothy intervened.

"Ye just don't want yer shortcomin's made known," Angus teased.

"Thanks for taking her with ye, Dad," Ben told his father as he closed the truck door. "We'll catch up later."

Angus chuckled at Dorothy's antics as Ben retrieved her purchases from the back of the pickup. "That lass is something else," he said fondly.

"I think she's a sweetheart," Macy replied, moving over some so she could breathe a little better. She didn't move too far because she didn't want him to think she was trying to get away from him, but at the same time, she didn't want to encourage him either by staying close when there was no need. Realizing how juvenile she was being, she rolled her eyes and looked out the window. She was too old for this kind of boy/girl anxiety. It would be a lot easier if she simply wasn't attracted to him. Unfortunately for her, she was.

"That she is," Angus replied. "Now let's talk about yer problems, lass."

"How far is it to Culloden?" she asked, trying to put him off.

"Not far at all." He shot her a stern glance. "Why do ye have a stalker, Macy?"

"I-It's a long story," she hedged.

"I've got plenty of time."

"We should probably get back to Neamh."

"Are ye mixed up in somethin' illegal?" Angus suddenly growled.

A FLOWER FOR ANGUS

"Of course not," Macy snapped back, shooting him a glance that could strip paint.

When Angus suddenly pulled into a small parking area that appeared to be a lookout for the Ness River, she held her breath. He did a U-turn, then parked facing the road from the small stand of trees nearby. "W-What are you doing?"

"I'm facin' the road to see if anyone appears to be followin' us," he growled as he turned toward her. "But I'm also giving ye a chance to start talkin' before I have to put ye across my knee."

She gawped at him. Was he for real? "Look here, Angus," she finally sputtered indignantly, "I'm not a young girl with stars in her eyes like Dorothy, or a child. I'll charge you with assault if you even attempt anything like that." Her pulse picked up rapidly when he didn't seem to be impressed.

"So, ye're goin' to go back on yer word? At the restaurant we had a deal. I wouldn't take ye to get a phone, and ye would tell me what was goin' on the first chance we got."

"I never promised," she protested. "I just told you what you wanted to hear and to avoid an argument." That ploy had served her well with both Sam and Julian in the past and had made life easier for her.

Angus's eyebrows threatened to escape his skull, then lowered with a warning glare. "That may have been the way ye treated yer husband but that won't fly with me, wee lass. I'll have answers or ye'll soon have a sore bottom."

"It's none of your business," she yelped, getting angry.

He didn't say anything, just stared at her as if he were planning his next move. It was very unnerving. She stared defiantly back.

When she'd defied Sam or Julian at this point in an argument, they had merely turned around and left the room. It seemed Angus was made of sterner stuff. Either that or he didn't intend to get out of his truck. The incongruous thought suddenly struck her as humorous in a crazy way as she imagined driving off and leaving him behind.

"Look, Macy," Angus began evenly. "Ye've been actin' like ye are hiding from somethin' or someone ever since ye got to Neamh. Ye don't talk about yerself unless it's an accidental slip, and ye guard yer words like they are the queen's jewels and can't be spent on the rest of us. Ye finally admitted ye may have a stalker and it's obvious ye're running scared. I want to know why. I'm ready to help ye. I know Darro will be willin' to help ye too, but ye have to let us in."

Macy almost crumbled. Almost. Until she realized that if they tried to help her, their inquiries would certainly lead Adrian right to her. If the man in the restaurant wasn't the man she'd seen in Toronto, then she was still safe. She couldn't risk it. Shaking her head at Angus, she replied, "I can't."

"Can't or won't?"

"Okay, won't," she sassed.

"Last chance, Macy," Angus said firmly.

"Or what?" Macy scoffed. She didn't believe he would actually follow through on his ridiculous threat. People their age didn't act like that.

Angus suddenly slid towards her in a quick efficient movement. Then he grabbed the back of her jean shorts with one hand, and with the other arm across her breasts, he suddenly lifted and tipped her over his broad lap where she landed face down in the driver's seat. The warmth of the leather where he had been sitting was suddenly up against the side of her face. His muscled arm was now effectively pinning her down. When the first of many spanks from his hard right palm burned through her jeans, it finally dawned on her that he meant business.

"Let go of me," she yelled as several unladylike curses assuring dire retribution sprang from her lips. "I mean it, Angus, I'll have you arrested," she shouted, her voice breaking as the heat and pain began to build in her rear. He didn't show any signs of stopping either.

Frantically, she pushed her knees against the seat, her toes against the floorboards, and tried to grab the steering wheel with her right hand, but all her struggles were completely ineffective. He didn't miss a spank in his steady rhythm.

"You have to stop," she finally wailed as tears spurted into her eyes. She couldn't take much more of the heavy-handed punishment. No one had ever spanked her before, not even when she was a child. Her butt must be glowing from the heat he was dishing out.

"Are ye ready to talk?"

He paused for a moment and she could feel the weight of his hand through her jeans where it lay on her bottom. When he squeezed her right cheek, she gasped in pain.

"You can't help me, you'll just give me away," she finally choked out. "I-I can't risk that, Angus."

"Can ye tell me if whoever ye are hidin' from is dangerous? Are ye in fear of yer life?"

Angus turned her red face sideways where she could look up at him. "I-I don't know for sure," she admitted desperately. "I just know there have been some unnerving incidents which is why I ran. I didn't feel safe in Chicago or Toronto anymore."

Angus's phone received a text notification and he took it from his shirt pocket and opened his messages. It was from his friend at the pub where they had eaten lunch.

'A tall stranger came in about 30 minutes ago and showed me a picture of you and claimed you were an old friend he'd lost track of. Wanted to look you up while he was visiting Scotland. Not positive but I think he was here earlier eating lunch around the same time you were. Had tourist cap on with a fake clan plaid.'

'Did you tell him anything?' Angus texted back. The stranger must have snapped his pic while they were eating.

'Nothing, but it's only a matter of time before someone will.'

Angus pulled Macy up and sat her beside him and then showed her the text message. "Now ye're no the only one in trouble, Macy, everyone at Neamh is at risk if this man is dangerous. Tell me what's goin' on, or I'll turn ye back over and ye won't sit for week when I'm done with ye."

"Oh no," Macy cried, her trembling hand covering her mouth as she read the messages. "Why can't he just leave me alone? I'm so sorry, Angus, I was just trying to put the past behind me and start new somewhere out of his reach. I wasn't trying to put anyone else in danger."

"Are ye talkin' about the stalker? Do ye know who he is?" Angus insisted.

"Not the stalker, I'm talking about my stepson," she replied, the tears running down her cheeks. "I got scared when the brakes suddenly failed on my car, so I left Chicago and moved to Toronto. I think the stalker is probably someone Adrian hired to find where I'd gone. Do you have a Kleenex in the glove?"

Angus handed her a napkin from above the passenger's visor.

Macy wiped her eyes and tried to get control of herself with a deep breath. "I'd seen someone who physically resembled the man we saw in the pub outside my home in Toronto driving by in a blue car. I saw the same man in the grocery store when I went shopping a few times. That same blue car would sometimes appear behind my car at random times before turning down a side street. I tried to tell myself that whoever it was must live in the area, but after my home had been entered, I really became suspicious and afraid."

"Did ye call the police?"

"Yes, I talked to them. Nothing was stolen and there was no sign of visible entry, so they couldn't make a report. But I knew someone had been in the house because things were out of place."

"Why is your stepson havin' ye followed?" Angus asked with a fierce frown.

She hesitated, staring up at him for a moment before she finally went on. "He's trying to contest his father's will," she admitted with a heavy sigh. "And he thinks I had something to do with Julian's heart attack, but I didn't." Tears welled up in her eyes again.

"There now, lass, steady on," Angus said softly, squeezing her hand.

She nodded and wiped her eyes again. "If I hadn't decided to go with my daughter to the mall the day Julian died, I think he would have succeeded in having me charged with trying to kill my husband."

If Angus's eyebrows could go any higher, they would have receded into his hairline. "Cripes, Macy!"

Macy focused straight ahead, the horrific memories of that day rushing back in on her. "I-I was actually supposed to be at home that day, but Julian made me go with my daughter Andrea. He said he would be fine by himself and didn't want me hovering over him, so I went. Oh, Angus, if I had been home..." Her words trailed off and she shuddered.

"Was yer husband murdered then?" Angus asked gently, putting his arm around her and pulling her in close. He expected her to pull away and was glad when she didn't.

"The coroner ruled it an accidental death," she droned on. "There was no suicide note, but his blood had triple the dosage of his heart meds in it. The same dosage that was missing from the pill bottle. Adrian found him several hours after I left.

"According to rigor mortis timing, I wouldn't have been at the house when he took his meds. And they knew he'd taken them because they found the bottle on the nightstand next to his water bottle. The coroner said he just fell asleep and didn't wake up. It was a suspicious death, which is why they did an autopsy, but Adrian had an alibi the same as me. With no other evidence of foul play, the DA quickly went with an accidental overdose ruling."

"Was Julian home alone that day?"

She nodded. "Normally his mother, Edna, would be home, but she happened to be playing bridge at a friend's house that day. She lives in a separate wing of the house and rarely came into the main part of the home. Edna didn't like me and considered me a gold-digger like her grandson, Adrian."

"Somethin' tells me yer nightmare didn't end after the death rulin'," Angus mused.

Macy shuddered. "Then the will was read and Adrian went ballistic. He became obsessed with having me charged with murder and insisted on dragging me into court to contest the will over and over. The tabloids were having a field day and making not only my life miserable, but my daughter and her family as well. He just wouldn't stop, so after several appearances in court, I tried to move out of his reach."

"Why would he contest the will?"

"Adrian never liked me," she confessed. "He was convinced I was a gold digger, but it wasn't true. When Julian left me with some really good investment portfolios and a nice sum of cash, Adrian was furious. He insisted that his father didn't want me to have anything according to the prenuptial agreement, which was true, so I didn't expect anything. But what we didn't know, is that Julian had his lawyer change the prenup so that I wouldn't be left penniless if something happened to him. Not that I would have been. Julian was very generous with a private allowance put into a bank account for me above and beyond what we shared as a couple.

"Adrian never realized it, but the investments Julian left me were ones I had advised him on. I was delighted that they had done so well. He left a good sum of ready cash because he was leaving the family ancestral home and everything else to his only child. It was all above board and Mack, that's the lawyer, insisted the will was ironclad. But Adrian wouldn't give up."

"And now here ye are, on the run, off grid, and takin' a housekeepin' job just to survive," Angus growled, shaking his head.

"D-Do you believe me, Angus?" Macy asked tentatively, peeping up at him. "Because if you do, you would be one of a select few. The papers didn't do me any favors when it all came out because Adrian kept dragging me back into court. Being crucified in the court of public opinion was devastating." She shivered again, her fingers trembling as she tugged a lock of hair behind her ear.

"COME HERE, LASS," ANGUS said gruffly, pulling her into his lap and hugging her tight. "I may not know ye, but I believe ye. It sounds like ye've been through the fires of hell."

Macy put her face in his shoulder and sobbed with relief. Her bottom hurt and she was getting a headache from crying, but this man she was attracted to was willing to believe her. That meant a lot. She knew she shouldn't be in his lap like this, but it did feel really good to be held. "Maybe I won't have you arrested after all," she croaked through her tears. "You just earned some forgiveness."

He tipped her chin up and smiled down at her. "Verra good to know, wee one, ye really had me worried."

She smacked his shoulder with her small fist and chuckled. "Jobbie."

"Now ye owe me," he replied with mock fierceness, his big thumbs brushing the tears away just before his mouth closed on hers.

His lips were warm and solid, nibbling her mouth slightly open to deepen the kiss. She could swear her toes curled as desire zinged right through her. Julian had never inspired her bloodstream like this and Sam had been a weak version. This was different altogether.

"Angus," she gasped when he finally lifted his head.

"Before ye continue to seduce me, I need to send a text to Darro and warn him."

She punched him again with her fist. "You kissed me."

"Umph," he grunted with a teasing grin. "Looks like I'll need to warm yer bottom again if ye keep that up."

She huffed and shot him a death glare but he missed it. She watched as Angus quickly sent a text to Darro that she had a stalker and to be on the alert for a stranger at Neamh. They were on their way home to explain the rest.

Angus dropped his phone in his pocket. "Jonny was right, it will only be a matter of time before yer stalker finds us. The Sangster and MacCandish families have been around for generations and everyone knows us, Macy. We need to get back to Heaven's Gate. As much as I'd love to continue this, we need to corner this guy and find out what he's doin' here."

Macy turned pale and nodded. "Do you think he means me any real harm?"

"That I don't know, but it's better to be safe than sorry."

"One more thing, Angus. My real name is Poppy Condoloro. Macy is just the name I've been hiding under," she confessed.

Angus's grin split his face. "Ye are a flower after all."

"Is that important?"

"I'll tell ye later, right now, ye need to relocate yer sweet bottom," he chuckled.

Happy to be Poppy again, she got off his lap so he could get back under the wheel. "Ouch," she complained as her bottom hit the leather seat.

"Are ye sore?" Angus asked, sliding under the wheel and starting the truck.

"I can't believe you did that, actually," she admitted. "I've never been spanked before, not by Julian or Sam."

"I have a lot of patience, wee one, but I don't make idle threats either. Ye were being unnecessarily stubborn and I called ye on it. Ye'd best remember that in the future."

Poppy didn't reply. There was too much going on in her life to consider she might have a future with another man. Did she even want that if she could? She was certainly attracted to Angus in a way she never had been to anyone, but she had never considered affairs either. Sex just hadn't been that big a deal in her life. It was nice, but not a hotbed of intense desire by any means. She wondered what he had in mind.

Caught musing, she started when he pulled on her arm to bring her closer to him. "I'm lonely over here by myself, and I need you to keep me warm. Curl in here and tell me who Sam is. I take it you were married before Julian?"

Why not? Poppy found she liked curling into his side. Being alone with Angus in the cab of his truck was surreal somehow. It felt like the outside world couldn't intrude while his arm was around her and she basked in that feeling. She'd worry about the ramifications later, right now her mind and body were enjoying their closeness. It had been so long since she'd felt so in sync with anyone.

As they made their way back to Neamh, she told him a little about her life and her family. Once she started talking, it was as if she couldn't stop. She suddenly realized how truly isolated she'd felt after Julian died.

She knew he kept asking questions to keep her mind busy so she wouldn't fret and worry, and she was grateful. His big warm body was comforting and made her feel safe—something she hadn't felt in a long time.

<hr />

"DAL!" DARRO BARKED as he strode out of the barn office. "Get Henry and a few of the boys from the fields. Medium alert status! Then get yerself and Henry to the house."

"Aye, boss." Dal dropped his medical bag and ran for the four-wheeler at the back of the barn. Like a well-oiled machine, Neamh would be quickly fortified. Neither he nor any of the other men would waste time asking questions. When Darro spoke, they just responded, already knowing the precautions that were strictly in place and well-practiced. The boss would explain when the time was right.

Darro hurried into the kitchen and locked the door behind him. His tone was a little less demanding, but an order just the same. "Lucerne, honey, I need ye to go to the study, please. Make sure ye have the key to the safe room in yer pocket. Use it if ye have any doubts as to what ye might hear. Angus texted me that someone is stalking Macy and may be coming here before they get back. That's all he knows right now. We were all correct though, there is something up with the lass," he added.

"Oh no," Lucerne squeaked with concern, turning off the stove and oven and taking off her apron.

"What's going on, Uncle Darro?" Delilah asked from the corner of the kitchen table, her face turning pale. Both children scrambled off the bench seats and she took Corey's hand, his big blue eyes wide with uncertainty.

Darro cursed silently. He'd forgotten the children had an early out day today and would be in the kitchen for their usual after school snack.

"I'm sure it's just a safety drill," Lucerne replied, taking both their hands in hers. "We've done them before, remember?"

They nodded solemnly, accepting her explanation and cuddling in close to her legs. "Can the two of ye help a pregnant lady into the study? I can't go much faster than a waddle, ye know." She smiled encouragingly at them.

"Aye, Auntie Lucerne," they chorused with eager smiles.

Darro smiled as the children immediately fell under Lucerne's calming spell. She was right, it was just a precaution, but the three, make that four, most important people in the world were right here with him. He didn't intend to take any chances with their safety.

"Aye, Lucerne is right. This is just a precaution and ye've no need to worry." He bent down to give them a hug and then patted Lucerne's rear to encourage them down the hall.

Lucerne hissed and shot him a killing glare over her shoulder, just before he kissed her. He chuckled as he watched her sassy bottom undulate down the hallway. He hadn't had to swat her luscious behind for several weeks, but interfering in his business with the hired help wasn't allowed. Of course, Macy was her hired help as well, but he still didn't expect her to countermand his orders or make excuses to an employee for his orders when he gave them. He wouldn't do that to her and he didn't expect her to do it to him. They had come to an agreement and she had apologized.

Besides, he knew she wasn't very sore because he hadn't swatted her very hard. She was just a stubborn little thing that liked to push her boundaries. The knock on the front door preceded Dal and Henry sticking their heads inside.

"Where do ye want us, boss," Henry asked.

Henry always reminded him of a beefed-up version of Peewee Herman, an old-time star of a children's show called Peewee's Playhouse. His slick black hair was cut short to his head and his eyes were perpetually wide open. He strode to the door and motioned the men outside. "Henry, you take the back door and Dal, you pretend to be busy here near the front door. I'll let ye know when I don't need ye anymore. If anyone ye don't know approaches, stop them. I'll be close by."

"Like whoever is in that car?" Dal asked pointing towards the outer road where dust was starting to rise behind an approaching vehicle. "I don't recognize that car, does anyone else?"

"Want me to stay up front boss?" Henry asked, watching the dust rise and the car get closer.

"No, watch the back, Henry," Darro replied. "There are plenty of eyes up front." His gaze narrowed and he checked around to make sure the men were putting something between themselves and the approaching vehicle as he leaned his own body against one large pillar holding the deck roof. The 9mm inside his vest pocket was just a precaution he'd grabbed from the barn after Angus texted. Never hurts to be prepared. He didn't normally wear a vest, but he kept this one handy in the barn for just such a purpose.

When the car drove into the circle drive and slowly made its way up to the front of the house, Darro watched the driver closely. When he finally pulled his tall frame out of the blue car and stood up, he could see the man matched Angus's description. The plaid on his cap didn't match any of the clans' tartans that Darro knew, which meant he'd probably bought it at a tourist shop. Dishwater blond hair, sharp eyes, and a lean figure, but no sign of a weapon.

"Turn around," Darro ordered.

"Is this Neamh?" the stranger asked coming around the front of the car.

"Bo, Misty, guard."

The dogs immediately bared their teeth and stalked towards the stranger. "I said turn around," Darro ordered again.

Holding his hands in the air with a shrug, the man turned around, calling over his shoulder, "I'm not armed, I just want to talk."

"Now ye can turn around and talk," Darro snapped after seeing there was no gun in the waistband of his jeans.

The dogs were still growling. "Can I put my hands down?" the man asked, watching them warily.

"Heel," Darro ordered curtly, relaxing his stance.

Bo stopped growling and returned to Darro's right side, Misty to his left.

"That's impressive, but do you treat all visitors this way?"

Darro ignored the compliment and asked his own question. "What's yer name and what do ye want?"

"My name is Vince Gallo. I'm a private detective and I'm looking for a woman named Poppy Condoloro, but you'll probably know her as Macy Kennedy. Is she here? And if so, can I speak with her? She could be in danger."

Darro's eyes narrowed. "From what I understand, that danger is ye, Mr. Gallo."

The stranger looked startled and disbelieving. "Me? No, no, you've got it all wrong."

Darro motioned towards the deck. "Ye can come up and have a seat whilst I text my second in command."

With Dal standing against one of the pillars and the rifle lying across his forearm, Darro was satisfied that Mr. Gallo was well secured for the moment.

Chapter 7

Angus plucked the cell phone from his shirt pocket when it went off with a text from Darro.

'He's here, how close are you?'

He quickly texted back. *'About 10 minutes out.'*

'We'll hold him for you.'

Poppy sat up straight with a worried frown. "Who was that?"

"Darro," Angus replied with a satisfied smirk. "Ye're stalker showed up and he and the lads are holdin' him."

She gasped. "He actually came to Neamh out in the open?"

"I would assume so, since Darro didn't report a shootout," Angus replied, his eyes twinkling.

Her brow furrowed. "Why would he do that?"

"I don't know, lass. I guess ye will get to ask him that. We'll be there in another few minutes."

"I don't like it," Poppy retorted, her eyes flashing. "I feel like knocking him out instead of talking to him."

"Were ye a boxer in another life?" Angus asked with a chuckle.

Poppy snorted. "For all you know, I might be a Taekwondo black belt."

"I'm looking forward to getting' to know ye, Poppy. Hopefully, you've given up yer prickly pear belt. Black belt I can handle—prickly pear not so much."

"Aren't you ever serious?" she asked, trying to keep from laughing.

"When it comes to food, I'm as serious as a judge waitin' on a jury so he can eat dinner," he assured her.

She cocked her head sideways, her pretty brown eyes bright with interest. "You are an interesting man, Angus Sangster."

"Does that mean ye are ready to move in with me?" he asked hopefully. "The offers always open and able to be upgraded with a ring. Just say the word."

She turned pink and punched him in the arm. "Dorothy's right, you are a jobbie."

Angus laughed and squeezed her hand, but he was keeping track of her punches. Maybe it was her nerves, maybe it was a habit with her husband, maybe she just wasn't sure what else to do, but it wasn't going to continue for long. Right now, he wanted to take her mind off her worries and troubles. He'd deal with her sassy habits later.

He did love the way she snuggled into his side, she fit him perfectly. He wondered how much she was actually worth in money? And would she be keeping the housekeeper's job if it turned out all her troubles were getting taken care of? Trying not to wish for miracles like rich girls falling in love with a lowly sheepherder from another country, Angus turned into the long drive leading up to the front door of Neamh.

"Would you look at that," Poppy observed. "He has a blue rental car. Do you think that's a coincidence?"

"I'd say the man likes blue," Angus responded dryly. "Was the car followin' ye in Toronto a rental?"

"I don't know, I never thought about it. I just know it was blue and it made me really nervous."

Angus could feel her hand squeezing his and he knew she was still nervous, and probably angry. He didn't blame her, but how would she react to the man?

He pulled his pickup in behind the blue car after noting Dal on the porch. A few of the other men were standing around the area with a piece of grass hanging off their lips. He knew they were armed; you just couldn't see anyone's weapon but Dal's. That was for intimidation purposes.

"Ye ready?" He turned to Poppy and she nodded, her lips pursed tightly. He helped her down from the cab of his tall truck.

When they walked past the blue car, the stranger on the porch stood up and Poppy gripped Angus's hand tighter.

"Just stay where ye are," Darro ordered the man as he stood up. "Ye can talk when she gets on the deck—provided she wants to talk to ye."

When they reached Darro, he turned to Poppy. "This man says he's here to talk to ye, Macy. Or is it Poppy?"

"It's Poppy, yes," she replied, her eyes narrowing.

"Mrs. Condoloro, I came here to warn you that you may be in danger," Vince quickly inserted.

Poppy took two steps towards him. "That's a laugh. I think Adrian put you up to following me," she bit out, temper creeping into her cheeks with a red wash. "Did you mess with the brakes on my car in Chicago? And did you come into my house in Toronto and move my things around? Were you following me everywhere I went in a blue car?"

He frowned. "My name is Vince Gallo and I'm a private detective. Yes, I drove a blue car. No, I did not mess with the brakes on your car."

"Who hired you, Mr. Gallo?" she shot back.

Vince flushed. "Your stepson did hire me to find you when you left Chicago, then asked me to stay up there and observe you. It was easy money so I took it. Now I wish I hadn't."

"Why?"

"When I returned from Toronto, your stepson was furious. He insisted I track you down and figure out where you had gone. I wanted to say no, but he made me nervous because he was armed and seemed so manic. So, I agreed to track you figuring I'd stay out of the country for a while once I found you and gave him your location."

"How *did* you find me?" Poppy asked through gritted teeth.

"Well...I did enter your home one day and looked at your photo albums. It was there that I found your picture of you and your cousin in Inverness. When I'm following a subject, I like to know all I can about them, and well...you didn't seem like a nice person based on the newspapers about your husband's death. I know that doesn't excuse it, but in my line of work..."

That was as far as he got because Poppy stalked the three steps forward to reach him and gave him a right hook in his mouth. Blood spurted immediately and he stumbled backwards with a screeching dynamo pummeling him in the chest.

Angus was as startled as everyone else, but he was the closest, so he sprang forward and grabbed Poppy around her waist and pulled her back.

"You slimy snake, you had no right to come in my home and go through my personal things," she screeched at him. "Let me go Angus, I'm going to wipe the deck with him."

"Hold on there, wee one, save some fer the rest of us. Ye got first blood," he chuckled, grabbing her arms so they would stop thrashing.

"I think ye had better talk faster, Mr. Gallo," Darro ordered with an amused grin. Dal was snickering behind him. "I don't know how long Angus can hold her off."

"Simmer down now," Angus whispered in Poppy's ear. "Don't make me have to swat yer wee bum in front of everyone."

Poppy ignored him. "If I'm such a horrible person, why are you here now? And it had *better* be good."

Vince glared back at her, nursing his bloody lip with a handkerchief. "Because after I called him to let him know where you were, he wanted me to arrange an accident. I told him no way in hell was I getting involved with hurting anyone and to do his own dirty work. He said he would and hung up on me," he snarled. "But after this, I'm not sure why I bothered to come up here and tell you."

"Did you tell him where I was?"

He nodded. "Yes, he paid me and it's my job. But I figured you could always arrange a flight out after I took off.

A FLOWER FOR ANGUS 101

He'll have to hire someone else to track you after this, I'm done."

Darro took charge after Vince's declaration. "Mr. Gallo, ye need to come inside where we can discuss this subject more thoroughly. Macy, as my employee and housekeeper, ye will control yerself and go fix us all a pot of tea, please."

"My name isn't Macy, remember?" she retorted. "It's Poppy. Poppy Condoloro."

Darro folded his arms and shot her a steely look. "Are ye still my housekeeper, or no?"

Poppy flushed and then finally nodded. "Yes, yes of course, sir. I apologize to you for my behavior in your home. I won't however, apologize to him." She flashed her thumb at Vince Gallo and then walked to the door.

"I wouldn't expect ye to, lass," Darro replied with a deep chuckle. "After ye, Mr. Gallo."

"I said what I came to say, why do you need me?" Vince asked, hesitating.

Darro's eyebrows rose. "Because I have more questions and ye aren't leaving here until I'm satisfied. One of my employees has been threatened and I don't take that lightly. While Ma...er...Poppy works for me, she is under my protection."

"Just make sure she keeps her fists to herself then," Vince retorted as he went through the doorway.

Angus snickered.

As Darro followed Vince, he turned towards Angus and curled his first finger. "Angus, reduce the men to normal status and then join us, please."

"Aye," Angus agreed.

"Woo wee...I think I'm in love," Dal exclaimed when the door closed behind Darro. "That Macy...er...Poppy...is a real scrapper."

"Keep it in yer pants, Junior," Angus snapped. "I done warned ye once, I don't want to do it again."

"Ye don't seem to be making much progress," Dal replied, practically running off the porch when Angus started towards him. "All right...I'm off."

"Get a couple of the lads ready to unload my pickup when I get back there," Angus called after him.

Dal waved his acknowledgement of the command and headed for the barn area.

Angus shook his head and climbed into his truck. "So, her real name is Poppy," he muttered to himself with a satisfied grin. "This must be a sign from the almighty. He's sent me another flower, and lord...what a red-hot flower she is."

He'd already suspected that the lass had a temper, but was throttling it with all the other things she'd been hiding. Having seen a sample of it, he found it exhilarating. Now, if he could just hang onto her.

Back in his younger days when he'd been full of piss and vinegar, Angus had left Heaven's Gate to find out what else might be out there besides working with sheep. He was the eldest of three sons, but he wasn't sure he wanted to work at Neamh, which was what his father was training his sons for in the tradition of past years. Not all of them would, but he was especially hopeful of Angus. Angus had been hopeful for more than sheep.

Working on a fishing ship in Ireland, he'd met his Dublin lassie and fell in love. She'd been a flower too, and they each knew they had found their fated love match. Their courtship had been intense and hidden from her family, her daddy being a man of the cloth with considerable influence and money.

His Aven had sworn undying fealty until her daddy found them together. Faster than you could whistle the bonnie banks of Loch Lomond, she'd pronounced him the evil seducer and Angus had seen the wisdom of leaving Dublin in his rear view. He'd set out for America to quench the painful heartbreak of undying love gone wrong.

Once he'd finally sown all his wild oats, he'd returned to Heaven's Gate, and to his family, much wiser to the ways of the lassies.

His father had put him straight to work at Neamh under Whipcord's tutelage where he'd remained ever since. He'd learned there was more than one kind of love as his dedication to the lord of Heaven's Gate and his loyalty to his native soil seeped deep into his heart and blood. His brother's had pursued their own lives' when he'd returned to the destiny he'd been born for.

No other lass had inspired his tadger to break free of his zip like Aven had until he'd met his Rosie. When it had arisen to salute the bonnie Rose McClanahan, he'd wooed and wed her within two weeks.

As he let himself in the kitchen door of Neamh, he knew Poppy was a woman he could fall deeply in love with, but how would they make it work when her family was in America? Would she even want to try?

WHEN ANGUS JOINED POPPY in Darro's study, she squeezed his hand when he took the chair beside her in front of the desk. Darro was seated at his huge desk with Lucerne on a chair beside him. Vince Gallo was on his left. Gallo was drumming his fingers where his arm rested casually on the wooden surface as he leaned up against the solid wood.

Now that she had made tea for all of them and calmed down some, Poppy tried to see things from Gallo's perspective. She was failing miserably, but she could concede that he had a job to do just like everyone else, and maybe he did help a lot of people who deserved his help. Adrian Condoloro wasn't one of them, so she was still bristling. He had come to warn her though, and she tried to give him credit for that.

Her mind raced, trying to figure out why Adrian would actually want her out of the way? She'd been afraid of the lengths he might go to force her back into court, but she hadn't expected this. It's not like her estate would go to him. He was only related to her by marriage, wouldn't it go to her daughter?

"Ye all right, lass? Ye're lookin a little peeley walley," Angus whispered in her ear.

A smile lit up her pale face, but she nodded weakly at him. She was anything but all right; she needed answers. Angus's soft Scottish burr soothed her though. Explaining the basics to Darro while Angus had been gone had left her drained. "I've been better." Angus squeezed her hand in support.

Darro shot a keen stare at Gallo. "Now that we are all here, can ye shed some light on why Poppy's stepson would want her dead? We've all heard her explanation of the will and it sounds rock solid. Since she has a blood child who would inherit her estate, how would he benefit?"

"He might be able to," Vince replied slowly, his brows furrowing. "I've picked up some things along the way when doing investigations for lawyers when stepchildren have come up. Legally, stepchildren have no inheritance rights. However, if the stepparent were to make conditions in the will that would include them, then they could inherit."

"My will doesn't have any provisions for Adrian," Poppy protested. "The man has enough money as it is, why would I want to leave him anything?"

Angus was quick to point out. "Aye, but what about his father's will? Did ye see the full copy of it? Mayhap there is a loophole yer stepson is trying to use, or plans to use if ye aren't around."

"Exactly my thoughts, Angus," Darro agreed, steepling his fingers together. "Poppy, I'd say the first thing ye need to do is order a full copy of the will and any added addendums that yer husband's lawyer may have included."

Poppy nodded. "I can get that from Mack, but I've never actually read a copy of the will. Mack has been keeping Adrian at bay for the last year in court. If not for him, I don't know where I'd be," she confessed. "I haven't had any contact with him since I left Toronto over two weeks ago."

"Did ye pick up a new phone in town?" Darro asked.

Poppy flushed. "No, sir. I had no intention of calling anyone so they could track where I was calling from," she confessed. "The cheap cell I bought with cash here was just to get a job with. I told my daughter before I left that I'd get in touch when I felt it was safe to call."

"I can understand yer caution under the circumstances. Do ye have yer lawyer's number? If so, ye can use my office phone to call until ye can get back into town and get yer own. If the man is meaning ye harm, it won't take long at all to get something in place. Mr. Gallo has explained yer stepson's mob connections, which means they could have contact resources right here in Scotland or at least in the UK."

Poppy hadn't thought of that and her face turned even paler. "I had no idea," she whispered.

Vince grimaced. "Trust me, Mrs. Condoloro, I didn't either. Not until I did some research of my own into Adrian's background. Given his attitude when you left, I wanted to know more about him and how to protect myself. I'm sorry for your situation and if there's anything I can do to help, I'd be happy to oblige."

"Are you trying to make me believe you aren't in his pocket," she asked scornfully. "I'd prefer to see you arrested and put into a Scottish dungeon where no one could get you out."

Angus grinned. "We don't do that anymore, lass, sorry to say."

Vince flushed and glared at her. "I'm not in his or anyone's pocket," he replied with enough zest that his declaration had a ring of truth to it. He ran his hand through his untidy hair. "Look, I did the job I was paid to do, but that's it. I won't apologize for the way I make a living, and I didn't have to come here to warn you either. So, if you all are finished with me, I'll just make my way over to the Netherlands or somewhere to take in some skiing for a while. Good luck, and I hope you find a way to solve your problems. And for what it's worth, I apologize for misjudging you, but no one's perfect." He stood up to go.

"I'd like ye to stay, Vince," Darro said quietly, standing up himself. "Ye seem like a good man and we could use someone who knows his way around these kinds of things. I'd pay whatever yer going rate is to keep an eye on the area, check new rentals, observe the arriving flights connected to the UK and other such activities ye do that might give us a heads up if trouble is arriving."

Vince looked surprised. "Well…I don't have a client at the moment, but I need a place to stay that's off the grid. Here wouldn't work because I'd be exposed if Adrian does come looking for Mrs. Condoloro."

"What about with my father?" Lucerne asked thoughtfully. "I'm sure he would be on board with the plan once he knows what's going on."

"You might be better off hiring a local detective." Vince frowned. "He knows the area better than I would."

"But he doesn't know Poppy's stepson like ye do," Darro replied.

"Dad could answer questions about the area and show ye where things are if ye need some help," Lucerne added.

"I need to turn in my rental because it's trackable," Vince replied. "I could always buy a bus ticket back to London and just make it look like I got on. I doubt he'd bother with me once he figures I'm not around anymore."

Poppy looked skeptical. "Why would you bother to help? What's in it for you?"

Vince grinned, the first one he'd shown them since he'd arrived. It actually made him attractive. "Besides the money, you mean? I do have my principles. I don't like being misled by someone like Adrian Condoloro. He flat out lied to me to secure my services, and I don't like that. I also don't work for criminals and he tried to strongarm me on this last deal. I figure I owe him a black eye."

"It's settled then," Darro said briskly, moving away from his desk. "Poppy, if ye would be so kind as to contact yer lawyer, please? After that, we'll leave ye alone to call yer family. I'm sure they must be quite worried about ye right now."

Poppy nodded and stood up. When she took Darro's seat at the desk, she sighed heavily and dialed her lawyer's number. Then she put the phone on speaker and waited for the overseas connection.

Mack DeNiro's voice came frantically across the line. "Poppy, is that you?"

"Yes, Mack, it's me."

"Where are you? Your family is worried sick! That jackass Adrian is trying to have you declared legally dead because they found your car at the bottom of the river in Toronto with blood in it. Morgan is trying to get Adrian declared a mob contact in order to investigate him and stop him," Mack spit out.

Poppy gave a horrified gasp. "Oh my god...why would he do that?"

"He's filed another motion with the DA based on a technicality with Julian's will that he thinks gives him immediate access to the inheritance his father left you."

"What technicality?" Poppy asked, thoroughly shocked and bewildered. "I thought the will was rock solid, Mack."

A FLOWER FOR ANGUS

Mack sighed. "I warned Julian not to add that last private clause in the will."

"What clause?"

"Because Julian didn't like the fact that your daughter Andrea is married to an FBI agent, he put a stipulation in the will that if you didn't access your inheritance within one year after the will was read, your inheritance portion would return to his son upon your death. He wanted you to be cared for, but he hated law enforcement and didn't want Morgan to ever benefit from his money.

"Neither you nor Adrian were supposed to know that, and he was positive you would need what he left you. But my office was broken into a few weeks after Julian died, and I think Adrian was behind the break in. I think he wanted a full copy of the will hoping to find a way to break it, which he did.

"He must need that money badly, Poppy, for him to have been so obsessive about it. When you disappeared and no one knew where you were, he decided to take this opportunity to get to the money very quickly."

"And since I've been living off my own savings so far, I haven't accessed the cash Julian left me," Poppy added.

"Exactly."

"But Julian left him extremely well off. I know because I saw the figures and the investments," she replied angrily. "How much money does one man need?"

"He acts like a man running scared, Poppy, and there have been rumors," Mack replied uneasily. "Rumors about him being in debt for illegal gambling. He has markers being called in that he apparently can't pay. If he went to his father's mob contacts for money and they are calling in his loans, that could explain his urgency for a big payoff. All I know is that it's a hell of a mess and you are three days short of the provision in the will. You need to access that money before it's too late."

Vince shot them all a thumbs up and nodded his head silently. The other's nodded as well, but no one was saying anything to interrupt Poppy's call.

"Maybe I should just let him have it, Mack," Poppy said slowly, closing her eyes and pinching her nose with her free hand. "After all, I don't really need it. I can find another way to buy some property once I don't have to hide anymore. I can authorize you to release it to him, can't I?"

There was silence for a moment. "Poppy...I could...but are you absolutely sure that's what you want to do? That money belongs to you, you've earned it, and Julian wanted you to have it."

"I'm tired of hiding, Mack," Poppy replied, her voice wobbling. "This has been a nightmare that money isn't worth living over. I've run halfway across the planet and he's still coming for me. I just want it to be over. I know investments; I can rebuild without that money.

"Besides, if Adrian really is in fear for his life, I still care about him as my stepson in spite of everything. We did make a few tender memories together over the last ten years."

"What do you mean he's still coming for you?" Mack asked suspiciously. "Are you in immediate danger, Poppy?"

"Maybe...I don't know for sure," Poppy hedged, glancing over at Angus. "I've got people looking out for me though, and I feel safe here. Just do me a favor and contact him tomorrow to release the money. I don't want to speak with him."

"I still advise against it, Poppy, but if that's what you want, give me an email where I can send you a DocuSign for authorization."

Poppy gave him her email. She was sure Darro would allow her to access it on a computer and she could get it right back to Mack. She was so done with all of this.

"This shouldn't take long, Poppy, even if you are out of the country. I can contact him in the morning after the paperwork is drawn up."

"Thank you, Mack."

"Call your daughter," he ordered before hanging up.

The room was silent as Poppy hung up the phone. Then she looked around at everyone apprehensively. "I know, you think I'm a fool for giving up the money, right?"

Impulsively, Lucerne came around to give her a hug. "Well…I don't think you're crazy, I think you're a very generous person."

"And I have to admit…I kind of like a lass that isn't obsessed with money," Angus added with a grin.

"Ye remind me of Lucerne, lass," Darro said gruffly. "I don't know how much money it was, but any woman with a generous and forgiving nature, even to those who don't deserve it, is worth her weight in gold as far as I'm concerned."

"That was really something, Mrs. Condoloro," Vince said in awe. "In one phone call you just saved me from fearing Adrian might be breathing down my neck for the rest of my life because of what he asked me to do. All I can do is say thank you."

"Call me Poppy, Vince," she replied. "After all, everyone else uses my first name." She threw Darro a wry grin.

As usual, Darro took charge. "Let's give Poppy some privacy to call her family," he stated briskly, ushering everyone towards the door.

They all filed out leaving Poppy alone.

Chapter 8

Angus wanted to stay with Poppy but he knew she needed the time alone to reconnect with her daughter. Reluctantly he followed Darro, Vince, and Lucerne into the kitchen.

"More tea, anyone?" Lucerne asked.

"No thanks, honey," Darro replied. He turned to Vince. "Now that ye're on my clock, why don't ye head into Inverness and see if ye can find out anything."

Vince looked surprised. "You still want to hire me?"

Darro nodded. "Aye. I think we should carry on just as we planned until we can be sure Condoloro hasn't sent someone to set up an accident for Poppy. It sounds like he is desperate and will do everything he can to achieve his objective. And for all we know, he may have had someone following ye here." He turned back to Lucerne. "Lucerne, can ye give Vince the address for Happy Housekeepers and explain to yer father?"

"Aye," Lucerne replied, taking out her cell phone.

"That's usin' yer head, Darro," Angus growled. "I was just thinkin' the same thing. I'll get the lads on white alert and put Sinh into action. He headed towards the door.

"Sin?" Vince asked, his eyebrows going up.

"Actually, it's Sin with an h. It stands for Sangster's Information Network Hub. Angus has a surplus of relatives and friends who keep him informed of things he might need to know. He helped me when Lucerne and I were dating, but he didn't put a name to his gossip clutch until after that," Darro chuckled. "It does work, that's how we knew ye were coming."

"I'm impressed," Vince replied as they walked to the edge of the porch. He turned and shook hands with Darro. "I'll let you know what I find out."

Angus joined Darro on the porch again and they watched as Vince got in his blue rental and drove away. "Do ye trust him, lad?" he asked.

"I think we can trust him, but it's best to be prepared in any case. What do ye think?"

"I think I should take Poppy to Thistlewind to be on the safe side until we know that sleekit basturt Condoloro has given up." Angus growled.

Darro stared. "Ye really got it bad," he chortled. "Ye're falling in love with the lass."

"Mind yer own business, ye git," Angus replied grumpily.

Darro threw his head back and laughed. "Now ye know how I felt when I met Lucerne."

Angus scowled at him. "At least ye didn't have to worry about her runnin' off to America on ye."

Darro's eyes twinkled and he stepped off the porch and headed for the barn, Angus falling in beside him. "Aye, there is that, but I'll still have to make trips there to visit Lucerne's mother's family from time to time. I'm actually looking forward to going to New Orleans, I've never been there before."

"If ye're expectin' me to say I knew a lass in New Orleans once, ye would be right," Angus replied, some of his usual humor returning. "Never caught her face because she had on one of them Mardi Gras masks. Never took it off the entire evenin' we spent together either," he added with relish. "Didn't need to, the rest of her made it a night to remember."

Darro just shook his head. "I don't know why, but I actually believe ye."

Angus just grinned. "Lord's truth."

"Well, I don't think taking Poppy to yer place is the best decision right now, Angus. Neamh is heavily guarded with plenty of willing hands fer ye to fire up. Ye would both be more exposed at Thistlewind right now and we don't need to be divided."

Angus sighed. "I know ye're right, but the instinct to hide her away where the world can't touch her is verra strong."

"That's yer heart talking and not yer head," Darro replied, his face softening. He clapped Angus on the shoulder. "Dinna worry, old neeb, we'll protect yer lass from this threat. After that ye'll be on yer own for her temper."

"That I can handle," Angus retorted.

"I'll remember ye said that when yer hanging out in the barn office with me instead of going home," Darro mocked.

"Just because ye ran from Lucerne's temper don't mean I would run from Poppy's," Angus snorted. "I got a few more years of experience when it comes to dealin' with the lassies than ye do, lad." Angus opened the barn door to find Dal just walking up.

"Ye will be happy to know, Angus, that I'm leaving ye to yer Poppy. I've decided I'll set my sights on the boss's little sister. Do ye know when that hot tidbit is coming for a visit?" Dal asked just before Darro stepped in behind Angus. Then his face went beet red and his tongue stopped working. "I...I..." he stuttered.

Angus snickered while Darro took Dal to task. "That hot tidbit has a name, ye young cock. It's Ainsley, and if I ever hear ye laid a finger on my sister, that won't be the only body part of yers that comes up missing. Ye ken me?"

He strode away leaving Dal still gawping helplessly.

"Stuck yer foot in it this time, didn't ya?" Angus taunted, his eyes dancing with laughter. "Ye're lucky the boss didn't bring out old Whipcord's bullwhip to snap yer backside. Now get out there and tell the boys we are on white alert and report back to me. Skitter, ye little walloper."

He watched fondly as Dal scurried away; his mocking retorts silent for once. It wouldn't do the lad any harm to get verbally spanked once in a while. The young cock needed taken down a peg now and then.

POPPY HELD HER BREATH while she waited for the phone to connect. Given that it was about a 6-to-7-hour time difference between Chicago and London, she knew it had to be around 10:30 pm Chicago time. Her daughter didn't answer phone numbers she didn't recognize, plus it was late to be receiving phone calls at all. She'd been lucky Mack had picked up on his personal line.

"Hello?"

It was Andrea's voice on the line she slumped in relief. "Andrea, darling, it's me."

"Mom! Where are you?"

The squeal was so loud and indignant that Macy flinched and held the phone away from her ear.

"I'm in Scotland."

"What are you doing in Scotland? I've been worried sick! We were told you might be dead and they were looking for your body. Oh God, Mom, I've never been so scared in my life. Are you hurt? Are you safe?"

"Calm down, honey, I'm not hurt and I'm very safe. I'm sorry I haven't called, but I didn't want to put you at risk. It's better you didn't know where I was going."

"When are you coming home?"

"I don't know, Andrea, not for a while though. I've found a safe haven and I plan on staying until things settle down for me in Chicago."

"I miss you so much, Mom..."

The catch in her daughter's voice made Poppy's own throat constrict. "I know, honey, I miss you too. Listen, I can't stay on the phone for too long, so I want you and Morgan to know what's going on before I hang up. My employer has been kind enough to allow me to use his phone until I can safely get my own."

"You're working?"

"Yes, for now. Is Morgan close by? Can you put me on speaker so you both get the information at the same time?"

Morgan's deep voice chimed in. "I'm here, Poppy. Go ahead."

"I talked to Mack a few minutes ago, so I know you've been trying to block Adrian's attempts to declare me dead, Morgan. You don't have to worry about that anymore."

Poppy went on to explain all that had happened since she left Toronto.

"It's not right, Mom, you shouldn't have to give up what Julian has left you for my lowlife stepbrother," Andrea declared indignantly.

"I feel very at peace with my decision," Poppy returned gently. "It's like it was a yoke around my shoulders weighing me down, and now I feel lighter and happier. I'll be perfectly fine without it."

They talked for a few more minutes and then hung up. Poppy regretted not getting the chance to speak with her grandchildren, but there would be more time later. Her thoughts drifted to Angus as she made her way to the kitchen. He was such a kind, teasing, growly, funny man. She'd never met anyone like him before, and she couldn't believe the way he made her body feel. It was as if he was something it had been craving all her life that she didn't know she even needed or wanted.

Andrea's father Sam had been a kind man, and very loving, but their relationship had been more like soulmate friends with benefits thrown in to make babies with. They had both wanted more children, and when it didn't happen, she'd turned to her education in financial investments skills to fulfill her life. She didn't regret a minute of her marriage to her Sam, but there had always been something missing. When his long battle with painful liver cancer had finally

A FLOWER FOR ANGUS 119

taken him away, she'd been relieved that his suffering was over.

Julian had come back into her life a year later at a time when she was very lonely, and had been going through some deep depression after the loss of Sam. He'd lost his wife when a chic restaurant in upper Chicago had been robbed while they were dining there, and some of the patrons had been shot by the unhinged gunman. Julian had been winged by a bullet and had come out of surgery to find out that his Lois hadn't survived her injuries.

They were both lonely and drawn to each other once again. They had drifted naturally together, and then Julian had asked her to marry him. Adrian had been 16 at the time and had resented his father's new wife. Julian's mother and his son had both insisted on a prenup agreement and Julian had apologized for it, but Poppy didn't care. She was comfortable with what Sam had left her and she hated being alone.

Julian was different than Sam. Where Sam had been open and friendly, Julian was closed and emotionally stunted, he could never laugh at himself. He had expectations of her as a society wife, in public and at home, and she'd dutifully done her best to be what he wanted. He did care for her though, even though Poppy hadn't married him for love.

They had a decent 10 years together despite the tension that Adrian and Edna had created most of the time. Adrian had made it plain that Poppy was not his mother and never would be.

Poppy had started working with Julian in investments to fill her life. Numbers was something she had a knack for. She loved it—and she was good at it.

After she'd lost Julian, Poppy had decided she didn't want to be with anyone again. Losing two husbands was hard enough for any woman. She wanted to create her own life this time instead of living in someone else's shadow. Blending families was difficult at best and the strain between Andrea and Adrian, and then Julian and Morgan, had put her off the whole idea. She'd just stay single.

She'd never in a million years expected to meet someone like Angus. Avoiding him was difficult at Neamh, ignoring him was impossible. The only time she'd been completely sure he meant what he said was when he was spanking her. Her face flamed at the memory and she furtively rubbed the curve of her butt cheek. She could definitely tell she'd been smacked. Hiding her feelings from a man like Angus would be very difficult because he simply wouldn't allow it.

Andrea had asked her when she was coming home. The answer to that was, she didn't feel like coming home yet. As much as she missed her family she felt at home right here, and she wanted to take the time to explore everything there was to see around Inverness. After the threat of Adrian was past anyway. She shivered, the shock of Adrian wanting to actually kill her still lingering. Why were some men so greedy?

She found Lucerne in the kitchen setting out preparations for supper. After all the excitement of today, making haggis with Lucerne seemed so normal that it was almost a letdown, but that was on the agenda for this evening. Besides, she needed normal right now to take her mind off the rest of it. Trying to concentrate on something normal should ease the nagging headache that had started in Inverness after spotting Vince. She'd had them from time to time after Sam had passed away. After Julian, they'd only gotten worse and she'd had to see a doctor for pain meds. She was out right now.

"I'm ready to learn how to make haggis," Poppy offered with a smile as she approached the kitchen counter to inspect everything.

Lucerne chuckled. "I'm ready too. I invited Dorothy for another lesson but she declined. That girl can't seem to get the hang of it."

Over the next hour Lucerne showed Poppy how to boil the bits of the sheep that she planned to use in her recipe.

"Traditional haggis uses heart, liver, and lungs of the sheep," Lucerne explained, giggling at Poppy's disgusted look. "But for tonight, we are just using the heart and liver which we will mix with toasted oats, suet, onions and spices. I'm leaving off the casing which is typically from the sheep's stomach. I don't want to overwhelm ye and honestly, there are many versions of haggis from easy and simple to completely traditional which can be harder to make at home.

"My mother taught me many wonderful American and Louisiana dishes to cook as well, and haggis can be similar to what Americans make as traditional meatloaf, except different meat. Ye can even use chicken or turkey hearts and livers to make a haggis if ye wanted to. Do ye like chicken livers or hearts?"

"I like breaded chicken livers that you can buy from Colonel Sanders," Poppy replied helpfully. "The gizzards are horrible."

Lucerne laughed. "Aye, I liked those livers too, and so did my mother, but my dad didn't care much for them like that."

Poppy screwed up her nose. "Sam, my first husband, always liked the giblet gravy at Thanksgiving to go on his noodles and mashed potatoes. I never cared for it, but I made it for him."

By the time they had the potatoes and turnips mashed, the loaf of haggis had finished its final cooking round and had a nice loaf shape that could be cut into slices. "You're right, it is similar to making meat loaf. Sam always liked to put ketchup on his meatloaf though."

Lucerne nodded. "Aye, some of my American cousins like that too, but don't even mention putting ketchup on haggis," she replied with a giggle. "I think Angus and Darro might have a heart attack."

"Is that so?" asked Poppy, mischief bubbling inside her.

"Don't even think it," Lucerne warned, but her eyes were dancing. The sudden pounding of feet had them turning to see Corey bursting into the kitchen.

"What did I say about running?" Lucerne scolded the 7-year-old affectionately and ruffled his blond hair.

"Sorry, Aunt Lucerne," Corey piped up, his little nose sniffing the air eagerly. "We could smell haggis cooking and it's making us hungry!"

Delilah came in at a more sedate pace. "I told him to walk but he doesn't always listen to me," she added, looking down her nose at her brother.

A FLOWER FOR ANGUS

Poppy smiled at the children. They were both blond-haired, and blue-eyed, with polite manners for the most part. It was plain who was boss in their relationship, but Delilah was also very protective of her little brother. Losing both their parents at the same time couldn't have been easy for any of the family, but she'd been impressed that Darro had elected to raise his brother's children. It had also impressed her that Lucerne had been willing to marry into a ready-made family. These were exceptional people though, and she was grateful they had been so kind to her.

"Dinner is almost ready, go wash yer hands," Lucerne instructed as she and Poppy set the table. "Yer uncle should be here anytime."

She'd no sooner spoken the words when Poppy heard the back door open. When she heard two sets of feet coming down the small entryway, her heart leaped. Angus was eating with them tonight. Her lips curled in a mischievous smile.

Like the children, Angus came in sniffing. She did like his hair neatly cut close to his head and the scruffy beard shaved off better than when she'd first met him. He was a very handsome man without all the grizzle. He'd flushed slightly when Darro had given him grief about finally cleaning up for the new housekeeper, but he'd taken it well, giving as good as he got right back at his boss. They did seem really close.

"The haggis smells delicious, Lucerne," Angus remarked, but his eyes were on Poppy. "Did ye make it or did Poppy?"

"I instructed and Poppy did the work," Lucerne replied.

Darro walked over and gave Lucerne a kiss. "Whoever did what, it smells wonderful as usual."

Angus sauntered over to Poppy. "I'd give ye a kiss too, but I don't want to embarrass ye," he teased in her ear. He did give her a hug though, which Poppy enjoyed. His strong body against hers made her knees tremble. She was relieved he didn't kiss her. She didn't know exactly what they were yet, but whatever it was, she wanted it to be private between her and Angus for now.

The kids came rushing in, excited to see their uncle and he scooped them up in his long arms. "Uncle Darro!"

"Umph...ye two are getting to be quite a handful together," he teased them, giving them a bear hug with his arms around them both while they squealed with laughter. He set them back on the floor and landed a playful pat on both their backsides to hurry them to the table. "Get to yer seats and let's eat."

After they were seated and everyone had a plate, Poppy jumped up. "Oh...I almost forgot." She rushed to the fridge and came back with a bottle of ketchup and set it on the table.

Angus eyed it suspiciously. "What's the ketchup fer?"

Poppy feigned surprise. "Why, the haggis of course. It's sort of like American meatloaf and some people like ketchup with meatloaf." She picked up the bottle and held it out to him.

Angus recoiled in horror, his eyebrows reaching for the sky and both hands in the air.

Even Darro and the kids were staring wide-eyed like they were watching a trainwreck they couldn't look away from as Poppy shrugged and shook the bottle. A quick glance told

A FLOWER FOR ANGUS 125

her Lucerne was hiding a smile behind her hand as Poppy poured a small puddle of ketchup beside her slice of haggis.

"Darro, are ye seein' this, lad?" Angus asked in disbelief.

When what sounded like a snicker from Lucerne turned into a cough, Darro's eyes narrowed. "I think we're being played, Angus," he replied, a smile hovering around his lips as Lucerne couldn't hold it in anymore.

Poppy joined her in laughter. "You should have seen your faces; you were right, Lucerne. That was too funny."

Angus's grin split his face. "Round one goes to the lassies," he said with good humor. "Are ye actually goin' to dip yer haggis in that ketchup?"

Poppy shuddered. "Of course not. I don't even use ketchup on my meatloaf. I am excited about trying Lucerne's recipe though. I'm not a fan of the ingredients, but it's not near as disgusting as I thought it would be. I do love mashed potatoes, but I don't know about the mashed turnips. I've eaten them raw as a kid on my grandpa's farm, but haven't touched one in years." She cut a slice of her haggis and dipped it in the mashed mixture, then placed it in her mouth. Again, they were all watching her intently, waiting for her opinion.

"Well, what do ye think?" Angus asked.

Poppy cocked her head sideways. "Needs pepperoni."

Angus choked, aghast. "Pepperoni?"

"It would add some spice to it. I'm an Italian girl."

Angus pointed his finger sternly at Lucerne. "Is this yer doin'? Ye done had Dorothy makin' habanero roast lamb and almost burnt my tonsils clean out."

Lucerne couldn't help it, she dissolved into giggles, Poppy right along with her. She'd already heard the story from Lucerne.

"Darro, yer lass is out of control in the kitchen."

"I have no complaints and neither should ye since ye didn't cook it, ye old git," Darro drawled lazily.

Angus grinned broadly. "Ye may be right about that, but my educated palate should be a learnin' lesson fer the lassies. I know good haggis."

"Educated palate my ar...rump," Darro mocked, side eying the kids.

"Uncle Darro," exclaimed both Delilah and Corey at once.

Both men burst out laughing and Poppy realized that they could have gone on forever. She was grateful for the chance to laugh and put her worry over Adrian on hold for the moment.

"Lucerne's haggis is a bit different than the bon bons we tried at The Waterfront, but I like them both. Not bad at all."

Angus nodded, and then looking as serious as a heart attack, he asked, "Think ye can make it on yer own?"

"I believe so," Poppy replied slowly, her eyebrow arching. "Why?"

He wiped imaginary sweat off his forehead. "Whew...that's a relief. I was afraid I'd have to take back my offer to hire ye as my housekeeper."

Poppy rolled her eyes and the children immediately threatened to throw scones at him if he even dared.

"Still trying to steal my housekeeper, eh?" Darro asked with a chuckle. "Why don't ye just hire yerself one?"

"Because it's more fun this way," Angus assured him.

The rest of the meal was fun, the feeling of close friends and family drawing Poppy in and making her feel safe. Neamh was slowly carving a place in her heart.

Chapter 9

Because of its remote location and the highland grasslands surrounding Neamh and Thistlewind, it was easy to spot vehicles that didn't belong in the area. And unless someone really planned on coming in on an alternate form of transportation, Angus felt it was safe to take Poppy for a moonlight drive and show her Thistlewind.

Vince had been talking to Darro after supper and had reported no suspicious activity that he could see or find so far. Dal and Henry were on horseback near the turnoff to the only road into Neamh and they had reported no activity either, not even a car passing on the main road.

Angus brought his pickup around to the back door and Poppy came to meet him dressed in those figure-hugging jeans lassies wore these days, a casual white blouse with the sleeves rolled up her forearms, and the brown loafers she'd had on that first day. She looked tense, cool and comfortable, not to mention beautiful. His heart tripped faster as she smiled at him and tucked one wave of her shiny brown hair behind a delicate ear.

"I'm ready," she said as she stopped in front of him, her eyes glistening in the moonlight.

His nostrils quivered with the wisp of the scent he'd caught on her before. "Ye look beautiful, lass, and ye smell good enough to eat. I've been meanin' to ask ye what that scent is, I've never smelled it before," he added as he lifted her into the seat of his pickup.

"It's one I had made up for me by a master perfumer," she replied. "I'm glad you like it because I love it and I wear it all the time."

"A what?"

She chuckled. "A master perfumer. You know, one of those people who create one-of-a-kind perfumes and other scents for people?"

"I didn't know they were called that but I have heard of it," he replied. She started to speak and he held up a finger. "Hold that thought while I get in or we'll never make it to Thistlewind."

She nodded with a grin and Angus shut the door and came around the truck to climb in. After he shut his door, he put his hand on her forearm and gently urged her towards his side. "Ye are too far away, lass. Come over here and tell me about yer master perfumer."

She hesitated. "Angus…I…I…"

"If ye don't want to, that's okay too," he replied stiffly, trying to stifle his disappointment. They already had a history. Okay, so it was just one real boner of a kiss, but maybe today hadn't meant anything to her.

Gently she put her small hand on his forearm. "I-It's not that, Angus. It's just that everyone is watching us, and I feel like a goldfish in a glass bowl. I'm more of a private kind of person, you know?"

Angus was relieved and he folded her small hand into his. "Aye, they are at that," he chuckled, noting the furtive glances from a few of the men stationed to keep an eye on the back of the house. He could care less who knew how he felt about Poppy but he would respect her wishes.

Once they started down the lane out of Neamh, Poppy scooted over immediately. Feeling much better now, he put his arm around her and hugged her in close, loving the feel of her warm contours. With the subject of her perfume forgotten, Poppy marveled at the sights around her.

"The highlands are beautiful in the moonlight, Angus. The stars are so bright, it's as if the land is closer to the sky in Scotland."

"Which is why Darro's ancestors started callin' this land Heaven's Gate," Angus replied with a chuckle.

"Angus! What are those white flowers among the grasses? I don't remember seeing those before," she exclaimed.

"Those are called Night Blooming Moon Flower, or fragrant Moon Vine, or other derivatives of that name. Some flowers only bloom at night and that's one of them. One evenin' I'll take ye to the waterfall just before twilight. There ye can see the night flowers open up all around ye. Wild Jasmine is especially thick around that area," he added.

Poppy's gaze caught him, her eyes bright and shining. "I would love that."

"Rosie's garden is full of the Blooming Cereus, also called Queen of the Night. If ye like flowers, I'll show ye."

"Yes, please. I love flowers but I've never been much of a gardener. Was Rosie your wife?" she asked gently.

Angus nodded and chuckled wistfully. "Aye, she was. That lass loved her flowers."

Poppy squeezed his hand sympathetically.

"Ye might want to duck now, or move over. Dal and Henry are coming up at the main road entrance," Angus quipped.

The awkward moment past, Poppy squirmed sideways and laid her head down on Angus's upper thigh with a giggle.

Angus immediately popped some sweat on his forehead. The lass was entirely too close to a certain part of his anatomy and it was quickly responding. Making a quick decision, he waved at Dal and Henry, who had been angling to the road to meet him, and gunned the accelerator on around the turn into the main road without slowing down. A quick glance to his right showed them just sitting on their horses staring at him as if he'd lost his mind. If he hadn't yet, he was going to if he didn't move Poppy.

"Ye can get up now, lass, we left them in the dust," he choked out hoarsely, pulling on her shoulder.

Poppy popped up just like her name and looked around, her face pink and excited. "That was close. I thought they were going to stop you to talk."

"It was close," he agreed, but not for the reasons she thought. He wondered why she wanted to keep their relationship private? He was too old for this nonsense. He liked her and he was pretty sure she liked him. Why hide it?

By the time he reached Thistlewind, his tadger had finally conceded defeat...for the moment.

"Thistlewind is absolutely charming," Poppy marveled as he drove past two concrete walls and into the courtyard where he parked in front of the house. "I love that the doors are painted with color in some of these old homes," she enthused as he lifted her out of the truck.

Angus was pretty proud of Thistlewind. "Aye, we've always had a blue door. Colors have symbolism, and for us, it represents peace and clan unity."

Fascinated, Poppy asked. "What does the red door at Neamh mean."

"Red means yer mortgage is paid off," he replied dryly, "but it can also mean rebellion and other things."

"Did you add onto the house?" she asked as he unlocked the door and opened it for her to precede him up the two stone steps and into the home.

"Aye. The front is pretty much the same as it's always been with the original white and gray stone," he explained. "I added the blue shutters on the windows on both levels and built a patio in the back made of the same stones. The back part of the house is made of wood and updated with a more modern kitchen and other facilities. My grandfather and my dad did that when we moved into the 21st century with electric and indoor plumbin'," he added with a chuckle.

"We still have a well and pump in the back garden though, that's been around for lord knows how long. Generations of Sangster's have lived on Heaven's Gate for as long as we have records." He turned the lights on and watched her as she perused his home. He tried to see it through her eyes.

Crofter cottages weren't very big back in the day. More people were stuffed into them than they could legally get by with under today's standards. The big fireplace that had once been the crofter family cooking center still took up most of the right wall of what was now only the living room. Just past the living room was his bedroom on the left. His study, converted from a smaller bedroom, was on the right. Then a step up and the add-on began with a staircase on the right. The add on sported a modern kitchen, dining area, and a bathroom. His modern areas weren't near the size of Neamh, but it had been plenty adequate for his family. The attic above the living room was used for storage and the two second level bedrooms were above the add-on.

"I'm not much of a home decorator," he explained, "that was Rosie's department."

"I think it's quaint and beautiful," Poppy replied, running her hand across a gorgeous antique sideboard made of mahogany that held family pictures on the base and delicate blue and white China in the doors above it.

She pointed to the massive fireplace. "I bet that's nice and warm in your Scottish winters."

He took her hand. "Come on, I want ye to see the Queen of the Night," he replied easily, trying to set aside the images of Rosie standing in front of the China and wondering whether to risk using it when the boys were little. Sometimes she had, but most of the time she hadn't. He never could figure out what China was for if it wasn't to eat off of, but he'd humored her. The China had belonged to her mother, and her grandmother before her, so that made it precious in her eyes.

He rushed her through the rest of the house and onto the rock patio outside where it sloped gently to the shimmering loch about 200 yards away. "There's the flower bed," he pointed off to his right as he led her towards a blooming array of white flowers that were cone shaped with spears of white leading away from the center.

"How lovely," Poppy gasped, reaching out and stroking a soft petal. "Thank you for showing me your home, Angus. It's truly beautiful."

Angus awkwardly ran his hand through his short cut. "I'm glad ye like it."

She tentatively reached out and took his hand. "Your Rosie must have been a lovely woman," she said softly. "If you've changed your mind about my being here with you, I'll understand. I might feel the same way if I were showing you around my house filled with memories of the love I'd lost."

Angus was at a loss for words at that moment. "Walk with me," he said gruffly, tucking her arm into his and heading for the path to the loch. They were both silent until they arrived at the small bench on a concrete square beside the loch where they could look out at the moonlight highlighting the undulating ripples in the water.

Angus absorbed the serenity of the water, the mountains in the background, and the sparkling ripples when a fish, or perhaps a turtle, popped a bubble up from beneath the surface, until he could formulate his thoughts. "It's not that, Poppy," he finally replied.

Poppy turned to face him with an inquiring look.

"I'm no verra good at explainin' feelin's," he said tensely, staring down at her. "We've both lost people we love in our lives. Aye, I did love Rosie. I loved her verra much, and she loved me in spite of my many imperfections. I'll always love her, but I no want to be alone for the rest of my life either. When I met ye that day on the road and held ye in my arms, I knew immediately that ye were someone I could love. Those special feelin's don't come along for just any lass."

A FLOWER FOR ANGUS 135

Poppy blushed and looked down at their clasped hands, then looked back up. "Angus, I..."

He put his finger on her lips. "Let me finish and then ye can have yer turn. I guess what I'm sayin' is that I want to court ye. I know that sounds old-fashioned and it is, but I want everyone to know that I like ye. I don't want to sneak around like I did when I was still tryin' to grow a beard and meet a lassie after school to steal a kiss. I'm too old for that, Poppy. If ye like me at all, then we can go as slow as ye like. All I ask is that ye be honest with me in return. And if ye don't like me, then I won't do this..."

He swooped down and took her mouth under his in a long searing kiss that had his toes curling and his tadger dancing. He didn't know about her toes.

"...anymore," he finished as he raised his head and searched her face. She didn't look repulsed, maybe there was hope yet.

"Is it my turn now?" she asked breathlessly, her grin taunting him.

"Aye," he replied reluctantly, his thumb brushing her soft cheek. She was so beautiful in the moonlight, he yearned to kiss her senseless until she couldn't find a way to refuse him.

"I-I felt a lot of things when we met," she confessed. "Confused, angry, afraid, and just about every other emotion you can name. Your arms around me made me feel like I'd been missing something in my life up until this point. That confused me."

She glared at him. "You made me angry because I'd had my fill of men running my life and I was now attracted to a complete stranger. And when you kept asking me questions and trying to get close to me, you made me afraid that my past would catch up to me if I let you in," she finished with a shake of her head and then stared out across the water for a few seconds before turning back to him.

"And now?" he prompted.

She lifted her soft palm to the side of his cheek. "I still feel confused, but not enough to keep me from doing this." She pulled his head down and reached up to kiss him.

Angus's entire body burst into flame as he groaned and took over the kiss. Her breast was soft and warm, fitting perfectly into his big hand as he explored the contours. He barely heard the first three times someone cleared their throat until Poppy finally pulled away.

"Dad?" a voice rang out, incredulous. "What are ye doing out here?"

"Ben," Angus replied evenly, "what does it look like I'm doin'? I'm courtin' a lass. What are ye doin' here?"

Poppy hid her face in his chest and he could feel the silent shake of her shoulders. Was she crying or laughing?

Ben strolled over. "I was taking a walk when I saw what I thought was a couple of kids necking in yer backyard. Given the situation, I thought I should investigate," he replied with a big grin. "I take it this is Poppy with ye?"

Poppy raised her head, her eyes twinkling with mirth. "Yes, it's me, Ben."

"I hope ye're okay with being out in the open now, Poppy, because if ye aren't, it means I'll have to hide my son's body under the Queen of the Night flowerbed," Angus inserted with a serious face.

Poppy's laugh rang out, giving Angus goosebumps. She had the most lilting laugh he'd ever heard, like a songbird.

"I can take a hint," Ben replied with a chuckle. "Although, I thought ye were supposed to be under lock and guard at Neamh. I'm surprised to find ye here."

"Vince reported in that he hadn't found anythin' unusual in town, so we decided to go for a short drive. It's pretty hard to arrange an accident when ye can be seen comin' fer miles around," Angus replied.

He'd already filled Ben in on what was going on in case any thugs came to check Angus's home. In fact, from the bulge under Ben's vest, he was pretty sure his son had been patrolling the perimeter.

Standing up, Angus held his hand out to Poppy. "Let's head back to Neamh, it's starting to get late for us farmers."

"Goodnight, Dad, Poppy," Ben said with a smile.

They chorused goodnight to Ben. Angus was gratified when Poppy let him keep her hand in his. She leaned in close to him as they made their way back through the house and out to the truck.

"Just think, Angus, by this time tomorrow, it should all be over with," Poppy said wistfully. "At least I sure hope so."

Then Angus got a text from Darro.

'I need you back at Neamh immediately. Holding a phone call for Poppy from Andrea. Hurry'

Angus grabbed the truck door, slung it open and then picked up Poppy and placed her on the seat before closing the door.

"Angus, what the heck..." she protested when he yanked open his truck door and jumped inside.

"Get yer seatbelt on, Poppy, Darro wants us to hurry. It's goin' to be a fast ride."

"WHAT'S GOING ON?" POPPY asked, her heart beating fast as she snapped the middle seatbelt into place. She felt safer next to Angus's big body and hadn't needed any convincing to move over this time.

"Darro said he's holdin' a phone call from yer daughter, that's all I know."

Poppy didn't try to talk so she wouldn't distract Angus's driving. He flew by Dal and Henry at the entrance to the Neamh cut off, his tires spinning gravel as he gunned it up the road. When they pulled up in front of Neamh, the door was wide open and Darro was waiting for them on the front deck, Lucerne standing in the doorway. Neither one was smiling.

Poppy released her seatbelt, her heart beating so hard she could barely breathe. She didn't wait for Angus; she already had the door open and was sliding out of the truck when he came around to get her.

They hurried up the steps where Darro said, "Ye have a phone call in my study, Poppy, from yer daughter Andrea. She's verra upset and insists on talking to ye. We held the call until ye could get here."

Poppy suddenly felt cold as a premonition of bad news raced down her spine. Without a word she brushed past Lucerne and ran for the study, the rest of them right behind her. Why would Andrea be calling at 3:00 a.m. Chicago time? Was one of her grandchildren hurt? Had Morgan been hurt? Or God forbid killed in the line of duty? In the study she picked up the phone where it lay on the desk with trembling fingers.

"Andrea? What's going on?"

"Mom? I'm afraid I have some bad news. Are you sitting down?"

"No, I'm standing."

"You might want to sit down. Are you alone?"

"Andrea, just tell me what's going on," she snapped. "Are you all okay?"

Poppy could feel the color draining from her face as she tried to take in what Andrea was telling her. "Yes, yes of course. I'll let you know what I decide to do. I-I need to think." She hung up the phone and stared at the three concerned people in front of her.

"I-It's Adrian," she whispered in a daze. "He's dead." She dropped into the office chair behind her and pinched her nose. This was about as close to fainting as she'd ever felt as points of light danced in front of her closed eyes. Her chest was heavy and she could barely breathe.

Lucerne gasped in shock. "Oh my God, Poppy."

Angus hurried to her side where he pulled her up and into his arms. "Easy lass, take a few deep breaths, ye look like yer about to pass out."

When her legs refused to hold her, Angus swept her up in his strong arms and took her to the loveseat in front of the fireplace where he sat down with her on his lap.

"Lucerne, can we get some hot tea for Poppy?" Darro asked. He took Lucerne's hands in his. "Are ye all right, lass? Ye're looking pale yerself."

Lucerne nodded her head. "Aye, I-I'll be all right."

"I'll come with ye," Darro decided firmly, and they both left the room.

Poppy's primary feeling was numbness now that the first horror of what she'd heard was past. Greedily she hung onto Angus, his solid body warm and comforting.

When Lucerne and Darro returned, Darro sat the tray on the coffee table and Lucerne sat and poured a cup for them all. Poppy took a grateful sip, feeling the warm liquid soothing her jangled nerves.

"Can ye tell us what Andrea said?" Darro asked gently.

"The police are saying it was murder," Poppy replied slowly. "I'm sure my son-in-law knows a lot more that he isn't saying. He has asked me to stay here until they know more. He doesn't think I would be in danger if I returned, but he said it's better to be careful at this point."

"I agree with him," Angus said slowly. "Until we know why yer stepson was murdered, considerin' the connections ye mentioned, ye are probably better off here."

"That's truly awful," Lucerne replied, shaking her head. "I'm so sorry, Poppy. I know ye weren't close to yer stepson, but that's a terrible thing to happen to anyone, let alone a member of yer family."

"What do I do now though?" Poppy asked woefully. "I can't hide here, I need to go home...I need to make funeral arrangements," she gestured helplessly at the air. "Julian's mother, Edna, will be devastated. Her heart is weak and this will be a huge shock. I know she didn't like me, but I don't want anything bad to happen to her."

"I'm sure the police will have notified her by now," Darro replied firmly. "Was Adrian married?"

"No, he's only 27 and hadn't married yet. He liked to date, but he didn't seem interested in anything permanent and has no children that I know of. Edna lives in one wing of the family home. It was one of the reasons Julian made sure Adrian got the house. I wouldn't have wanted it anyway, it's too big. It always reminded me of a museum or a mausoleum." She shuddered.

"Ye do realize that it's yers now whether ye wanted it or not," Angus remarked, squeezing her hands in his. "Eventually, ye will have to decide what to do with it."

Poppy suddenly sat straight up. "I need to talk to Mack. Do you mind if I call him, Mr. MacCandish?"

Darro's eyebrow shot up. "Is there anything he can do at 3:00 a.m. in Chicago?"

"Darro's right. Besides, ye need to get some rest," Angus added firmly. "There's nothing more ye can do tonight. Ye should call him first thing in the morning."

"How about if I send him an email cancelling the DocuSign papers? That way he'll have it when he first gets up and won't waste time drawing up papers," she replied.

Darro nodded. "Great idea."

Poppy sent the email, feeling sad that Adrian had missed the chance to pay his obligations by a few hours. Was that why he was killed? She walked outside to say goodnight to Angus before he left. When he took her in his arms, she went willingly in spite of the eyes around her. With her head against his shoulder, she found herself wishing she could just hide there and not have to face anything else.

She couldn't believe Adrain was actually dead. So young to die for his mistakes.

No—murdered.

There was a world of difference in those two words in spite of the same ending. She shivered; she'd never get any sleep tonight.

Chapter 10

The next morning, Vince Gallo sat across from Darro and Angus in the barn office sipping a cup of hot coffee.

"Did ye find out anything?" Darro asked, taking a drink from his own cup.

Vince nodded. "Yes, I contacted my office partner after you called last night and he did some checking around. He said the word among the street cops is that it was an execution style murder. No one is giving out many details, but it's a typical on-the-knees shot to the back of the head used by mob enforcers."

"Meant to send a warnin," Angus inserted slowly.

"Exactly," Vince replied with a grimace, "which is why they left the body in an alley to be found. If Adrian was heavily in debt to some of his extended family on his father's side, they may have gotten tired of waiting. Even family members have a time limit if they are foolish enough to borrow, especially if they add nothing of value to the organization.

"If Morgan Kincaid managed to get the FBI to look into Adrian, he probably knows a whole lot more than he's going to say, and it could have caused Adrian to become a liability as well."

Angus nodded. "Poppy indicated somethin' like that last night."

"I know for sure he was a gambler and had a lot of markers," Vince replied with a shake of his head. The man was desperate to get his hands on his stepmother's inheritance. He was obsessed with the two million cash his old man left for Poppy in a separate account."

Angus's eyes widened. "Did ye say two million? That's a lot of money."

Poppy had never mentioned what her inheritance was and he'd never asked. He felt deflated suddenly. Poppy was actually a well to do heiress. Hard to compete with something like that. Thistlewind must seem pretty simple back country to her and would be even more so now.

Angus also suspected that the part in the will about her accessing her inheritance before a year was up would become null and void. As Julians widow, Adrian's inheritance would revert to her unless he had left a will. Which he could have, but most young people in their twenties didn't normally have anything like that in place yet. He sighed inwardly.

Even Darro was surprised at the money Vince threw out there. "That's a lot of gambling debt," he observed.

Vince nodded. "I also followed my trail backwards to see if I could find out if anyone had followed me over here like you asked," he added. "I can't be totally positive, but it doesn't look like it. So, are you finished with me?"

"Are ye in a hurry to leave?" Darro asked mildly.

Vince grinned. "Not particularly, but it's your nickel I'm playing on now. I'm just giving you my honest opinion."

"Then I'd like ye to hang around a few more days just to be on the safe side, and check into mob connections between Chicago and Scotland."

Vince's eyes gleamed. "That's pretty generous of you."

"She's my employee and I do what I can for those who work for me."

"I'll see what I can find out and get back to you." Vince stood up and shook hands with Darro.

Darro stood up too. "Ye're welcome to stay for breakfast if ye like. I think Lucerne is teaching Poppy a full English breakfast if that's still on for this morning."

Vince's eyes bulged. "Would I ever. I haven't tried one of those yet, it's been on my list."

"Ye won't find any better than Lucerne's," Angus bragged. "Darro got lucky when he married that little lass."

"Luck had nothing to do with it," Darro mocked.

"It wasn't yer good looks or yer personality, so I'm still tryin' to figure that one out," Angus hooted.

They all laughed and headed for the house.

―――⁂―――

THE NEXT WEEK WENT by like a blur for Poppy. Phone calls, decisions to make, and sorrow all played a part in her not sleeping well. Lucerne tried to relieve her from her housekeeping duties but it was the only thing that kept the worry at bay.

Some success came out of all the doom and gloom...she learned how to make good pie crust. That one had always escaped her. Besides that, the house was full of the scent of her home-made yeast rolls and pies, much to the delight of

Darro's crew with whom the boss shared what the family couldn't eat.

For Poppy, the simplicity of daily life with Lucerne's Scottish cooking classes, keeping house, and playing with the children soothed her jangled nerves and kept her mind occupied.

After speaking with Edna, it was decided that Adrian would be cremated like his father and his ashes placed in the family mausoleum in the cemetery next to his dad. There would be a memorial later on in the year, which Edna would organize with the help of one of her nieces.

Adrian didn't have a will, which was no surprise. Mack had convinced her that an immediate audit of the corporation was standard procedure and needed to be done now that the reins were in her hands. Funds for Edna weren't near as healthy as Julian had left since Adrian had taken over. She'd followed his advice and told him to make it happen. She had no clue how to run a corporation and would have to promote someone from within or hire someone. Now they were waiting for the audit results. Poppy rubbed her forehead at the nagging headache that seemed to come and go since Adrian had been killed.

Mack wanted her to return to America and run Julian's corporation herself. Without someone at the helm, it was floundering. He was afraid that the audit would reveal that Adrian had drained a lot of the company funds to pay for his gambling habits. The investments that were really showing a good profit were the ones Poppy had advised on and inherited. Without Adrian's hand in the till on those, they were flourishing. Had Julian known about Adrian's gambling habits and embezzlements? Was that why he'd designed the will the way he had?

Vince was still staying with Jamie at the moment, but had given the all clear here. His partner hadn't heard anything on the streets of Chicago about Poppy being targeted, and he hadn't found any connections in Scotland that might be of concern. If Adrian had hired someone, the word of his death would have made it to all ears involved by now and it was no longer a live contract. Simple mathematics. No money to be paid—no hit.

She hoped.

"Are ye goin' to make the scones or just keep on kneadin' that big ball of dough?"

Poppy started and turned around to see Angus and Lucerne grinning at her. "I-I didn't hear you come in," she replied. She gave a brittle chuckle. "You are right, I'm worrying this to death, aren't I?" Her hands trembled as she reached for some butter to pat the top of the ball.

"I'll take over that, Poppy," Lucerne said gently, moving Poppy aside. "Angus wants to take ye out today, and Darro and I agree that ye need the break."

"That's right. Ye've been wantin' to see Loch Ness, so that's where we're goin' to spend the afternoon. Mayhap pick up some lunch from The Waterfront and take with us."

Poppy started to argue but the steel in Angus's brown eyes made her think better of it. He was a stubborn man and she'd learned to recognize when he meant what he said. He might pose his decision as a question, but after a few not-so-gentle spanks to her backside now and then, she'd learned when to just give in. Especially since it was always out of concern for her.

She smiled and nodded her acceptance. There was no good reason not to. "Alright, that sounds lovely. Let me change my clothes and I'll be right out. Should I bring a swimsuit?"

Angus smiled back. "Ye don't want to swim in Loch Ness, it's verra cold and deep and there's other things that swim there."

"Like the Loch Ness monster?" Poppy asked flippantly, shivering slightly at his ominous tones.

"Aye, Nessie, among other things," he teased. "We can take a boat ride out onto the Loch though if ye like."

"I'd like that. Be right back."

Poppy's hands trembled as she dressed in white cotton shorts and a pink Chicago bears T-shirt. She was a sports fan after all. She felt brittle, as if one more bad thing would crack her into shards and leave her body lying in pieces on the floor. Maybe she did need to get out.

She prayed there still wasn't a lone wolf out there determined to end her existence the moment she popped up. Sequestered here at Neamh with big protective Scotsmen all around her would have made it difficult to get to her, but back in the public with strangers all around she would be easy prey. Trying to shake off her jitters, she resolved to stick close to Angus and try to relax.

When she returned to the kitchen, Angus's eyes lit up and he took the last swallow of his tea and placed the cup in the sink. "Ye ready, lass?"

He was looking particularly handsome today with a white shirt open at the collar and tucked into dark blue khaki shorts. He had really nice-looking legs, tanned and muscular with a light covering of fine blond hairs.

"Do you ever wear a kilt?" she asked impulsively.

He grinned. "It's been known to happen."

Lucerne laughed. "Supposedly he and Darro have participated at times in some of the local dances for the tourists, but I have yet to see that."

"I'd love to see that," Poppy enthused. "I wonder who can step the highest?" she teased, knowing their competitive bent with each other.

"Depends on the way ye look at it. Since Darro's taller, naturally he would step higher, but if ye mean high as in knees above the waist, that would be me," Angus assured her with pride, folding his arms and stepping high.

Darro came around the corner from the back hallway and eyed Angus with an arched eyebrow. "What the devil are ye doing? If ye need exercise, there's plenty of work to be done outside."

"Demonstratin' my high step to the lasses, of course," Angus responded frostily.

"He assures us that his step is higher than yers in a kilt jig," Lucerne goaded the situation.

Darro rolled his eyes. "I thought ye were taking Poppy into town. If that's changed ye can perform for the sheep in the north pasture. They need a scary sight to make them move south."

Angus grinned. "Always the slave driver, and he wonders why I eat so much." He held out his hand to Poppy. "Come on, lass, before he changes his mind."

Poppy giggled as Angus pulled her out to his truck and lifted her into the cab. Sometimes she really envied their easy camaraderie.

Lucerne had told her that Angus had always been there for Darro when Whipcord would come down hard on his son. Darro MacCandish senior had not been the gentlest of men and could use a whip with deadly accuracy. The name Darro meant *'the hard one'* in Scottish and he'd lived up to his name. He'd been nicknamed Whipcord because he hadn't been above landing the tip of his lash on a backside to get them moving faster. He'd set a high standard for his sons and Darro had responded.

When Whipcord had passed away, the transition of her husband to lord of Neamh and station master had gone smoothly, thanks to Angus. They were completely loyal to each other in spite of their good-natured squabbling.

"What would ye like fer lunch from The Waterfront?" Angus asked as he climbed into the cab and took out his cell phone. "I'll order and have it ready to be picked up when we get into Inverness."

"I take it The Waterfront prepares picnic baskets for tourists?"

"Aye, that or we can order right off the menu if ye want hot food."

"Then I'll have a cheeseburger and chips this time," she responded enthusiastically. "I can see how their burgers compare to McDonalds."

Angus snorted. "That's easy, they don't. Cheeseburgers it is."

After the order was placed, Poppy laid her head on Angus's shoulder while he held her hand on his thigh as they headed to town. She tried to relax but she couldn't help glancing furtively around her as if something or someone was going to come out of nowhere and start shooting at them. Each time they passed another vehicle, she tensed.

In town, she had to bite her tongue when Angus told her to stay put in the running vehicle while he grabbed their lunch. As soon as he left the truck, she slammed the door locks down and kept vigil all around her as people moved up and down the street, mostly ignoring her. No one gave her a second glance. Finally, she relaxed a little and picked up the brochure on Loch Ness. When Angus tapped on the window, she nearly jumped out of her skin. He pointed at the locked door button.

"I-I'm sorry," she muttered, her face pink when he climbed into the truck and handed her the basket. "I didn't see you coming, I was looking at the brochure."

"Ye need to relax, lass," he replied gently, staring at her face. His big thumb brushed across her cheek. "Ye're safe now."

"Am I really? How can you know that?" she snapped suddenly, then dropped her gaze to her trembling fingers on the picnic basket. "I-I'm sorry, that was uncalled for."

"I can see ye're needin' the Angus special stress reliever," he declared, his eyebrows sky high.

Undecided if he was teasing or not, she bit, albeit suspiciously. "I highly doubt that I'll want that, but tell me what it is anyway."

"What a lass wants and what a lass needs are usually two verra different things," he replied, waggling his eyebrows. "Ye'll just have to wait and see. Hand over a few of those chips to eat on the way."

Within a few minutes, Angus was pulling off road and following a bumpy track until he finally came to a stop. "Grab the burgers and I'll get the bag from the back," he instructed as he helped her out of the truck.

"Aren't we a long way from the loch here?" Poppy asked, shading her eyes from the bright sun.

"We'll walk down a bit from here," he threw over his shoulder before grabbing a canvas bag out of the back. "Ye ready? It's this way."

Poppy followed him down a well-trodden path among the brush and small trees until they came out much closer to a pretty area where water flowed over small rocks and pebbles before merging back into the larger body of water. "This is lovely," she exclaimed, her eyes darting around to take in the grassy bank and the soft gurgle of the flowing water.

"One of my favorite places to avoid the tourists," he replied with a chuckle, opening his bag. He began taking out blankets and pillows, plus another smaller bag, and spreading things out.

"Did you bring the tent too?" she teased. "You have enough blankets and pillows for a harem there."

"Always prepared for a lass's comfort," he quipped.

A FLOWER FOR ANGUS

Poppy wondered how comfortable she was supposed to get in this secluded spot? They'd had so few chances to be alone...really alone...since she got here that she had no idea what Angus might have on his mind. Watching his muscles ripple in his arms and thighs she decided if it was the same thing her mind was turning to, they might be in trouble.

"We should have brought swimsuits," she said, as he took his shoes off and stepped onto the blanket.

He took the food out of her hands so she could take her shoes off. "Nay, ye don't swim wild in Loch Ness," he replied, shaking his head. "It's the coldest and deepest loch in all of Scotland. Most of the sides are cliffs and if ye are brave enough to get in, ye might not be able to get back out. The undercurrents can move ye and the risk of hypothermia from the water is too great. If ye want to swim, I'll take ye to Loch Duntelchaig sometime. Ye can snorkel there too."

Poppy took her sandals off and stepped onto the blankets where they both sat down cross legged to eat their burgers and chips.

Angus opened a small soft-sided cooler and took out a bottle of cold ice tea and handed her one. "Nothing like cold ice tea on a hot day," he added with a lazy grin.

Hot was one word for it, she thought as their knees and shoulders nestled close enough to touch each other. Her body was beginning to tingle, aware of his every time he brushed against her.

"Let's wade on the rocks when we finish eating," she said impulsively.

He nodded. "Aye, we can if ye want to. Ye can dip yer toes in where the rocks end at the darker waters and feel the differences in the temperature. But I warn ye, it's going to be cold."

Poppy chuckled. "I think I need something cold about now, I'm getting pretty warm." She lifted her bottle and took a big swig of her ice tea.

"Is that literally or figuratively speakin'?" he asked, holding her gaze captive when she turned to him.

Her eyes widened and she licked her lips with her tongue. "Both?" she managed to whisper hoarsely. His soft Scottish accent was super sexy and so were his eyes as they searched her face and finally landed on her lips. Inching closer, she raised her mouth, yearning for him to kiss her…wanting him to crush her aching breasts to his hard chest.

"Ye are so lovely, lass," he whispered just before he tenderly kissed her mouth.

"I need…more," she demanded when he lifted his mouth mere inches from hers. She was barely aware that he'd taken the little bit of food left and set it aside. What was he waiting for? She grabbed the front of his shirt in both fists and pulled him down hard. "Kiss me like you mean it, Angus."

He pulled her closer, one strong arm around her back as he pressed her into his body, the other in her hair as he controlled her mouth in a searing kiss that had her throwing caution to the wind. Nothing mattered in that moment. Angus would make her forget her terror, make her forget the horror of Adrian's awful death, make her forget everything but the overwhelming desire setting her body on fire.

"What do ye want, lass?"

"I want you," she begged. "Make me forget, Angus."

A FLOWER FOR ANGUS

ANGUS STARED DOWN AT Poppy's flushed face, her desire echoing his own. He could see the deep shadows in the pale skin beneath her eyes indicating her lack of sleep. He was afraid her nerves had her teetering on the brink of collapse.

Lucerne told him that Poppy drove herself harder since Adrian's death than she ever had, and she could barely get her to take a break. She was always the last one to bed and the first one up, beating even Darro. When Lucerne would wake to go to the bathroom, as her pregnancy often drove her to do, she would sometimes hear Poppy moving in the hall. To be blunt, Lucerne was really getting worried about her.

Angus could tell she'd lost some weight; he could feel her ribs more pronounced than when he held her that first day. But was this something she would regret as soon as her bodies needs were met? The last thing he wanted was to take advantage of her weakened state of mind. He wanted to be here for her and to help her, but he was also in love with her and he didn't want to have any regrets.

As sorely tempted as he was, Angus sighed and leaned back as her eyes popped open and she stared accusingly at him, a blush creeping up her face.

"Y-You don't want me?" Suddenly she was fighting to get out of his arms.

"Hold on there, lass," he said soothingly. "Of course, I want ye, but that's not what ye need right now."

"Let me go, Angus, I want to leave," she yelled. "Take me back to Neamh right now."

"Settle down, wee lass," he said firmly, holding her upper arms.

"I'm not staying here with you," she replied, suddenly rounding on him with a fist in his stomach. "Let me go."

"Oomph," Angus grunted, his brows slashing downward. For such a weak thing, she had a good right hook. "Now ye did it," he snapped, his patience spiraling.

"Let me go, I'm warning you," she snapped, trying to headbutt him when he grabbed her wrists.

"The only place ye are goin' is over my lap," he retorted as he slipped his arms beneath her body and flipped her over his legs before she realized what he was doing. Then he simply held her against his body as she wriggled and swore words that should never come from a lass's mouth. He glanced behind him to make sure no one was approaching to invade their privacy. He was glad he'd chosen this spot. If they were in public, he'd be arrested as soon as someone called the local constable. It was time to settle her down a bit. He lifted his right arm and landed several stinging spanks on the seat of her cotton shorts, then paused.

"Let me up, Angus, you can't do this to me, I'll have you arrested."

Angus rubbed the rear displayed so enticingly over his thighs. "That was to get yer attention. Have I got it?"

"You're going to get something all right," she threatened, "and it won't be my attention once they arrest you and throw your as..."

He landed several more stinging blows. "No swearin'," he admonished. "Ladies don't swear."

"I never claimed to be a lady," she panted, sounding like she was trying not to cry.

He began rubbing the seat of her shorts now that she wasn't wiggling all over the place. "It's not that I don't want ye, Poppy," he said gently. "I want ye with everythin' in me right now, but when we make love for the first time, I want it to be special. I don't want it to be somethin' ye'll regret because it was spur of the moment and ye just wanted to forget everythin' that's hauntin' ye. I didn't mean to embarrass ye." He slipped his hand inside her shorts and slid them over the rounded contours of her cheeks and down to her thighs.

"D-Don't do that," she squeaked, reaching back to try and grab the sides of her pants.

"Why?" he asked, admiring the now pink curves in the thin silkie panties. He rubbed his palm over them reverently, loving the satiny feel. Then he slipped his hand inside those and they joined the panties on her thighs.

"A-Angus, stop," she squealed. "What are you doing?"

The full cheeks trembled beneath his rubbing palm. "What I wanted to do to begin with before ye attacked me," he replied with a teasing chuckle. He glanced down at her red face.

"I can see ye are embarrassed, wee one, and all I'm doin' is lookin' at yer gorgeous bum. Ye asked me to make ye forget, and I intend to. But not the way ye wanted to go about it. I don't want ye to have any regrets, and I'm afraid ye would have if we'd just went at it like rabbits."

"Oh my God," she whispered, sounding completely mortified.

"Trust me, Poppy, and I won't leave ye wantin'." He felt her body relax under his soothing ministrations, so he lifted his palm and gave her several more smacks, though not as hard as before.

Her body tensed up. "Oh," she gasped.

"Did that hurt?"

"Well...not like before," she replied uneasily, glancing back at him. "Are you sure you know what you're doing?"

"Oh aye. My special stress reliever works like a charm."

"That remains to be seen," she moaned as he began kneading her back and shoulders with both hands.

Slowly, Angus worked some of the knots out of her shoulders and moved down her back, allowing the sun's rays to help heat her body. Then he moved his hand back to her rear and began all over again, spanks, rubs, and massaging. Chuckling, he slowly slid his palm up her inner thighs checking for the moisture he was sure he would soon find there, if it wasn't already. He was pleased to feel plenty of her sweet heat, but he also felt her tense slightly.

"Relax, wee one," he crooned, landing more spanks and then rubbing, each time teasing closer and closer to that inner core with his fingers. When she finally began a gentle undulation of her hips to meet his next foray into forbidden territory, he knew she was climbing that long slow rise to ecstasy. Right where he wanted her.

"Angus," she keened, her body arching for more.

He gave it to her and sent her spiraling among the clouds of heaven. Then he grinned with satisfaction when she lay spent across his legs. She didn't move when he gently slid her clothes back in place and placed a pillow under her head. Reaching behind him to grab the sunshade he'd brought out of his large canvas bag, he set it up over her upper body, then set about cleaning up while she slept.

For a long time, Angus just watched Poppy sleep, happy to hold her hand when she seemed restless and reached over as if searching for him. When she would relax again, he'd go back to the book he was reading on his phone kindle.

Beside him and beneath a pillow, he had his knife at the ready should it be necessary to protect his lass, but he didn't think he'd need it. He would have liked to sleep beside her, but he wanted to be absolutely sure he wouldn't be caught with his pants down, so to speak. Poppy was his to protect and he'd make damned sure he did.

Chapter 11

It was getting late in the afternoon and the sun was beginning to wane when Poppy finally rolled onto her back and yawned so wide it brought tears to her eyes. Then it all came rushing back and she sat up, moving aside the sunshade. "What time is it?" she asked softly. She could feel a flush heating up her face at his knowing look.

"Hello to ye too, sleepyhead," he teased. "To answer yer question, it's getting' close to suppertime. Are ye hungry? We can stop at The Waterfront for some seafood on the way back to Neamh if ye like."

Poppy shuddered to think what she must look like. She reached up to smooth down her hair. Her shorts and cotton shirt were sporting wrinkles. "I don't think I'm ready for polite society," she replied. "I must look a fright." She rubbed her chin. "Do I have drool lines?"

Angus's eyes popped. "Drool lines?"

She smirked. "Just making sure you know what you could be getting into."

He threw back his head and laughed. "I'd still get into it, drool lines, snoring and all. I'm glad to see ye feelin' less tense, lass."

"I guess I do have you to thank for that," she replied, reaching up and giving him a quick kiss. Thank you, Angus."

"The Angus special...works every time," he teased. "And ye're welcome." He dropped a return kiss on her lips. I can come over every night if it helps ye sleep like a baby," he offered helpfully.

"Uh...I'll take a raincheck on that."

He pointed at the rocks. "Did ye still want to walk on the rocks and dip yer toes in the loch?"

Poppy shivered; the air was getting a little cooler off the lake. "I'll take a raincheck on that too."

"Then let's get things back in the bag."

Poppy picked up a pillow and gasped when she saw the wicked looking knife laying there. She stared at Angus. "Didn't you sleep while I was sleeping?" she asked suspiciously.

He picked up the knife and shook his head. "Nay, but it was just a precaution, lass. I never truly expected anyone."

Poppy couldn't believe it. Her heart swelled with feelings that threatened to turn to tears. This man had watched over her while she slept. Just to be on the safe side. "Oh, Angus," she breathed softly. "You are an amazing man."

He actually blushed. "Nay, lass. Just doing what any man would do fer his lass."

She slipped her arms around his waist and laid her head on his chest where she could hear and feel his heart beating. "Not just any man would do what you did."

He held her close and Poppy loved the feel of his arms around her. Hope blossomed with tentative tendrils as she realized she was starting to truly feel safe again. It was something she'd despaired of ever feeling when she'd left Toronto.

Finally, Angus turned her around and landed a spank on her backside. "Let's get goin', wee one, before the sun sets and it gets as black as the lake out there."

Poppy hopped to it with a mocking salute to her forehead. "Sir...yes, sir!"

Angus chuckled in those rich deep tones that she loved.

"I like that. Ye can call me sir anytime ye want."

She arched an eyebrow as she folded a blanket and handed it to him. "Don't get used to it."

They did stop for seafood at The Waterfront, which was everything Dorothy and Angus had promised it would be, and they arrived back at Neamh with Poppy feeling satiated, and in a much better mood.

"Ye are looking more relaxed," Lucerne noted with approval as they made their way into the kitchen for a nightcap of tea. "Ye need to take more time off."

Darro was sitting at the table and he leaned forward as Poppy and Angus sat across from them. "We were just discussing exactly that and I'm afraid I agree with my wife. After all, it's not like ye need to work, Poppy. What would ye say if I hired another housekeeper? Ye are free to stay here as long as ye like as our guest, but it would give ye breathing room to consider yer options instead of blocking everything out by focusing on working yerself into the ground," he added sternly.

Poppy gawped at him. Guest? That meant short-term. Options? That equated to they didn't need her anymore which equated to the bottom falling out of her safe haven. Where had this come from out of the blue? Didn't they like the work she was doing? She'd thought they were happy with her. Why were they trying to get rid of her?

"Y-You don't want me as a housekeeper anymore? I'm being fired?" She finally stuttered, unsure of what to say.

"Ye could always be my housekeeper, Poppy," Angus inserted cheerfully.

Like a lightning bolt of revelation, Poppy gave Angus a very suspicious side eye. Had Angus asked Darro to fire her so she'd move in with him? "Did you put Darro up to this?"

"Up to what?" Angus looked genuinely confused.

He looked completely innocent and Poppy felt a twinge of regret and confusion. Was she just being paranoid?

"It's not like that, Poppy," Lucerne replied in concern.

"No?" Confused, Poppy stood up, knocking over her cup of tea as she did so. It ran right towards Darro and he jumped up as Lucerne went to grab a towel.

Darro growled. "Look, Poppy..."

Poppy waved her hand to stop him, her feelings suddenly overwhelming her. "I don't know what's going on, but if I'm not wanted here, I need to find someplace else to be," she sputtered.

She didn't want to make accusations that might not be real, but she couldn't help feeling that the bond between the two men could have Darro trying to push her and Angus together. Did Angus really not know about it? Or was he just good at pretending innocence?

She liked Angus, more than a little, but she wasn't ready to move in with him. Angus tried to grab her hand but she shook him off. Her entire life had been controlled by men and although she might be falling in love with Angus, this time she wanted life on her terms. "Just leave me alone," she cried as she climbed over the bench seat and ran to her bedroom. She needed to be alone and think this out.

As she sat on the bed, her new cellphone rang and Andrea's name popped up. "Hello, Andrea," she said in a wobbly voice after sliding the green button aside.

"Mom? I'm sorry to be bearer of bad news, but you might want to come home. I'm putting you on speaker so Morgan can talk."

Poppy's heart dropped and her mouth immediately resembled a day in the Sahara Desert. Home was the last place she wanted to be. If they didn't want her at Neamh, then she'd move back into Inverness now that she was supposed to be safe.

"Why? What's happening now?" she asked bitterly. Her head was already starting to ache again and her body tensed as she waited for the next announcement of never-ending bad news that had seemed to take over her life for the last year.

Morgan's voice came across the line. "Poppy, the FBI did start an investigation of Adrian and his activities over the last year. His alibi has fallen through. The secretary who vouched for him the day Julian died said he paid her to do so. Sarah Solano said she was afraid of Adrian before, but now that he's dead, she's coming forward with what she says is the real truth. I'm not going to lie to you, Poppy, it's looking more and more like he's responsible for Julian's death."

"Oh my God," Poppy whispered. The nightmare was nipping at her heels again. Would she get dragged back into court for repeated testimonies? Would she be subpoenaed as

A FLOWER FOR ANGUS

soon as her feet landed on Chicago soil? Would they try to charge her and say she was complicit if Adrian had done it?

Edna might jump at the chance to implicate her in any wrong doing. Her mother-in-law hated her and would do anything to get revenge over the way Julian had negated the prenup.

And the media vultures—they would be circling once again wanting more flesh. They never stopped hunting her.

Morgan's voice droned on. "And the audits Mack has been doing are starting to filter in and it looks like the corporation is nearly broke. The only ones that are healthy are the ones Julian left to you."

Poppy could feel the big red target on her back as if Morgan had reached through the phone and painted it on her. The media would have a field day when this came out.

'Black widow eats her way into millions and leaves the country.'

It was more than Poppy could bear.

"I-I don't want to come home, Morgan. What if the DA tries to drag me back into it again? Or worse yet, Edna accuses me of something I didn't do? I won't come back—I can't do it," she groaned painfully as the pressure in her head increased.

The room started to spin and Poppy slid off the edge of the bed and landed on the floor. Moaning at the splitting pain in her head, she pulled her knees up and tried to shrink herself into a tiny ball where nothing could get to her. The phone landed on the floor a few feet away from her but she was beyond hearing Andrea's frantic voice calling to her.

Where could she turn? Even the safe haven of Angus's arms now seemed suspicious.

Who could she trust?

ANGUS STARTED AFTER Poppy but Lucerne stopped him. "Let me, Angus. I'll talk to her."

He sat back down and stared accusingly at Darro. "What was that all about, lad? Ye aren't tryin' to do me any favors are ye? Because this isn't the way to earn Poppy's trust if ye are. I can only imagine the hell that lass has been through this last year."

Darro ran his hands through his dark hair with an exasperated sigh. "Not at all, Angus. Lucerne and I just want to help Poppy and we didn't want her to feel obligated to stay on as a housekeeper now that she doesn't have to hide anymore. She seems to have an over developed sense of obligation to her job commitment, and she's been working herself to the bone since she got here. Frankly, Lucerne has been very worried about her because she seems so fragile and brittle, especially since Vince showed up."

Angus nodded with a worried frown. "Aye, she's told me a bit about the media feedin' frenzy after her husband died, and then being stalked for months until she finally left the country in fear for her life. It's the stuff horror stories are made of. She passes it off as just uninterestin' history that she wants to get past, but I think it goes deeper than that. She's a private lass though, and I no want to press her."

Darro nodded. "Of course, I have to agree. Poppy can keep her position if that's what she really wants to do. We just wanted her to have options but it apparently didn't come out right. For that, I apologize."

"Darro! Angus!"

Lucerne's frantic cry had them both jumping up from the table and running to where Lucerne was urgently motioning them into Poppy's room. "Angus, ye need to get Poppy off the floor and Darro, ye need to talk to Andrea and Morgan." She handed Darro the phone, her pretty eyes filled with worry.

Seeing Poppy curled into a fetal position had Angus's heart jumping into his throat. He rushed forward and gently lifted her up in his strong arms. She was incredibly cold and moaning. "I'm takin' her into the livin' room where I can hold her and get her warm," he said, striding out of the room.

Once in the living room, he grabbed a warm throw from the back of the couch and tucked Poppy's head into his shoulder as he covered her up. He wondered what the hell had happened now? What had her daughter told her that had caused this reaction?

"Docs on his way," Darro announced as he and Lucerne came into the living room and sat down across from Angus. Doc MacCandish was Darro's uncle who'd gone into medicine half a century ago and had a practice in Inverness. His given name was Evan, but everyone just called him Doc in deference to his profession. He'd preferred medicine to sheep and had left Neamh to seek his own fortunes when he and Whipcord were young men. Whipcord had stayed with Neamh.

Angus scowled. "What did Andrea have to say?"

Poppy stirred in his arms and he glanced down. She was warming up finally, he could feel the bare skin of her thigh and arm heating where he held her. One small hand reached out and pushed the cover off her chest as she tried to get up.

His arms tightened and he growled possessively. "Where do ye think ye are goin'?"

Eyes seeming the size of Canada stared mutely up at him. The doubt he saw in those depths made him want to strangle whoever had put it there. Before Darro had, that is. Then she tried to put her legs down off the sofa.

"Unless ye want to be turned over and warmed up from an up-ended position, I suggest ye sit still, wee one."

Poppy glanced over at Darro and Lucerne and then blushed. "I don't want to sit on your lap," she hissed.

"I didn't want to find ye collapsed into a ball of ice on the floor either, but then we don't always get what we want, do we?"

She closed her eyes, but not before he saw a flash of fire in those brown orbs. "My head was aching and I slipped off the bed. It just seemed more comfortable to stay on the floor than move at the time," she scoffed, rubbing her forehead.

"This isn't the first time ye've mentioned havin' a headache. How long have ye had them?" Angus asked in concern. "Is it still bad?"

"I don't remember," she replied wearily. "And no, it's not as bad, but it still hurts."

"Have ye seen a doctor?"

"Not for a long time," she quipped facetiously. "It tends to give hidey holes away when you do things like that. Besides, Ibuprofen and Tylenol are cheaper."

Her sarcastic comments told Angus a lot. One, she was trying to shut him out. And two, she'd been through a lot more than she wanted to admit. Maybe it was time to take the kid gloves off. The feelings he had for Poppy grew deeper every day and he knew she cared for him as well. He wasn't about to let her run away from him or hide.

"Let me explain somethin', Poppy," he growled. "Darro and I are not plottin' together, ye are not fired. Ye jump to conclusions without listenin' more often than I'd like. Ye need to calm down and show a little faith and trust in us instead of flyin' off the handle. And if ye don't, I'm goin' to see that ye start sitting a little sorer than ye're used to."

When she opened her mouth for what he assumed would be a scathing retort, he held up his forefinger and waggled it at her. "Think verra carefully about what ye are goin' to say next, because havin' company in the room won't save yer backside if ye're determined to be a brat."

Darro cleared his throat and tried to hide a smirk until Poppy turned to glare at him. "Uh...Poppy, I spoke with Andrea and Morgan."

Poppy shivered suddenly as her thoughts were refocused. "I'm not going to Chicago," she spat out defensively.

"Why do they want Poppy back in Chicago?" Angus asked Darro with a scowl. His eyebrows tried to crawl off his head when he heard that they suspected Adrian of murdering his own father.

"This just keeps getting' worse and worse," he finally replied, his grip on Poppy tightening. "I'm sorry ye are goin' through this, lass. What a nightmare."

Poppy sagged against him, suddenly deflated and fragile. "It's never going to end. Edna will take this opportunity to put me in the middle of it again. Especially if the company really is broke. Without Julian's coffers to fund her lifestyle, she'll come after my inheritance. I've always wondered if she put Adrian up to charging me with Julian's murder. She didn't realize I was leaving the house that day."

"Are ye sure about that?" Angus asked in disbelief once he'd picked his jaw up off the floor.

"Can ye prove any of this, Poppy?" Darro asked, his eyebrows nearly as high as Angus's.

Poppy shook her head. "Of course, I can't prove it. But after living with that harridan for the last ten years, I wouldn't put anything past her. She was another one of the reasons I left Chicago in the first place. She kept inviting her press cronies over to the house where she would secret them away in her wing for hours at a time. I even caught them sneaking around the mansion trying to take pictures of me."

"Did Edna and Adrian get along?" Lucerne inserted.

"Oh, she spoiled Adrian ridiculously. Julian actually had very little control over his own son. She insisted Julian take Adrian into the family business, which he wanted to do anyway, but it wasn't something Adrian ever enjoyed. He liked the money; he just didn't like to work. He was crap at investments and the board didn't care for him either. He was always thick as thieves with Edna," she added bitterly.

"The detective on Julian's death investigation was also a friend of Edna's. He never missed an opportunity to make me look bad if he could. I guess that makes me a coward, but I finally just ran away from it all," she confessed.

"What ye did is understandable, lass. What about Morgan? As an FBI agent, wasn't there anythin' he could do?" Angus asked.

"What about him?" Poppy flashed back. "Morgan's hands were tied. Besides, he is my son-in-law, so he wasn't allowed anywhere near the murder investigation. The case wasn't FBI jurisdiction and attempting to stick his nose in could have cost him his job. There was nothing he *could* do.

"I suppose since Adrian's death looks like a mob execution, that finally gave the FBI the chance to exercise their jurisdiction and investigate Adrian's connections. I never expected the murder investigation to be re-opened though. Whatever happens, I'm not going back there," she vowed adamantly.

Angus thought it wise not to point out that she might have to; he knew she was aware of that fact despite the way she felt. He didn't like anything he was hearing. The Condoloro family had a lot of secrets and he wondered how deep the corruption went. Could Edna be as vicious as Poppy said she was?

The doorbell ringing in the sudden stillness made Poppy jump. "Who can that be?"

"That will be Doc," Darro replied, heading for the front door.

"Who is Doc?" she asked.

"The man who's goin' to check ye over and speak with ye," Angus replied firmly. "And don't forget to tell him about the headache tablets ye need, or I will."

Poppy's eyes narrowed. "I don't know who made you the boss, but I don't need to see a doctor."

Angus grinned and pointed at Darro as he came around the corner. "He's the boss and he's the one who called Doc. Since ye're still employed, I suggest ye listen to him"

Poppy huffed as she glared at the distinguished looking man behind Darro. He had a full head of neatly cut graying hair, a trim mustache, and a striking resemblance to Darro. He was dressed in casual dark slacks and a white polo and carried a black bag in his hand. His blue eyes landed on Poppy and he smiled appreciatively.

Darro looked down at Poppy. "This is Doc MacCandish and I want ye to speak with him, please."

Seeing the mulish look on Poppy's face, Doc's eyes twinkled. "Well now, lass, as comfortable as ye might be on Angus's lap, I think I'd like to talk to ye in the kitchen where we can have some doctor patient privacy. Would that be acceptable to ye?" He held out his hand to Poppy with an engaging grin.

Poppy surprised Angus by taking the Doc's hand and allowing him to help her up as he boosted her with his hands on her waist.

"Since you've so kindly *rescued* me from my current predicament, I'll follow you anywhere," Poppy retorted. "There's nothing wrong with me though, just so you know you've wasted your time."

"Poppy," growled Angus. "Tell him about the headache tabs ye need."

Darro chuckled. "She's a feisty one, Doc. Think ye can handle her?"

"Beautiful lasses aren't handled, Darro, they are thoroughly appreciated," Doc replied, ushering Poppy ahead of him with a wink and a grin.

Chapter 12

Poppy had to admit, Doc was easy to be around. He was professional and thorough as he went through her basic vitals. She answered most of his questions regarding her stress level in the last year as briefly as possible. She knew his sharp mind was reading between lines to understand the parts she wasn't saying, but she didn't want her horrible reputation in Chicago to follow her over here. Especially if she decided to live here in Inverness.

Finally, he laid his stethoscope on his bag on the table and folded his arms. "My diagnosis is that ye do appear to be in reasonably good health, too far on the thin side so I'm guessing ye don't eat when ye're stressed, and judging from the deep shadows under yer eyes, ye don't sleep well. Plus, ye've not seen a therapist but ye've seen yer regular doctor," he summed up nicely. "Do ye remember the names of the tablets he gave ye? Were they supposed to be pain pills or sleeping aids?"

Poppy screwed up her forehead, the low throbbing pulse in her head making her want to keep her eyes closed. "Both? I just know that when my head really began to ache, I'd take one and then I'd go to sleep. When I woke up, the headache was usually gone. I don't remember the name of the medicine." She rubbed her temples, trying to ease the current pain.

"Is the script he gave ye still good?"

"I don't know, I threw the bottle away after it was empty while I was in Toronto," she confessed.

Doc took out a script pad and began writing. "I'm going to give ye a script that will do the same thing. Ye can take it for either, a good night's rest or pain. Since the headaches are obviously stress related, which happens more often when ye are overtired, ye need to get more sleep. If this doesn't address yer headaches as well as ye'd like, I want ye to make an appointment with me for a CT scan. I doubt we will find anything, but it's always better to rule out anything wrong inside yer head other than the normal lassie stuff." He grinned down at her and winked.

"Is this an addictive narcotic?" Poppy asked suspiciously, ignoring his teasing comment. "I don't want to take oxycodone or something like that."

"No, I don't think ye need anything that strong at this point. Let's see how ye fare with this first. The next time I see ye, I want those shadows gone and few more pounds on ye. Get more rest."

"I hope there won't be a next time," she replied with a scowl.

Doc snapped his bag closed, one eyebrow arching higher than the other. "That remains to be seen, young lass. If ye're staying at Neamh for any given amount of time, I wouldn't count on it unless ye take care of yerself. My nephew has strict rules about his employee's health. And Angus always made sure Rosie had her annual checkups as well," he remarked.

Poppy could feel the blush creeping up her cheeks. "Scottish men are over protective—noted."

"Nay, lass. Scottish men are protective of their women and families. They consider them a duty and a gift."

"All Scottish men?" she scoffed in disbelief.

He studied her briefly. "Not all, nay. I'm sure in America there are protective men as well, but just like here, they have their share of evil men too."

"I guess the trick is figuring out which is which then," she retorted, rubbing her forehead again.

He handed her the script and then reached in his bag and pulled out a sample packet. "Here. Take this sample and go to bed. At the risk of sounding cliché, ye should feel better in the morning. And for the record, Angus and Darro are some of the good men."

He grabbed his bag and strode out leaving Poppy to stare after him. He was right, they were good men, she just had a hard time trusting *any* man.

With a sigh, she went to the fridge and grabbed a bottle of cold water and opened the packet. She could hear the rumble of voices coming from the living room and made her escape to her room while she could. Her head was pounding and she didn't want to face Angus and Darro again. She owed them all an apology but she couldn't think clearly right now. All she wanted to do was hide and not have to think about or discuss what was happening in Chicago. With the tablet, maybe Edna would stay out of her nightmares.

She could only hope.

A FLOWER FOR ANGUS 177

THE NEXT MORNING, ANGUS arrived at the barn office a little earlier than normal, his worry about Poppy pushing him to get his rear end in gear. Not that Angus was ever late to work. In fact, he didn't have a schedule at all, he just spent the majority of his time at Neamh and it was a second home.

Usually, he arrived before Darro most mornings, especially now that Darro was married. Up at 5:00 a.m. and out to the barn by 5:30 a.m. had been his schedule. He'd pushed it back by a half hour, or sometimes more depending on various things that Angus was happy to give him grief over or torture him about. Women had a tendency to change a man, and mostly for the better in his opinion. Lucerne had certainly taken some of the sharp edges off the lad.

He glanced at the kitchen door as he drove around the backside of the house to see if he could detect any sign of movement. No one should be in the kitchen to fix breakfast at 5:00 a.m., especially Poppy. If she was, then she needed her little arse tanned. Breakfast was at 7:00 a.m. and she didn't need to be up at 5:00 a.m. for that.

Doc had assured he and Darro last night that the tablet should help Poppy get a good night's sleep, and that he'd given her a script to be filled in town today. Which was exactly where Angus intended to take her once she was up and around.

The closed sign was still facing out in the back door window and he chuckled with satisfaction as he drove on behind the big barn. The sign in the window had been Lucerne's idea. If the sign had a bright sunflower with a big smile on it, then the kitchen was open for him to come in and get coffee and a tart on his way to the barn office. If the board was on the blank side, then the day hadn't begun for the MacCandish household.

He glanced at his watch. It was just now coming up on 5:00 am. He pulled his truck in and parked, then headed into the office to make a pot of coffee. A stash of Lucerne's sugar biccies was stored in his desk drawer. He totally loved those delicious, sugary biccies, or cookies as the American part of her sometimes called them. Apparently, the yanks loved their sweet treats too. Sometimes Lucerne would flavor hers with a bit of lemon or even a slight orange flavor and he really liked that as well.

Fifteen minutes later with a cup of coffee in one hand, and a biccie in the other, he'd been staring at the papers in front of him and seeing nothing when the door behind him suddenly opened. He whipped around to see Dal standing there with a sheepish grin on his face.

"Uh...ye are here early," he stammered, looking guilty as hell, as if his hand had been caught in a cookie jar. That's when the light bulb went on.

Angus's eyes narrowed. "So, ye are the mouse what's been into my biccie stash, are ye? Here I've been accusin' Darro for weeks."

"Ye have plenty of cookies," Dal protested, his unrepentant grin giving him away.

"Why don't ye just ask Lucerne fer yer own?" Angus growled.

A FLOWER FOR ANGUS

"She's the boss's wife. I don't think he'd take it too kindly if I turned up at the kitchen door begging. Everyone knows the sunflower is only there for ye," Dal complained, folding his arms and leaning in the doorway.

"That doesn't excuse yer thievin'," Angus scolded. "Nothin' worse than the employee who takes someone else's lunch out of the cooler when no one is lookin'."

"I don't take lunches. Besides all's fair in love and treats," Dal taunted with a mischievous grin. "I hope Ainsley can cook as well as Lucerne when I marry her."

The sudden sharp crack of the whip was like a gunshot going off just before Dal leaped two feet forward and grabbed his arse.

"Arrghh," he yelped in shock as he turned around and then paled.

Angus roared with laughter when Darro stepped into the doorway, coiling the horsewhip in his hands back into a circle.

"Consider that yer only warning," he growled with a fierce look. "Thieving is no tolerated here on Neamh, even if it is limited to sugar biccies. And it had best be, or ye'll be holding yer arse for a lot longer on yer way off the property."

"Y-Yes sir...I mean no sir. I don't steal," Dal assured him, rubbing his backside furiously.

Darro folded his broad arms across his chest. "Ye just admitted to stealing Angus's biccies."

"I-I might have borrowed a few," he confessed, his pale face now turning red.

Darro's eyebrow shot up. "Borrowed? Were ye planning on putting them back then?"

Dal finally shot Angus a ferocious glare. "All right then, I ate them without any intention of putting them back. But it was no with the intention of stealing, it was just a practical joke on Angus because he takes so much pride in having them."

"And are ye the only one eating Angus's biccies?" Darro asked, a thread of amusement seeping into his words.

Dal hesitated. "Aye, I'm the only one who took them and I apologize, sir."

Darro nodded, satisfied with the explanation. He walked to the drawer and took out the bag of sugar biccies and handed two of them to Dal.

"What are ye doin'?" Angus protested.

"Thank ye for yer honesty and yer loyalty, Dal. Tell Henry to stop by the house before he leaves and Lucerne will have a box waiting for his granddaughter." He gave Dal a wink. Now get to yer work."

"Aye, sir. Thank ye, sir, ye are very kind." Dal left in a hurry, still rubbing his arse cheek.

Angus eyes narrowed at Darro. "Care to explain what that was all about, lad?"

Darro snorted, his eyes twinkling as he headed for the coffee pot. "When ye accused me of taking yer biccies, I made it my business to find out who had. When I learned that Dal had given a few biccies to Henry now and then to give to his granddaughter who's been sick with RSV, I admired his charitable intentions, but not his method of delivery."

Understanding dawned. "Ah, I see." Angus shook his head. "That lad is always surprisin' me. Somehow, I missed that, I should have known about Henry."

"A man tends to miss more than he otherwise would when a lass is turning him inside out," Darro replied with a chuckle. Then he turned serious. "I sent Vince back to Chicago to see what he could find out about the situation there. I suspect Poppy will have to go back at some point."

"Aye," Angus agreed with a frown. "But when she does, I'm plannin' on goin' with her. Can ye get by without me for a while?"

Darro nodded. "Of course. If ye are sure that's what ye want. Poppy's life is in shambles and has been for the last year. If ye have marriage on yer mind, how can ye be sure ye won't be a rebound?"

"The real problem is gettin' her to even let me court her, yet alone marry her," Angus scoffed. "She's no lookin' fer another husband."

"Are ye sure she's the one?"

Angus cocked his head sideways. "At my age, lad, there is no *'the one'* any more. "That's fer the younger generations just startin' out. They haven't figured out that there might be more than one. We are no promised tomorrow, lad. Life is full of twists and turns that sidetrack us from our original goals." He shook his head ruefully. "I told ye about my Dublin lassie. Back in the day, I thought she was *'the one'* until her daddy rode me out of town on a rail, so to speak."

Darro chuckled. "Aye, ye told me."

"I had a lot of good years with Rosie and she blessed me with my bairns and a good life. She's gone now, somethin' I never expected to happen. Now, I've been handed another flower, thanks to the good lord's mercies. Right now, she is *'the one'*, and if I can find a way to convince her that she's mine, she'll be the one fer the rest of our lives," he finished. "And now, that's enough of the mushy stuff, there's work to be done."

"Well, it's time fer breakfast, so let's head to the house. Lucerne and I intend to set down some rules fer my employee and she may not like it much, but it might give ye more opportunities to convince her."

"I'm starvin', let's see what the lasses have fer us this morning," Angus replied with relish.

"Ye're always starving, ye old coot," Darro replied with affection.

"Like I said, ye're a slavedriver."

THE PILL DOC HAD GIVEN Poppy worked a miracle. When the sun peeked through her curtains and bathed her face in warmth and light, she stretched and rolled languidly onto her back. For a few precious seconds she was at peace—until the previous night came rushing back, dragging her miserable life to the forefront of her mind once again.

With a groan, she swung her legs over the side of the bed and glanced at her watch. It was almost 7:00 am. She was supposed to fix breakfast this morning!

Now that she was awake, she could smell coffee and the heavenly scent of bacon on the air. Lucerne hadn't awakened her on purpose, for which she was grateful. It had been a long time since she'd been able to sleep in, mostly because her mind wouldn't let her rest at night.

She padded to the dresser and picked out some clothes to take into the bathroom with her. First a hot shower, then she'd head to the kitchen for some toast and coffee. Maybe she'd add a few slices of bacon this morning. It did smell good and Doc wanted her to eat more.

After getting dressed in modest jeans and a cool blouse for her housekeeping duties, she headed to the kitchen.

She could hear Angus talking before she got there, teasing the kids and bantering with Darro. What he'd done for her at the lake yesterday brought a pink blush to her cheeks and she had to admit, it had put her to sleep immediately. She wondered if that type of massage would do it all the time or if she was just so tired that the blissful after affect had knocked her out?

That she could get used to.

In fact, she could get used to Angus on a full-time basis. She carried so much baggage though, he didn't deserve that. His dominant, protective attitude was actually a part of his charm, although she would never admit it. It's when men got really bossy that their over protectiveness became annoying. So how would that work long-term? Was spanking her for punishment a part of his personality too? One thing she knew for sure, she had no intention of getting married anytime soon, if ever. Even if Angus was growing on her.

As she rounded the corner and took a left into the kitchen, he stood up to greet her. "Good mornin', lass. Did ye sleep well?" The corners of his mouth tipped up with his usual grin.

"Very well, thank you." He was dressed in a red shirt and jeans this morning and looking good enough to make her pulse race faster. "You look dressed up, are you going somewhere?"

He nodded his head. "Aye, I'm takin' ye into town to get yer script filled."

Annoyance shot through her as she headed to the coffee pot. She hadn't asked him to do that, and he hadn't asked her if he could. Besides, she was perfectly able to drive her rental into town alone. "I can manage on my own, thank you."

Darro intervened at that point. "I'm glad ye slept well, Poppy. When ye get yer coffee and sit down, Lucerne and I need to go over a few things with you."

She glanced at her watch with a frown. "Isn't Lucerne dropping off the kids and headed into town in a minute?"

"Aye," Lucerne replied, "but this will just take a few minutes. We need to do some rescheduling. Delilah and Corey, ye need to get yer shoes on and get your backpacks ready to head towards the car."

Once all the goodbyes were said, Poppy seated herself at the table by Angus where she could face Darro and Lucerne across from her. "Okay, I'm ready."

Darro cleared his throat. "Poppy, Doc was very clear about ye needing to get more rest. Last night ye misunderstood and I don't want that happening again, so let me be perfectly clear. Ye can be our housekeeper for as long as ye like, but there will be no more working the hours ye have been.

"This job is very versatile, mostly revolving around mealtimes and when the kids are home but Lucerne isn't. That being the case, she will tell ye when she needs ye on a weekly schedule, and ye will have three-day weekends off. If ye need other times off for whatever reason, ye need to coordinate with Lucerne. Like this morning. Lucerne needs a short list of items and I need Angus to pick up a few things.

"Doc said ye had a script to fill as well, so I'm sending the two of ye in together. Since this is Friday, the rest of today and the weekend are yours to do as ye wish."

Poppy frowned, trying to think fast. Was Darro trying to push her and Angus together? It had seemed that way last night, and now this made her suspicious again.

"I-I was actually planning on stopping in at a realtor's office while I was in Inverness to get some ideas of properties for rent," she supplied. "You don't normally have a live-in housekeeper, do you? And since I plan on staying around Inverness for an unspecified period of time, I thought I should get my own place."

"I'll be happy to help ye with that, Poppy," Angus replied earnestly, his gaze looking like he was trying to read her thoughts on a page in her brain.

"Since Lucerne is the first actual housekeeper I've hired, and I married her, I haven't given it any thought," Darro replied with a teasing grin at Lucerne. "But if ye are here through the winter it would be impractical, not to mention impossible at times, to drive up here when the roads are bad."

"Oh, you're right. I hadn't thought that far ahead," she confessed. "I'd still like to look around and get some information. I'll need a place of my own eventually, I can't stay here all the time, and I probably won't work as much once all this stuff in my personal life is past."

"Ye aren't planning on going back to Chicago when all this is settled?" he asked.

"I-I don't know. I like it here in Scotland. I've always wanted to come back since I was a young girl. But I do have my daughter and her family to think of."

Afraid of getting any deeper into the conversation, she gave in and looked at Angus. "I'll go into town with you then, if you don't mind."

"Of course, I don't mind," Angus replied, patting her leg under the table.

Darro nodded. "Good, it's settled for now."

Poppy drank her coffee and nibbled her bacon, trying not to feel like a paranoid fool. What was wrong with her? She liked Angus, more than a little bit. Just because he had a bossy way about him didn't mean he and Darro were plotting against her. Being with Angus was something she wanted anyway, so why spoil the opportunity by being a suspicious brat?

Chapter 13

Angus noticed Poppy biting her lip as she sat beside him in his truck. He hadn't allowed her to stay away from him on the seat, losing ground he'd already gained wasn't an option. "What's troublin' ye, wee one?" he asked gently, squeezing her small hand.

"I-I just wanted to say I'm sorry about being so paranoid last night, Angus. Sometimes it's hard to trust when you've been burned before."

"Aye, I can understand that. It happens to all of us for different reasons."

"Yes, but I shouldn't have had a meltdown and accused you and Darro of plotting against me," she confessed. "My temper gets away with me when I least expect it, and you didn't deserve it."

Angus chuckled. "I believe in women's rights. A lass has the right to speak her mind, and then apologize fer it over a lap," he educated her.

"Angus!" she complained, punching him in the shoulder. "Is that what you had in mind for me today? Is that why you wanted to take me into town?"

Angus winced. That last punch might be from a little bit of a lass, but her knuckles did leave an impression. And

Vince's lip had been cut by her punch, although he'd deserved that.

"It was no what I had in mind to begin with, but I'm thinkin' verra seriously about it now. That's the third time ye've punched me. Three strikes and ye're out, isn't that the rule?"

"What rule?" she asked innocently. "I didn't know we were playing a game." She peeked up at him, devilment in her chocolate eyes.

Angus whipped over to a small hamlet and put the truck in park. Then he turned to her *cat-that-ate-the-cream* face with a stern gaze. "Ye are a naughty wee lass, aren't ye? Thinkin' ye can get out of consequences by pretendin' ignorance?"

"What?" she protested uneasily. "You never said anything the first time. Besides, I was just playing."

Angus reached out and smoothed his long finger down the side of her creamy cheek. She was such a pretty woman. Just touching her made his tadger dance with excitement. Merely sitting beside her was an intimacy he thoroughly enjoyed.

But she was also an onery little mite.

"Ye can consider yerself as havin' one foul ball left, and then ye are goin' over my knee for some postgame instructions of how to play," he replied firmly, chuckling as the tenseness left her body and she practically slumped into his chest. That was a guilty slump if he'd ever seen one.

"S-shouldn't we get going?" she quavered.

Angus looked around with a grin. "Oh, I don't know. This private hamlet looks like a good spot fer a guilty conscience to be cleansed. After all, ye said ye felt bad about losin' yer temper when ye jumped to conclusions."

"Not *that* guilty." She wiggled in the seat.

Angus threw his head back and laughed. "Then get up here on yer knees fer a good hug and kiss. Ye owe me that much at least."

Poppy quickly folded her legs beneath her. Then she put a hand on either side of his face and bent down to give him a searing kiss.

Angus held her small waist and kissed her back, but as she lifted her head, he slipped one long arm around her tightly, and with his free hand, landed several spanks on her plump backside before she could twist away.

"What was that for?" she asked indignantly, rubbing her rear and then plopping down on the seat with a ferocious glare.

"Love taps," he responded with a teasing grin.

"They didn't feel like love taps."

"Neither did yer punches, but like ye, I was just playin'," he mocked, turning her own words back on her.

"You...you...you did that on purpose," she accused.

"Aye I did, so be forewarned. I love yer bottom and won't hesitate to spank it, pat it, massage it, pinch it, rub it or otherwise engage with yer delightful wigglin' cheeks every chance I get. And if the occasion warrants, I'll give it a good hidin' if it means keeping ye safe and happy. How do ye feel about that, lass?"

He arched his eyebrow in question as he waited for her answer. Protecting his woman was as bone deep in Angus as was his Scottish heritage. He could give a lot of leeway with a willful lass, but in the end, he would still do what he deemed necessary. Rosie had understood that and he hoped Poppy could as well.

Poppy smoothed a lock of hair behind her ear with one slender finger. "I-I'm not sure," she admitted. "I love what you did for me yesterday, but I'm not comfortable with being seriously punished. That first spanking you gave me hurt a lot."

Angus understood what she was saying. No one likes to get their arse tanned. "I guess the bottom line is, ye have to decide whether ye trust me to always have yer best interests at heart or not, Poppy. And for that, ye can take all the time ye need." He tipped her chin up and dropped a kiss on her soft lips. "Let's get headed into town, we have shoppin' to do."

Poppy didn't say anything but she placed her small hand on his thigh as he restarted the truck and got back on the road. Then he placed his big palm over hers and gently squeezed. She'd become very precious to him already and he didn't like the thought of her moving away from Neamh, even if it was just to Inverness.

"Poppy, were ye serious about movin' out of Neamh? Because ye can always move in with me. Ye would still be close to yer job, if ye plan to keep it."

"And how would that look?" she scoffed. "You and I shacking up together at our age? I'm sure yer family would love that and I know Andrea would have a heart attack."

Angus looked pained. "I didn't offer to *shack up* as ye so nicely put it, I was offerin' to rent ye a room. Or hire ye as my housekeeper and business partner if ye like keepin' house so much," he offered innocently.

She raised her fist to punch him, then thought better of it and lowered her hand. The lass was learning.

"Angus Sangster, ye are such a jobbie," she exclaimed with a sudden giggle. "I don't believe ye meant that at all."

"There ye go again, accusin' me of dire things." He shook his head woefully. "What am I to do with ye, lass?"

She huffed with folded arms, but her eyes were twinkling.

Angus grabbed her hand again and shot her a serious side eye. "Just so ye know, the offer to '*shack up*' is verra real if I thought ye'd accept it. I'm too old to worry about what my family thinks. All I care about is the lass I'm fallin' in love with, and I'll take ye anyway I can have ye."

"And that's me?" she ventured as if trying to reassure herself that he was serious.

"Aye lass, that's ye." He squeezed her hand once again. "Take as long as ye like. Marriage would be my end game, but the game is in yer court. I'd be proud to have ye in my home and at my side without the ring if that's what ye want."

Angus was silent then as he drove towards town, and Poppy didn't speak either. He'd put it out there and there was no taking it back. The rest was up to her.

POPPY DIDN'T KNOW WHAT to say. Marriage was the last thing on her mind and she couldn't believe Angus had just declared his intentions so bluntly. They'd only known each other for about five weeks and yet he wanted to marry her.

The warmth and joy that was spreading through her was undeniable though. Her body was responding to him even if her mind was at war with itself. In a few short sentences he'd proposed marriage, or living together, or anything else she wanted to consider. He was open to anything. She marveled at his honesty and willingness to face possible rejection so quickly.

Her eyes narrowed as a thought popped into her head. "You don't have a terminal diagnosis or anything, do you?"

His eyebrows reached for the sky. "What? Nay, of course not. Why would ye think that?"

She sat up straighter. "I've never met anyone like you, Angus Sangster. You're so perfect it's hard to believe you are real." She reached up and pinched his cheek.

He smiled down at her. "Oh, I'm real all right, lass. My hand on yer butt for that pinch will make that clear soon enough."

She reached up and kissed the spot she'd just pinched. "I think I might be falling in love with you too, but it terrifies me," she confessed. "I didn't want this, I'm not ready for another relationship."

Angus pulled to the side of the road again.

"We're never going to get to Inverness at this rate," she giggled.

He put the truck in park and pulled her in close to his body. "I know ye aren't ready, honey," he said softly, palming her cheek. "There is a lot goin' on in yer life right now, I understand that. It's why I said take all the time ye need, just don't shut me out. I want to be here for ye and support ye through it all."

Tears spurted into Poppy's eyes. "Angus…I-I don't know what to say."

"Then don't talk, just feel," he growled as he put one big palm behind her head and held her while he kissed her breathless.

The sound of a horn blaring outside his window made them jerk apart and he whirled around to see Dal and Henry slowly passing him in one of Neamh's trucks with big grins and thumbs up.

"That Dal is a pistol," he growled, some red creeping up his neck.

"I think he's cute," she laughed. "When he has you as a role model, how can he help being a tease? I don't know Ainsley, but Lucerne said Dal is interested."

He's never even met Ainsley," Angus snorted as he released her and started the truck again. "He's always got a girlfriend stashed away, that lad, and on the prowl for another one at the same time."

"Maybe he just hasn't found the right one yet."

Angus shot her a grin. "Well Ainsley is one lass he'd better be sure he's ready to tangle with because she'll tie him in knots and laugh while she's at it if he isn't careful."

"She sure is a beautiful young girl in her pictures."

"Aye, she is at that. But she's dedicated and driven, just like Darro. Dal will have to work night and day to keep up with her."

Her phone sent a notification and she glanced down as she took it from her pocket. It was from Mack—again. Closing the screen, she put in back in her pocket.

"Any news?" Angus asked.

"It was just Mack asking if I had considered coming back to run the company again. He's been bugging me since Adrian died."

"And have ye given it any thought? It sounds like they need someone at the helm now."

"I don't know anything about running a company, Angus," she replied. "I thought I might try hiring someone or promoting someone from within the board to run it for me. Nevil Hanrahan is the senior member, so he's the most likely candidate."

Angus nodded. "To do that properly though, ye need to be there to interview yer candidates."

"I know," she sighed. "I said I wasn't going back last night, no matter what, but I have been giving it some thought." She looked up at him. "Maybe it's time I stopped running and face this all head on. After all, I do have a solid alibi for when Julian took that medicine. How can they possibly charge me with colluding with Adrian when there's no evidence? What do you think I should do, Angus? Any thoughts?"

"Didn't ye say last night ye thought Edna might accuse ye?"

Poppy nodded with a shudder. "Yes, she hates me."

"Then I'd start with her," Angus replied simply.

"What do you mean?"

"I mean I'd start makin' some phone calls when we get back. Call yer mother-in-law and be blunt. Tell her ye suspect her of pushin' Adrian to have ye charged and then see what she says. Right now, she must be feelin' the pinch for money and not much chance of gettin' any if the company is about to go broke. She may be more reasonable than ye think."

Poppy was intrigued. "And what else?"

"Check in with Morgan and see if they've found anythin' new. Call Mack and ask him for the complete files on Condoloro Enterprises and what the auditors have found so far."

She frowned. "But I don't know anything about accounting."

"But ye do know investments and numbers. Ben is about to graduate in accounting and finance, and Darro and I have been involved in Neamh's books for years. He believes in knowin' what his hired help is doing on all levels. Mayhap between all of us, we can see some discrepancies ourselves, or spot where the money is leakin'."

"Isn't that tantamount to telling Mack we don't trust him to hire someone competent?"

"Not at all. If anythin', he should respect the fact that ye want to get involved. He's been tryin' to get ye to do that from what ye've said, so I can't see him objectin'."

Poppy sat up straight, hope filling her breast making her feel lighter. "You are right, Angus, thanks for the pep talk. I'm going to text Mack right now and ask him to send the files to my email. We'll look them over when I get back." Her fingers flew across the screen and his reply was almost instant.

'Thank God, Poppy. Will advise the board that you are getting involved now and they should hear something soon. Files are on their way.'

Poppy bounced in her seat and read Angus the text. "He's sending the files! And he's not defensive or angry at all, just relieved."

Angus shot her a worried glance. "I hate to say it, honey, but ye really need to consider goin' back and run Condoloro Enterprises yerself. Interview and get a feelin' for each board member. Sometimes corporations have rats in them that get to nibblin' the cheese when they think no one is lookin.'"

Slowly Poppy nodded. "You've given me a lot to think about, Angus. So much of what's been happening, based on what I know of Adrian, seems off somehow. Maybe you are right. Maybe I have been running scared for long enough. I thought I was through with Julian's family when his will was read, but Adrian has been chasing me like a horrific nightmare ever since."

Impulsively she grabbed his arm. "Did you mean it when you said you'd go with me if I went back? Can you get away from Neamh for very long?"

He nodded. "Darro and I have already discussed it. I told him I'd be goin' with ye when ye decided to return. It was inevitable, Poppy. It's a mess ye need to face and clean up fer yerself, even though none of it is yer fault. Ye had no right in Adrian's business before he was murdered, but now ye have every right to investigate what happened to yer stepson, and to take over Condoloro Enterprises if that's what ye decide to do."

"I don't want to stay in Chicago," she retorted adamantly, "or in that mausoleum of a house any longer than I have to."

"Ye don't need to," Angus said with a teasing grin. "Ye can run a corporation from anywhere in the world if ye have good people in place. Ye can live right here with me and be my housekeeper part time, and run yer business from my office the rest of the time."

Poppy laughed. "You really are determined, aren't you?"

"Of course. I always mean what I say," Angus assured her.

Poppy settled back in her seat, her mind whirling. Angus was right, it was time she took the reins of the runaway horse she was riding instead of clinging to its neck and waiting for it to throw her off. Condoloro Enterprises was going down the tubes if someone didn't do something. It belonged to her now, and she had stock in it as well, so it was up to her to do what she could to save it. She glanced up at Angus.

"I think I'll put a hold on looking at properties in Inverness for now, and start checking for flights to Chicago instead. You sure you're in?"

He grinned down at her. "I'm in, wee one."

O'HARE INTERNATIONAL Airport was as messy with crowded lines of people, bustling foot traffic, and rolling luggage carriers as Poppy remembered it. As she and Angus waited for their bags to appear on the baggage carrier, the butterflies were going nuts in her stomach. That slight nagging headache that always signaled tension building was more prevalent now than it had been on the plane. She rubbed her temples pensively as she took a few calming breaths.

Was it just five days ago that she and Angus had been talking about her coming back to try to get Condoloro Enterprises back on its feet? It seemed longer.

At first Poppy had grown a backbone and felt ready to take on Edna, the press, and the corporate world, and then had changed her mind. Then she changed it back again after another night requiring a headache tablet to sleep. She finally decided she really was tired of being a victim. She didn't want the headaches and the haunting memories to keep plaguing her.

After more intense soul searching, she'd finally made the reservations and plunged ahead. Now here she was, a nervous wreck, and desperately hoping she'd made the right decision.

Morgan had assured her that no one was trying to press charges against her for anything. The investigation was all about Adrian, his connection to the mob, the possible murder of his father, and the likely hood of embezzlement of funds within the corporation itself.

There were some very suspicious things going on. For one thing, one of the board members, Ace Ducat, had retired six months ago and moved to Florida. His wife had divorced him earlier and hadn't moved with him. But no one had been able to reach him since then for questioning.

Poppy also knew the auditors were wondering why the investments left in her name from Julian were quite healthy when none of the others were. If she had to guess, anything regarding those investments had to be signed off on by her. She hadn't been available to do that.

"Ye holdin' up okay, lass?" Angus asked in her ear. His arm was around her, sheltering her from the crush of the crowd.

She nodded. "Yes, just nervous. Vince said he's waiting outside to take us to the house."

"Are ye sure not tellin' Edna ye were comin' was the best course of action? What if she's had the locks changed," he teased.

"Then I'll just ring the doorbell," Poppy snorted. "When Ralston answers the door, I'll just go right in. Besides, I want to see her unprepared reaction when she sees me. I think that might tell me a lot."

Angus shook his head. "Ye Americans. Ye say ye are broke, but ye don't fire the waitstaff."

Poppy laughed. "For someone as spoiled as Edna, the butler, cook and maid are necessities. To be fair, she wouldn't be able to keep up with all of that anyway and she would never move to something smaller. That house has been in the Condoloro family since the last years of the gilded age of Chicago. Wait until you see it."

"Well, ye do own the house, ye have every right to be there," he replied.

Seeing her bag near Angus's, she grabbed hers off the carousel and he did the same, then they headed out the massive glass doors and into the bright Chicago sunshine where Vince hailed them from a blue car several vehicles down.

"How was your flight?" he asked as he opened the trunk.

"Reminded me why I don't fly any more than I have to," Angus grunted. "I prefer the silence and beauty of Neamh than the madhouse of international travel."

"Anything new, Vince?" Poppy asked as she got into the back seat so Angus could sit with Vince in the front.

"Not really," Vince replied, his eyes glancing at hers in the mirror and then back to navigate the traffic that would take them out through Rosemont and headed towards Lincoln Park area on the northeast shores of Chicago. "I've been keeping an eye on the house for the last three days like you ask, but I haven't even seen Mrs. Condoloro. The only people coming and going seem to be a few delivery people."

Poppy frowned. "I wonder what happened to Ralston, Molly and Martha? Her staff," she clarified at Vince's raised eyebrow.

"Maybe she actually let them go," Angus volunteered.

"I can't imagine she would. Especially Ralston. He's like a member of the family. Julian told me he was the butler his father hired when he and Edna were first married," Poppy said.

"Is it possible he lives in the house in exchange for wages?" Angus asked. "Or smaller wages anyway?"

"He could, I guess. He never married that I knew of." Poppy's cell phone notification popped up Andrea's name.

'Are you in Chicago yet?'

'Yes, Vince is taking us to the house right now.'

'See you later for dinner then. Love you.'

Andrea wasn't happy that Poppy was staying at the mansion, but she felt like she needed to. Unless someone had thrown them out, all her business suits, shoes, and other clothing had been left behind when she ran from Chicago to Toronto. She highly doubted anyone had bothered to clean house. Her bedroom wasn't in Edna and Adrian's way, so they would be inclined to ignore it.

She and Julian had been in separate bedrooms after Julian was diagnosed with sleep apnea and heart disease over three years ago. It wasn't like they'd had much of a physical relationship anyway. She wrinkled her nose. As long as she was available to be seen on his arm and play social hostess, he didn't need her in his bed. The most time they spent together was in his study or in the office working with the company portfolios.

Lost in her own thoughts while Vince and Angus chatted, it wasn't long before they finally pulled into the drive facing two wrought iron gates where the immense golden stone structure loomed.

"The code is 6789876," she instructed Vince as he opened his window to push the buttons on the door entry box. "That is if it hasn't been changed."

It hadn't. The iron gates swung open and Vince proceeded up and around the concrete circle to stop in front of the three-story structure. Monstrous 4-foot square stone pillars held up the upper balcony of the second floor. Above the second-floor balcony, a massive letter C had been etched into a section of stone that jutted out from the main wall. A raised rock flower bed in the middle of the drive held daylilies of all colors swaying in the slight breeze.

Angus opened his door. "I see what you mean about it lookin' like a museum or a mausoleum," he remarked to Poppy when he opened her door to help her out. In her ear he growled, "Why did ye put me in the front seat? I wanted to sit in the back together."

"Because Vince would have been lonely in the front with no one to talk to," she glibly replied.

"He can find his own lass then," he growled, hugging her into his side.

Poppy chuckled nervously as Vince came around with their bags from the trunk. The butterflies were getting worse. Then she turned to face the mansion.

Taking a deep breath for reinforcement, she started up the steps and made her way to the huge front door. She tried the big handle of the door first, but when it didn't open, she took the keys from her shoulder bag and inserted one into the lock above the door handle, then pressed the lever. It opened.

"Here we go," she whispered to Angus, looking over her shoulder with trepidation.

"Once more into the breach," Angus teased. "Ye can do it, lass."

Poppy shoved the door wide open and stepped inside. As she slowly walked into the mansion, it was if nothing had changed. To her right and left were huge coatrooms for guests to leave their belongings. Directly in front and across a broad expanse of gleaming dark wood flooring were two staircases with landings halfway up, one on each side of the room, that led to the next floor. There was a step down into the main floor where a long hallway stretched toward the back of the house. A huge crystal chandelier hung above them.

A FLOWER FOR ANGUS

"I'd hate to be the maid who has to clean that," murmured Angus in her ear as he pointed upward towards the glittering crystal.

They were all startled when a voice suddenly exclaimed from the doorway to the left side of the room. "Poppy! What are you doing here? Come to gloat, have you? And who are these people with you?"

Chapter 14

Poppy whirled to face Edna standing in the doorway on her left, her mouth dry and her heart racing. To her amazement, Ralston stood right behind her dressed in casual dark slacks and a white polo instead of his neatly pressed butler's jacket and suit pants. He looked angry and protective of Edna with a hand on her frail shoulder, his dark eyes glaring at them. They had come from the direction of the library and Julian's study.

"What's Ralston doing out of uniform?" she asked bluntly.

Edna lifted her aristocratic nose. "It's his day off and he's been helping me with the budget. Now again, what are you and these men doing here?"

Bracing herself for the onslaught of verbal abuse to come from her nemesis, Poppy replied with a firmness she didn't feel inside. "I've come to find out what's happened to Condoloro Enterprises and get it back on its financial feet if that's possible." She waved her hand at Angus and Vince. "These are my friends who are going to help."

Even from ten feet away, Poppy could see the elderly dowager with her snow-white hair, patrician features, and slender figure open her mouth in an attempt to speak. The expected vitriol didn't come. Instead, her mouth tightened in disbelief as she walked slowly towards them in a smart, cream-colored pantsuit and flat black sandals. "Why...why would you do that?" she finally croaked.

"Because it was Julian's company," Poppy replied simply. "And I'll be blunt. If Adrian murdered Julian to pay off his gambling debts, then he's left not only you high and dry, but a lot of stockholders who need their money. Not to mention the hundreds of employees who will be without a job if it goes completely under. Since I'm in charge now, I feel like I need to do something about it."

"You got your cut and took off," Ralston exclaimed bitterly. "I'm sorry if I can't believe you are here on a charitable mission. I would be more inclined to believe you're here to siphon the last dregs of a dying corporation, although there's hardly anything left."

"And how would ye know that? Ye are just the hired help," Angus drawled.

Poppy's eyes narrowed at Ralston. "I don't care what you believe, Ralston," she replied firmly, her fingers trembling in spite of herself. "I never wanted anything from Julian, it was his choice to leave me with my own work. After what Adrian did to me, I finally left to get away from him...and you, Edna." Her eyes swiveled back to her mother-in-law. "I always believed you put him up to trying to have me charged with murder and contesting the will over and over. Did you put him up to tampering with the brakes on my car too?"

Edna gasped, her face turning pale. "What? No...no...I would never do something like that. And I didn't put Adrian up to anything else either. You and I had our differences I admit. I was very upset to find out that Julian had negated the prenup when the will was read, but I never wished you harm."

The ring of truth to Edna's words had Poppy suddenly unsure of herself. She looked over at Angus, a question in her eyes. Did he hear it too?

Angus's eyes narrowed when Ralston took Edna's hand in his own. "Looks to me like Ralston's been busy featherin' his own nest," he accused bluntly.

Ralston flushed, but Edna jumped to his defense. "Ralston and I have known each other for years; our relationship is nothing new. It's just been...private," she finished.

Poppy glanced at her watch. "I need to make some phone calls and let Mack know I'm in town. I plan to have a board meeting tomorrow morning. Nevil already knows and is notifying the board members to plan on being there."

Edna nodded, then she reached out and put her trembling fingers on Poppy's arm. "For what it's worth, Poppy, I'm glad you are here. Julian always spoke highly of your business skills and it looks like my future may well depend on it," she confessed dryly. "With all the changes, the will is a complete mess."

Again, Poppy was surprised at the uncertainty Edna displayed in her words and actions.

"We will talk about that, Edna. I know I now own the mansion and the company, but Julian wanted you to live here and I respect that."

Ralston growled. "Just know that if you try to evict Edna from her home, we will take you to court to enforce Julian's requests for his mother."

Poppy looked surprised at his outburst, then her eyes narrowed. "I have no intention of evicting my mother-in-law from her home, Ralston. I'm trying to make sure she can maintain the lifestyle she was promised. It was Julian's wish for his mother to live here as long as she wanted, and I will honor that."

Edna looked like she was about to pass out in relief. "If there is anything you need, Poppy, let me know if I can help. Will you require a meal this evening? I can't cook, but we could order something in."

Poppy shook her head. "No, I'm having dinner with Andrea and Morgan tonight. But I would like to interview any employees you still have besides Ralston."

"I don't have any employees," Edna admitted ruefully. "And Ralston doesn't get paid to stay here, he stays because it's his home."

"Are you married?" Poppy asked, her eyebrows searching for the ceiling.

"Not because I haven't asked," Ralston replied defensively. He ran a hand through his thinning hair. "What Edna and I do is our business anyway."

"You can do me one favor, Edna," Poppy decided impulsively. "If you want Martha and Molly back, call them and tell them they are hired. I'll pay their back wages too if there are any. If they don't, then can you take care of hiring someone you will like? With a house this size, I think you need them."

Edna's throat worked painfully again as if it were closing up. "T-That's very generous of you, Poppy. I've been selling off a few valuables to take care of the most pressing needs and that hasn't been pleasant. Martha was with me for years and still comes by now and then to prepare a nice meal for me. I hated to let her go, and I haven't paid Ralston in months. Y-You have every right to gloat, my dear. I certainly gave you a hard enough time while you were here. I misjudged you—I'm sorry."

Poppy cleared her throat, feeling a little embarrassed and a little bewildered. "I don't understand. Before Julian died, everything seemed to be going well with the company. Of course, I had no influence or ability to look at anything except my own investments once Adrian took over. Do you know what happened?"

Edna's face started to flush. "All I know is that Adrian said he'd had to pull money from household accounts and others to cover a multitude of debts that Julian had amassed for you and others he didn't even know. He was frantic to contest the will because he needed the influx of the cash Julian had left you to keep the corporation solvent."

Vince stepped forward. "That's not entirely true, Mrs. Condoloro. I'm Vince Gallo. I'm a private detective and your grandson hired me to find Poppy. I did a little checking into his background and found that the cash he needed was for his gambling debts. It looks as if he was the one draining money from the corporation in huge amounts after his father died, but when it wasn't enough to cover him, he went after his stepmother's inheritance."

Edna gasped in outrage. "That's a bald-faced lie! I know Adrian had a gambling addiction; his father was well aware of it. But Julian always covered Adrian's debts and left him well off. And for the record, there is no way Adrian would have killed his father. He loved him and respected him. He hadn't gambled in over a year before he passed away. I don't know why Julian's bitch of a secretary implicated Adrian after he was dead, but she was lying too," she denied hotly.

Poppy frowned at this unexpected revelation. What Edna said made sense. "Well, right now, I have a full audit taking place and we should know something soon."

"There's certainly somethin' rotten in Denmark," Angus observed.

Ralston and Edna both glared at him.

"Oh...this is Angus Sangster, a friend from Scotland." Poppy introduced him. "He and Vince are here to help me sort things out."

Edna stared and then finally she seemed to pale and wilt. "Let's hope you can find some answers, Poppy. This has all been such a nightmare." She pressed trembling fingers to her temple.

Ralston leaned down. "You really need to lie down, Edna. You've been on your feet too long as it is."

"You're right as usual, Ralston. I was just trying to figure out what bills to pay and which ones to put off in the study," she replied wearily. "Can we talk later, Poppy?"

"Of course," Poppy said with a nod of relief. She needed some time to absorb what she'd learned. It certainly wasn't what she'd expected.

"Oh, one more thing, Edna. No press members are allowed in the mansion. I'm not going through that again, and they have no business in here snooping around any of us," Poppy added firmly.

Surprisingly enough, Edna nodded her head. "I agree. It seems those we think of as friends often turn out to be the enemy, and vice versa. I have no friends in the press anymore, so that's not an issue."

Poppy was still suspicious of Edna's motives, but she felt surprisingly lighter as Edna walked away. Coming here had been the right thing to do. With each small success she felt more in control of the chaos that had been her life this past year. Facing her nemesis and her subsequent mild reactions had been huge. Being the stone in the lake creating the ripples instead of the victim in the path of the ripples was invigorating.

"WHERE ARE OUR ROOMS, Poppy?" Angus asked, picking up the suitcases as Edna and Ralston headed towards what looked like an elevator near the stairway on the right. "Is that an elevator?"

"Yes. Julian had it put in years ago when Edna wanted the third-floor suite of rooms. She wanted to be completely away from the family parts of the home and feel like she was living alone. I'm surprised with her age that she hasn't moved closer to the main floor. Especially with just her and Adrian in the house after I left."

"Ye haven't said much, Vince," Angus remarked as they followed Poppy up the stairway on the left side of the house.

"Just taking it all in," Vince grunted. "Something is off about that Ralston guy. Poppy, you don't have to put me up here, I can stay in my own bungalow just fine."

"I want you here, Vince, if you don't mind staying. The more eyes to observe, the better I'll feel. Investigate whatever you think needs investigating because we need to figure out what's going on. I'd really like to know who killed Julian, or if he was murdered at all. I still have a hard time wrapping my mind around Adrian doing it. He loved his father, I know that. I know the police have already been here, but the house is yours to poke around in."

"I'll do what I can. You said you wanted me to see if I could find out if the brakes on your car were messed with? I'll need the name and place of the mechanic who repaired them. You can also point me in the direction of the security room. I'd like to know what the set up was and if anyone backed up the tapes from a year ago."

"Wouldn't the police have that?" Angus asked.

"I'll have to find that out," Vince replied. "They might not have collected the data if they declared it an accidental overdose due to lack of suspects from the beginning."

"Here's your room, Vince." Poppy opened the door to a neatly laid out room and stepped back to let him in. "I have no idea about the sheets and such. Some of these rooms were rarely used and the sheets are probably clean. That's all I can say without a maid to refer to. Julian's room is right next door to yours. You can investigate all you like."

"It'll be fine," Vince rumbled. "I've got some work to do on my computer. Don't worry about me for dinner, I'll take care of myself."

She moved down the hall to the right. "This first door is your room, Angus, and the next one is mine. You can put your bag in there." She leaned up to whisper in his ear. "I'll meet you between the rooms."

Angus's eyebrows crawled off his forehead and he grinned as she shot him a furtive look and went to her own door.

Angus opened the door and stepped inside his room. It was neat and elegantly furnished with a queen-sized four poster bed sporting gender neutral quilts and pillows in a blue and cream design. The window by the right side of the bed was decorated with heavy cream drapes.

The room also sported a walk-in closet that was bare, an overstuffed chair by the marbled fireplace on the right wall, and a door on the left between the mahogany dresser and chest. The carpet in thick beige was a nice blend of modern style with the antique furniture and the desk on his left as he came into the room.

If he wasn't mistaken, the massive painting on the wall with dogs, riders and hounds looked like real art. He wondered who the artist was. Then again, there was plenty of artwork everywhere he'd looked, from vases to paintings to figurines standing on little tables. There was still a fortune in this mansion, even if Condoloro Enterprises was going broke.

He placed his bag on the bed, strode to the door on his left, and turned the old-style metal knob. It was locked so he tapped gently with his knuckles.

A giggle was his reply as the chain was unbolted and the door opened to reveal Poppy smiling up at him. "Can I help you, sir?"

"Do ye know a lass named Poppy? I'm supposed to meet her here," he growled as he stalked her backward.

"She's not here, will I do?" Poppy asked, batting her eyes at him like a fem fatale. He decided he liked her in this mood.

He shook his head woefully. "I'm afraid I can't be seen with the likes of ye. Only the lass I want will make me happy. Unless ye've got a big pot of haggis and tatties in there," he teased. "I might be convinced if ye can cook."

"I'm afraid not," she sighed woefully, "but I'll help you look for her." She grabbed his hand and pulled him on through the bathroom, which was huge with a sunken tub and a walk-in shower. No expense had been spared to modernize the old mansion with comfort conveniences, much like some of Scotland's old homes.

"Then I'm afraid I'll have to stay loyal," he apologized. "I can't have her thinkin' I'd stray."

Poppy giggled. "You just said you would if I could cook."

He waggled his finger at her. "Nay, lass. I said I *might* be convinced. It would be verra difficult I admit, but I'm also verra determined."

She batted her eyelashes again. "Then I guess I'll have to admit that my name is Poppy and I can cook. Now what will you do?"

Angus growled and swooped his arm down around her legs and picked her up. "Then I'll just have to turn ye over my knee fer lyin' to me."

Poppy squealed with laughter as Angus strode across the room to her neatly made bed and sat down with her on his lap.

"Don't you dare!"

He wrestled her over his lap and pinned her in place as he spoke. "Ye shouldn't have said that, lass. Those three words are a direct challenge to any man worth his salt. One they can't afford to ignore lest their manhood be in question." He lifted his arm and landed three hearty spanks on her wiggling bottom. "One spank for each word," he said with relish as he pulled her up to look into her laughing eyes.

"That wasn't so bad," she purred, snuggling into him and kissing his chin.

"Come here, brat," he replied softly, taking her chin in his big palm and devouring her mouth. Silence reigned until her cell phone rang.

With a sigh, Poppy, took her cell out of her pocket and frowned at the name. "It's Hanrahan," she explained to Angus.

Angus nodded as she got off his lap and took the call from the board director.

"He wants to meet with me privately at Julian's office," she told him as she put the phone back in her pocket.

"When?" Angus growled. He didn't like it. Arranging a private meeting didn't sound safe for Poppy.

"At 9:00 p.m. tonight," she replied. "He said there are some things we alone need to discuss in person before the board meeting tomorrow."

"Ye're not goin' anywhere alone, lass," he said sternly. "And if I find out ye have, I'll be givin' ye that skelpin' I promised.

Her eyebrow shot up. "I'm quite capable of handling Hanrahan."

"Mentally, aye, I'm sure ye are more than his equal."

"He's not about to attack me," she scoffed. "Why would he? I'm here to help."

"Maybe not everyone wants ye here," Angus growled. "Things are no adding up. If it's no Adrian, then who killed Julian?"

"Or was he even murdered," Poppy added. "I hate to say it, but what Edna told us makes sense. I would never have pegged Adrian desperate enough to murder his dad for any reason. He did love him and they were close. I think it was an accidental overdose."

Angus folded his arms. "Let's say that yer husband was murdered. Who stands to gain if it wasn't ye or Adrian?"

"That's what I'm hoping Vince will find out," Poppy replied uneasily. "I've given him free reign to look into anything or anyone connected with all of us."

"Aye, but whoever's been embezzlin' funds won't want to be found out. That could put ye in danger and brings me back to my original statement. I don't want ye goin' anywhere alone."

"That's where I intend to focus my energy," Poppy replied, "hence the meeting with Hanrahan tonight. But you are welcome to come if you like." She leaned up to kiss his cheek, her eyes twinkling.

"Just try and stop me," he vowed, enforcing his tone with a hard slap on her delicious rear.

She rubbed her butt and pouted up at him. "That wasn't necessary."

He held up her chin and planted a kiss on those pouty lips. "Just a reminder. Ye are mine and I don't want to lose ye by takin' risks that ye don't need to. Let me help ye, wee one."

"Even you couldn't stop bullets, Angus Sangster," she taunted.

"Nay, but I could stop one long enough for ye to get away."

He watched her shiver as the thought hit home that she really could be in danger. He meant what he said. If he had to protect her with his life, he would.

He had a bad feeling about this meeting request at night, and in a building where all the staff would have already gone home.

While Poppy was freshening up, he mentioned it to Vince and he didn't like it either. Vince promised to call him and Poppy if he found out anything they might need to know before the meeting.

Chapter 15

Poppy hugged her daughter with joy, little Maddie and Josh both clamoring for Gramma's attention. Andrea had been on the patio of her brick ranch home in a suburb of Naperville before Poppy and Angus had even made it to the door. The patio sported half barrels of colorful Dahlias, Marigolds, and other summer flowers beginning to blossom in abundance. Children's outdoor tricycles and other toys dotted the patio.

It was a madhouse for a moment, then Poppy pulled Angus forward. "Andrea, Morgan, this is Angus Sangster, my very good friend from Scotland. Without him, I don't know if I would have had the courage to come home."

"She'd have found it without me, she's a brave lass," Angus inserted easily, taking Morgan's hand as he held it out to him.

Then he was surprised when Andrea suddenly pulled him into an energetic hug. "Thank you so much for getting her back to us, Angus," she enthused. "Any friend of Mom's is always welcome."

"Mister...hey, mister."

Poppy watched with interest as Angus hunkered down to talk to her granddaughter who was tugging on his pantleg.

"What can I do for ye, wee lass?" he asked with humor and patience.

Now that four-year-old Maddie had the full attention of the man in front of her, she didn't seem so sure of what she wanted to say. Her long brown curls were parted neatly on the side but were trying to escape their designated path. She was a pretty little thing in her princess pink dress and slippers. Her wide hazel eyes stared in wonder. "You talk funny."

"Do I now?" Angus chuckled.

Six-year-old Josh wasn't about to be undone. He puffed out his little chest in the striped t-shirt and pushed his unruly mop of hair out of his eyes, the same color as his sisters. "I like the way he talks, Maddie. Mom told us he was coming and would talk funny, didn't you, Mom? But I like it."

"I like it too," protested Maddie, her lip pouting as if it were a contest.

"Ye know what?" Angus asked, taking each of their hands. "I like both of ye wee ones more than ye can like me, I'll bet. Which one of ye can show me where dinner is? I'm starved."

And just like that, Angus fit in because the children wanted all of his attention from then on, each one sure they could like him more than the other, or more than he could like them. Poppy shook her head. She'd never seem him with any kids except Delilah and Corey, and to them, Angus was just another family member they loved and hugged on.

Dinner was quite the affair with Andrea's eyes widening the first time Angus put his arm over the back of Poppy's shoulder and hugged her. And with Angus teasing the children every chance he got. They loved the attention of course.

A FLOWER FOR ANGUS

"Okay kiddos," Andrea finally addressed the kids after they had finished their chocolate pudding dessert. "I need you to play in the playroom for a while so we adults can talk. After that we'll get your baths and pajamas on."

The kids whined until Morgan scolded in his firm voice. "That's enough complaining now, you heard your mother. Josh, you and Maddie go play for a while and no fighting or you'll both end up in bed early."

"Okay, Daddy," Josh agreed and took his sister's hand.

"Would anyone like some coffee?" Andrea asked as Poppy helped to clear away the dishes from the table.

"None for me," Angus rumbled. "That's a pre breakfast drink fer me while I'm in the office at Neamh. Water will be fine, thank ye."

Poppy knew he accepted water because Andrea didn't have any tea, which she thought was really sweet of him to take note and not request it. Here in Chicago, Poppy usually drank ice tea, not hot tea. Cultural differences.

Morgan started right in as soon as Andrea sat back down. "I'm not going to lie to you, Poppy, the FBI isn't getting very far at the moment. I'm not on the case itself for obvious reasons, but Mike Docent is and he said everyone is coming to the same conclusions. With Sarah Solano's testimony, it's enough to cast suspicion on Adrian for murder, but not enough to actually prove he did it. Only that he had motive and opportunity.

"We did have one informant who gave a written statement that Adrian did owe a lot of money to bookies connected with the mob. But the bookies have legitimate markers to show money was lent and paid back freely and without force. On the surface, they are legitimate money lenders. And they all firmly deny there was any hit placed on Adrian. If one of them is lying, they are all sticking together. Undercover operatives say they don't know anything either, so Mike says he tends to believe them."

He frowned. "The one interesting thing in all of this is that there doesn't appear to be any other suspicious instance of either Julian or Adrian doing any other sort of business with the mob or any of its connections. The corporation's books are legitimate and so are their sources and investments. It's a puzzle, really."

"Who's the informant?" Angus asked casually. "Vince might want to speak with him."

"Who's Vince?" Morgan asked.

"Vince is the private detective Adrian hired to find me," Poppy said dryly. "I now have him investigating the board and all concerned with the company. It's almost bankrupt and no one appears to know why."

"I thought you hired auditors to do that?" Morgan said.

"I did, but they are just concerned with the books. I wanted someone who could check out the people. I want to know who I'm dealing with and who I can and can't trust. It's my corporation now and someone's been helping themselves to it," Poppy said firmly. "I'm not about to let that continue."

They talked until it was time for Poppy and Angus to leave with Poppy explaining everything that had been going on and what her plans were.

"You know, Poppy, meeting with this fellow at night doesn't seem like a good idea to me," Morgan said with a frown. "What could he possibly want that couldn't wait until the morning?"

"That's what I said," Angus agreed.

"There is a security officer in the building," Poppy argued.

"Just the same, I'd feel better if Mike knew about this and stopped by there. Two owners of Condoloro Enterprises dead within a year aren't good odds in my experience."

"And the company bleedin' money like a fresh slaughter," Angus snorted.

Poppy stood up, glaring at both men. "I don't care if you notify Mike, that's fine with me. But just so you know, I do have my 9mm in my purse just in case. I don't intend to take any more risk than I have to. This whole thing has me spooked too, but I can't let it scare me from doing what I have to do," she declared adamantly. She glanced at her watch. "It's time for us to go. Are you ready, Angus?"

Angus got to his feet, his studied gaze making her lift her chin defiantly.

"Aye, ready as I'll ever be."

VINCE WAS STUDYING the coroner's report for Julian with a frown. He'd done a background check into every board member and every employee in the office building, but he had the distinct impression he was missing something. Something important. Then it hit him.

Flipping to the end of Julian's report he found the sentence he'd read before that hadn't stuck with him. *Possible DNA match.*

The one thing he hadn't checked out was Adrian's death report from the coroner. Was it even ready yet? Quickly, he got online and checked in the coroner's data base. It had just been submitted today. Flipping to the last page, he found it. *Positive DNA match.* Following the link included to reveal the source, he struck pay dirt. Now he had something to go on.

He glanced at his watch. It was 8:45 p.m. and Poppy was due to meet Hanrahan at 9:00 p.m. He tried to call her, then he tried to call Angus and all he got was static. That meant they were in the building and their calls were being blocked.

Frantically, he grabbed his car keys and dialed the number Poppy had given him for Morgan Kincaid as he raced to his car. He hadn't met the man, but he assumed he was competent and could act quickly with his status as an FBI agent. When Morgan answered, he practically yelled into the phone. "This is Vince Gallo, the detective Poppy hired. Poppy is in danger. I think I know who the killer is. I'm headed to Poppy's meeting at the Condoloro building, send back-up."

He started his blue Trax and hit the gas, ignoring Morgan's return call. He needed to get there fast and without distraction.

POPPY SLIPPED THE KEY into the door of the sleek, chrome two-story building and opened the door. "I wonder where the guard is?" she murmured uneasily, looking around. "He must be making his rounds."

Angus slipped the folded piece of napkin he'd taken from Andrea's dinner table and folded it into an even smaller square. Then he slipped it between the door lock to keep if from closing completely. Just a precaution in case Vince wanted to check on them later. They had prearranged it while Poppy was freshening up.

Every instinct Angus had was on high alert. The knife he'd taken Julian's study was in his casual dress boot for easy access. He hadn't known Poppy had a 9mm or he might have asked for one himself, but it was too late for that now. If there was any trouble, they would search him first anyway for a gun. That might give her a few moments to reach into her purse if needed.

The low lights in the foyer cast shadows from the dark corners where the light didn't reach. All was quiet. Too quiet in his opinion, as if a pall of doom hung heavy in the atmosphere.

The clicking of Poppy's low heel on the gleaming silvery tiles of the floor made him wish she'd worn something with a soft tread, like his boots.

The reception desk was silent as they passed, no machines humming, no fingers pecking on keyboards or phones ringing. There were only a few security lights for the guard above the hallways and the elevator straight ahead.

"Is Julian's office upstairs?" Angus hissed in her ear, making her suddenly jump.

"You scared the crap out of me, Angus. Yes, but why are we whispering?"

"For the same reason I want ye to take yer shoes off and take the stairwell," he whispered back. "It's so quiet in here it's like the silence is screamin' at me. Where's yer guard?"

"I don't know," she said uneasily. "When I was here, the guard stayed in the foyer and did a security check of both floors on the half hour, which took about 15 minutes. If that's still the schedule, he should be back by now, so he's 10 minutes late. It's almost 9:00 p.m. Just because that's the way it was doesn't mean things are still the same though."

"I think we should call the police and ask for an escort through the building," Angus said uneasily. "It doesn't feel right."

Just as Poppy seemed ready to agree, the elevator dinged and the doors slid open with a soft hiss. A young woman stepped from the elevator and smiled at them. "Hello, Mrs. Condoloro, I'm Abby Nesbitt, one of the board members. Nevil sent me down to escort you to Julian's office. The security guard called in sick tonight so we didn't have anyone in the foyer to meet you. I'm so sorry about that." She came forward to shake hands with Poppy.

"Oh yes, Abby. I remember you now. It's been a while, hasn't it? I didn't realize you were going to be here. Nevil didn't mention it when he called me today. This is my friend, Angus Sangster."

Angus held out his hand as he eyed the pretty young blonde in a sharp business suit. "It's a pleasure to meet ye, Mrs. Nesbitt. Ye're a mite young to be on a board of a corporation aren't ye?" If he had to guess, he'd say Abby Nesbitt wasn't out of her twenties yet, but some young people were highly motivated and driven these days, especially in the corporate world.

"It's Miss Nesbitt, but you can call me Abby. Thank you for the compliment, but somedays 35 feels ancient," she replied with a soft chuckle. "Please, this way." She held the elevator for Poppy and Angus to get on, and with one swift sweeping glance around the lobby, she stepped inside and hit the button for the second floor.

It was the smear of red on the collar of her cream jacket just beneath her ear that had Angus's instincts twitching. Was it lipstick? Or was it something else. The elevator doors slid open and she waved them out. When they traveled the few steps to the office door, Angus put a hand on Poppy's arm to hold her back from entering the doorway. With a gallant sweep of his arm, he motioned Abby through before them. "After ye, Miss Nesbitt."

"No, after you, Mr. Sangster," she replied coldly as she drew the gun from inside her suit jacket pocket and pointed it at them both.

Poppy gasped. "What are you doing?"

She eyed Poppy with disgust. "It's really too bad you chose to bring your friend with you tonight. It's a complication I could have done without, but then I'll manage. Now get inside, both of you." She waved the gun at the doorway and stood back. "Don't try anything, I won't hesitate to kill you immediately," she warned Angus.

***

WHEN ANGUS FOLLOWED Poppy into the interior of the office she gasped in shock. In the low lights they could see Nevil Hanrahan lying back in the office chair with a bullet hole in his forehead.

"What's going on?" Poppy cried. "Did you kill Nevil?"

"No, you did," Abby spat back at her. "If you hadn't decided to stick your nose in and come back to run the business, he would still be alive. As it is, you and he got into an argument and he shot you and your friend, but not before you got one shot off and killed him. Nice little ending, don't you think? Especially when they find out Nevil was the one who embezzled the funds from the company."

"And did he?" Angus asked grimly, glad he'd turned his cell on silent and set it to record just before they came into the building.

"Of course not," Abby snorted. "He's not clever enough to do that."

Beside him Angus could feel Poppy trembling. He glanced sideways to see her face was pale but a determined light in her eyes. She might be afraid, but she wasn't down for the count yet.

"But you are," Poppy said decisively, stiffening her back. "Were you and Adrian in this together? Did you both kill Julian as well?"

Abby laughed and then jeered, "Adrian was a weak, pathetic fool. His rich father gave him everything life had to offer. Julian bailed him out of trouble time after time and then he gave him the company...everything that I should have had. No, Adrian never even saw me coming."

"Ye killed Adrian and Julian," Angus guessed, trying to keep the woman talking. It was obvious she'd been planning all of this for a long time. The light of insanity and obsession was evident in her eyes. He knew she was going to kill them both, it was just a matter of time. Bracing himself, he watched for his opportunity.

"I killed him and his loathsome father," she taunted with a smile of satisfaction.

"Why should you have what Adrian had?" Poppy asked, bewildered.

Abby's eyes narrowed. "Because if he'd done right by my mother, I would have been the heir to Condoloro Enterprises. It's *my* birthright! Instead, he used my mother like a common whore and then refused to acknowledge me," she raged. "My mother died a horrible death and I didn't even know who he was until she told me on her death bed. He used women until he was ready to have a *nice* marriage with a *nice* girl who would give him a legitimate child and life would be lemonade and rainbow stew for the handsome billionaire. Money always wins and the rest of us are dispensable."

Abby started pacing and Angus's arm slipped protectively in front of Poppy's body.

"After my mother died over 12 years ago, I started making plans. I would dismantle his perfect little world one piece at a time, starting with his perfect wife," she hissed.

At Poppy's gasp Abby shot her an evil grin. "I made friends among the family connections he refused to acknowledge. They accepted me, but he would have nothing to do with them, as if he were the perfect human being himself," she jeered. "Adrian met me many times in different disguises, the kid was a complete idiot. I helped him revenge himself on dear old dad by acquiring a gambling habit. The pathetic, whiny brat with everything had no idea how to use it to his advantage. Given the world on a silver platter he still wanted more without expending any effort to cultivate what he had. What a waste of human space on the planet."

Angus had to give the woman credit, in spite of her manic rant she kept the gun steady and pointed right at him. If she'd engineered Julian's first wife's death in a mass casualty situation, and executed Adrian in cold mob style, then she was a groomed killer. Deadly and determined. He wondered who else was on her kill list besides Hanrahan behind them?

"Did ye kill Julian too?" Angus asked carefully. If they made it out of this alive, this was his opportunity to clear Poppy once and for all.

"Of course not," she scoffed. "Going to the house myself would have been a mistake. His retired friend gave him the extra meds in a drink and a chat between old buddies," she scoffed. Her eyes twinkled with nasty mirth. "Everyone has a price, don't they? Secretaries, board members, and even old friends. And if they can't be bought, they always have secrets to exploit. He retired to Florida six months later, but leaving loose ends isn't my style, so he retired to a bayou instead."

"W-What about the funds going missing?" Poppy stuttered.

Abby waved the gun impatiently. "While this has been fun having an audience to appreciate all my efforts, I don't have time to explain anymore and you probably wouldn't understand if I told you. Now move behind the desk, both of you."

Angus tensed. It was now or never.

A FLOWER FOR ANGUS

POPPY FELT FAINT. THIS was it…this was where she and Angus were both murdered by the diabolical killer in front of them. When Vince's head suddenly popped around the corner, Poppy's eyes widened. She couldn't help the involuntary gasp, which alerted Abby that someone was there.

When Abby instantly whirled partially around and shot automatically into the darkened hallway, Poppy grabbed for the 9mm in her purse with shaking hands.

"Step out where I can see you or I'll kill them both right now," yelled Abby.

When a knife hit her in the left shoulder, Abby huffed and fell back a few steps, her gun hand slipping down. Recovering, she screamed in rage and raised the gun back towards Angus to fire.

Poppy was faster. She pulled the trigger on her 9mm and watched in horror as Abby's shot went into the floor while the gun slipped from her hand. She slumped to the carpet while blood gushed from just below her right shoulder.

Oh. My. God. She'd killed someone. It all happened so fast.

Unable to take her eyes off Abby's still body, Poppy just stared, the gun shaking in her hands. She was frozen in the two-handed shooting stance she'd been taught at the local gun club.

Suddenly Angus was there and easing the gun from her trembling fingers.

Vince stepped inside the office where he cautiously made his way to the woman on the floor and kicked her gun away. Then he knelt down and checked for a pulse in her neck. "She's alive, I'll call 911." He nodded to Angus. "You better have Poppy sit down before she falls down."

"Ye're right about that," Angus agreed, helping Poppy down into one of the office chairs in front of the desk. He sat in the other chair and held her cold hands. "Are ye all right, lass? That was a damned good shot, ye just saved my life."

"I-I was aiming for center mass but I missed," she croaked inanely. When the room started spinning Poppy dropped her head between her knees. "I think I'm going to be sick." Whether it was the fact that she thought she'd killed Abby, or relief because she hadn't, Poppy wasn't sure. She just knew she felt like losing the contents of her stomach. There was so much blood everywhere. The metallic odor burned in her nostrils.

"Close yer eyes and take a few deep breaths, lass. Breathe out slowly. Ye got this," he crooned, moving as close to her as he could get and rubbing the back of her neck. "Steady on, wee one."

Morgan suddenly appeared with piercing eyes in the doorway with his service weapon drawn. With a huge sigh of relief, he put it away. "Looks like it's all over, thank God. You must be Vince, I'm Morgan Kincaid. Is she dead?" He indicated the woman on the floor.

Vince nodded. "No, I've called 911. The man in the chair wasn't so lucky, she killed him."

"Did any of you sustain injuries?"

"No, we are all good," Vince replied.

The ding of the elevator and the clumping of boots in the stairwell sounded in the room as Morgan finally switched the lights on. He held up his FBI badge at the approaching officers. "It's all over, men. I'm with the FBI and the scene is under control. No need for weapons. One dead and one suspect with life threatening injuries. Scene secured for the emergency unit arrival."

The next hour passed in a blur of questions as the local chief of police, whose jurisdiction the crime was in, sorted out the basics.

"I want to go home," Poppy announced once some of the numbness began to pass. She'd tried to avoid looking at the blood everywhere for as long as she could, but the stench of it was clinging to the insides of her nostrils like a permanent visitor. The pool where Abby went down and the splatter on the desk and wall behind Nevil was macabre against all the silver and white of the modern office.

"We need to get a full statement from you both," the chief replied.

Poppy felt increasingly nauseous from the stench and stress which increased the pain in her head. "If I have to endure all this gore any longer, I'm going to puke all over your crime scene," she shot at him. "I've told you what happened, now I need to go home." She turned to Angus with a pleading look. "Angus, get me out of here."

"Look, Chief," Angus growled. "Ye have all the facts ye need right now, can't ye get the rest of the story when Mrs. Condoloro has had a chance to recover from the shock of all this?"

"I'd prefer to get it tonight," the chief replied, his eyes narrowing with suspicion. "Mrs. Condoloro was already implicated in one murder not that long ago."

Angus stood his ground. "She was never indicted, so unless ye are charging either of us with a crime, we'll be leaving. Ye know who she is and where she lives. I'm her guest so

I'll be there as well. Ye can get our written statements in the morning at the house, or we can come down to the station and give it to ye tomorrow. What will it be?"

The chief waved his hand irritably. "Fine, I'll expect you both at the station tomorrow. Don't leave the country," he warned Angus.

"I wasna plannin' too," Angus replied testily.

They had just stepped outside the door amid all the flashing lights from police cars and ambulances when Poppy couldn't hold it any longer. She ran to the hedge beside the front entrance and lost everything in her stomach. Angus held her hair as she wretched miserably. Then he took off his nice white dress shirt and gently wiped her face.

"Oh...my head is pounding," Poppy bleated. "Your poor shirt, it will never be the same."

"Don't ye worry about my shirt. It gives me a chance to show off my abs for the ladies," he teased.

One of the ambulance drivers approached. "Are you all right, Mrs. Condoloro? Why don't you lay down for a minute." The young girl motioned Angus towards the back of one of the ambulances where a gurney stood at the ready.

"How do you know my name?" Poppy asked suspiciously. "Angus, don't let them kidnap me and find out later that supercilious bitch upstairs was behind it."

"I recognize you from the papers and we are at your building," the pretty medic replied with a smile. "The bitch is on her way to the hospital. I heard you shot her. You should have aimed another inch to the right and it would have been more effective," she added helpfully. "I've been hearing stories of what she's done for the last hour."

Poppy finally laid down on the gurney with Angus's help. "I was aiming a whole lot further to the right," she confessed with a wobbly grin.

"Do ye have a bottle of water so Poppy can take her pain pill?" Angus asked.

"I can do better than that," she replied eying his tanned abs in the lights around them, "I'll give her something for the nausea too. It's from the shock most likely, but it will pass."

Poppys eyes were closed against all the flashing lights. They didn't help her head any. "Here I finally get to see you without your shirt on and I'm too nauseated to appreciate it," she joked feebly.

"If I'd known ye wanted to, I'd have done it before this," he teased.

The young medic came back with a pill packet and a bottle of water. "Take this, it will fix you right up."

Poppy accepted her offerings and sat up to swallow the tablet the medic gave her and her pain pill Angus had retrieved from her clutch.

"I love your accent, by the way," the admiring medic told Angus and then handed him a plastic drawstring bag. "You can put your shirt in this. Good thing it's not too cold out tonight."

"Thank ye, lass." Angus smiled down at Poppy. "I'm goin' to call a cab, wee one. Ye're in no shape to drive us to yer house."

"No, wait. You don't have to do that," the helpful medic replied. An earsplitting whistle and a hand wave later and one of the young policemen standing around hurried over.

"Arty, can you take Mrs. Condoloro and her friend back to the mansion?"

"Of course I can," Arty replied, eager to help too. "I'll just call it in. Thanks, Pete."

Angus raised his eyebrows. "Pete?"

She nodded. "Yep. Short for Petunia, but everyone calls me Pete."

"Well, Petunia, I thank ye for all yer help," Angus replied as Arty brought the car around.

"No Pete?" she grinned.

Angus winked at Arty. "Flowers are the best, lad. Ye need to get one like Petunia here in yer life. Ye'll never be sorry."

Arty blushed, Pete giggled, and Poppy groaned and tried not to roll her eyes. It hurt when she rolled her eyes.

Chapter 16

It was after midnight by the time Angus had finally gotten Edna and Ralston back to their quarters and Poppy settled in bed. Edna had been very distraught over the whole thing and she didn't know the half of it. Ralston had helped her back to their quarters where Edna had meds waiting for her.

Andrea called on Poppy's cell and he was telling her that rushing over wouldn't solve anything except to disturb the children. Poppy had taken a pain pill and was in no shape to see anyone anyway.

"Is Mom really all right, Angus? I was so worried when Morgan got that call from Vince and went running out. If it hadn't been for the kids, he would never have been able to keep me from going with him. Thank God you were with her."

"She will be, Andrea," Angus assured her. "Yer mum is an amazing woman. She saved my life tonight, ye have every reason to be proud of her." Angus could hear her snort of derision and grinned.

"It would have been better if she hadn't gone at all, but that's Mom for you. She never was one to back down from a hard choice. Her life has been crazy this last year; I'm surprised she's still sane."

When the doorbell chimed, Angus rang off and went to answer it. That should be Vince and Morgan. He looked through the peephole, saw it was them and opened the door to let them in. He led them through to Julian's study where he closed the door behind them.

Morgan was the first to speak. "What's up, Angus?"

Vince eyed the liquor cabinet. "Any possibility of a drink?"

Both men were looking tired, but then so was he. "It's no my house, but I'm sure Poppy wouldn't mind if ye wanted to help yerself," Angus replied. "I asked ye here because I wanted ye to listen to something before I turn it over to the police chief in the morning. When ye are ready, gents."

Vince poured himself a shot of whiskey and sat down in the conversation area in the study near the fireplace where Angus and Morgan had seated themselves. "What's this all about, Angus?"

Angus held up his cell phone. "I took the precaution of settin' my phone to silent and record just before Poppy and I went in. Let's just say it answers a lot of questions ye didn't even know ye had yet." He pushed the button and sat back as the men listened to what had recorded.

"My God." Morgan's stunned expression echoed what they were all feeling as the recording ended.

Angus nodded. "Morgan, I especially wanted ye to hear it because I'm no convinced that the chief will share with yer organization. He's already sniffin' up Poppy's tree even when he has Nesbitt in custody. How well she's covered her tracks could be the difference in no bein' able to clear Poppy of all

A FLOWER FOR ANGUS

suspicion of her husband's murder. I want that fer her," he added simply.

"Can you send a copy of that to my cell phone?" Morgan asked.

Vince spoke up. "I haven't had a chance to tell you, but I got to see the coroner's report regarding Adrian. It's how I suspected Angus and Poppy might be in serious trouble."

Morgan frowned. "How did you get that already?"

Vince grinned. "I have my ways. Anyway, it states right in the report that a DNA match had popped up with a positive for Adrian. I followed the link and found that a Carma Michelina had requested it, and that it was a sibling match to Adrian.

"I knew there was going to be trouble at this meeting, so I called you, Morgan, and went to Condoloro Enterprises as fast as I could get there. Abby Nesbitt, who just happens to be a member of the board for Condoloro Enterprises, changed her name over ten years ago from Carma Michalina. She's the one board member whose credentials were very sketchy. I couldn't link Carma to anyone connected to Julian until I read the coroner's report and followed the link."

He looked at Poppy. "The statute of limitations never runs out on murder, which was why Abby didn't want Poppy looking into anything.

"Not only that, but someone isn't going to want Abby talking, Morgan," Vince told him with a steely look his way. "You might want to get her into protective custody before the locals lose their prize."

"Did you download any of the coroner's files?" Morgan asked Vince.

Vince nodded. "They can't keep this secret, even if they try to do damage control by eliminating Carma, ergo Abby Nesbitt. It will come out, but just how deep her ties go into the mob will be something they will want to cover up."

"Now that we have the mob connection, we'll take over the entire case," Morgan replied, standing up. "I need to get moving on this immediately and get this recording to Mike Docent, the agent on the case."

Angus and Vince stood up and walked with him to the door. "Be careful, Morgan," Angus warned. "People like that tend to move fast once a breach has been committed."

"Don't worry," Morgan replied as he shook hands with Angus. "No one knows about this recording but the three of us yet. By the time you go to the police station tomorrow, Carma should be in our custody."

Angus shook hands with Vince. "Thank ye, Vince. Ye saved our lives tonight. There's no telling how this might have turned out if ye hadn't distracted Nesbitt long enough fer Poppy to get her gun out."

"I'd say that knife in her shoulder was a pretty good distraction, Angus. Is that where you aimed to hit her?" Vince joked.

Angus chuckled. "Like Poppy, I was aimin' more fer center mass, but it looks like we both got a shoulder without killin' her. I'm glad Poppy doesn't have to deal with takin' another person's life."

Vince and Morgan nodded soberly in agreement.

A FLOWER FOR ANGUS

THE NEXT MORNING POPPY and Angus were in the study where Poppy was going over the newly arrived auditors report in her email. It was only 7:00 a.m. but the cook and the maid were both back and she would be sitting down with them later on. Right now, she was enjoying the luxury of having someone preparing her breakfast and bringing her a pot of fresh coffee.

She heard the doorbell but she knew Ralston would get it because he had decided to resume his duties as well, which was fine with her. He still seemed resentful of her, and why he should be was lost on her. He hadn't been when Julian was alive. Like so many other things, it would have to wait. Condoloro Enterprises was her first concern.

Her head shot up when a knock on the door distracted her. "Come in."

Ralston opened the door and behind him was Chief Flinders looking like a thundercloud. "Chief Flinders to see you."

She and Angus both stood up as the Chief entered the room and immediately announced, "Abby Nesbitt is dead."

Poppy gasped. "Dead? How? Did she die of her injuries?" she asked, her heart sinking.

"How did that happen in yer custody?" Angus growled.

"There's also a dead FBI agent," Flinders snapped. "Nesbitt was in their custody at the hospital as of 2:00 this morning, so the investigation as to how she died is in their hands and they aren't talking. They've taken her body to their lab, and Nevil Hanrahan's as well. I'm here to take your statements."

"Ye couldn't wait until after breakfast?" Angus asked mildly.

Poppy plopped back down in the office chair. "Does that even matter now?" she asked bitterly. "The chance to get any more information from Carma is gone."

"Who?" Flinders eyes narrowed.

"Never mind," she said hastily. "If it's not your case, why do you need statements?"

Flinders eyebrows shot up. "A crime happened in my city. I need detailed reports on everything that happened up until the time I'm no longer investigating it. I was pulled off at 2:00 am, so that means I still need statements from witnesses until then."

"Would you like some coffee, Chief?" Poppy asked, indicating the tray with the hot pot of coffee and extra cups.

His gaze softened slightly, making him look younger than his fifty something, even though his salt and pepper hair was thinning badly, and his paunch hung a few inches over his belt. "I'd like that, thank you, Mrs. Condoloro."

Poppy noticed that his uniform looked permanently wrinkled as if he hadn't been to bed yet, and there were dark shadows beneath his gray eyes.

After he poured his coffee and took a seat by the desk, he studied her as he stirred cream into his coffee. "Just so you know, I never thought you had anything to do with Julian's death. I've always thought someone was feeding the media frenzy behind the scenes, but I never could prove it," he growled almost kindly. "So, how do you know about Carma?"

The question caught Poppy off guard and she flushed. "I might have been doing some investigating on my own," she replied, lifting her chin.

"The coroner's report is classified information," he said mildly taking a sip from his cup.

"I haven't seen the coroner's report," she replied truthfully. She hadn't seen it but Vince had.

He nodded. "I know you have a private detective, Vince Gallo, working for you. Gallo's an excellent detective. He could have been a lot better if he'd stayed on the force, but he didn't want to operate by the rules. He does get results though. As long as he stays away from my cases, I have no quarrel with him. What else did he tell you?"

"Why do ye want to know, Chief?" Angus drawled, shooting Poppy a warning look. "And for the record, we neither confirm nor deny anythin' ye just said."

Chief Flinders actually chuckled mirthlessly. "Just because the FBI interfered with my case doesn't mean I've stopped hunting. I don't like anything about the mob, and I especially don't like mob hits in my jurisdiction. And I really, *really* don't like dirty law enforcement—in any agency."

"Ye think Nesbitt was killed by dirty cops?"

He shot them both a steely look. "I will neither confirm nor deny that question."

Angus grunted and took out his cell phone. "I do have somethin' I'd like to share with ye then. There was so much goin' on last night that I thought I'd save it for our statements today." He took out his cell, flipped it to the recording he'd made and pushed the play button.

The Chief was silent for a moment after the recording ended. "What you have there is dangerous, and you need to give it to me or get rid of it. If the wrong people were to know you had that...well...you get the idea."

"Ye seem like an honest man, Chief," Angus said tersely. "So, I'm goin' to give ye this recording and then I'll delete it."

"Did you give it to anyone else?" he asked shrewdly.

"Why do ye want to know?"

Flinders sighed heavily. "I know Mrs. Condoloro's son-in-law is FBI, but he isn't the agent investigating Adrian's connections with the mob. If you gave him this recording and he passed it on, then that could mean someone in the FBI is dirty."

"By the same reasoning, if we'd only given it to the police and she wound up dead, you could consider there is a dirty cop on mob payroll," Poppy snapped, her eyes flaring.

"There's safety in numbers, Chief," Angus replied. "The more people who know about this tape, the less chance of anyone trying to tie up loose ends. If it were me, I'd use my media contacts and get it out to the public. Carma's mob contacts will scarper for holes like moles exposed to the light. And if they are dug out, they'll just lawyer up as ye yanks say."

Flinders stared. "What do you do in Scotland, Mr. Sangster?"

"I manage Heaven's Gate, a sheep farm more or less."

Poppy snorted. "He's too modest. Heaven's Gate is a highland sheep station near Inverness covering more than 250,000 acres, Chief."

Flinders grunted. "I'd have pegged you for law enforcement. Your talents are wasted on sheep."

A FLOWER FOR ANGUS 243

"I prefer wrangling sheep to wranglin' the miscreants of society," Angus drawled. "Sheep are much cleaner."

The Chief's laugh was more of a bark than anything else. "You have a point there." He drained the last drop of his coffee and stood up. "If you will send that tape to my phone, Mr. Sangster, I'll be heading home for a few hours of sleep."

Poppy stood up. "What about our statements?"

His gaze held hers as the corners of his mouth quirked up. "I just came to hear the tape. You can give your statement at the station where it can be officially recorded whenever you can have time to get there."

Angus shook his head. "So, Morgan already told ye."

Flinders cell phone dinged and he gave it a quick glance. "Not Morgan, the agent he gave it to. I'll need to be on my way. I just wanted to see if you would tell me without prying it out of you," he replied with a grin. "He just didn't tell me exactly what all was on it or I'd have been here before now."

"We'll see you out," Poppy replied as she and Angus followed him into the foyer and to the front door.

Chief Flinders turned to Poppy as he opened the door for one parting shot. "If I were you, Mrs. Condoloro, I'd fire the entire board or let the company fall into bankruptcy and completely clean house. You have no idea who has been compromised, or what all Carma has been up to."

"I'll take that under advisement," Poppy replied. She closed the door and turned to Angus. "Well, that was interesting."

"Aye, it was."

When Poppy turned around to go back to the study, she saw Ralston glaring at her from the middle of the foyer. Deciding she'd had enough of his attitude, she marched right up to the man.

"What is your problem, Ralston?" she enquired. "I don't have time for your resentful stares and nasty attitude. I didn't have to rehire you, and make no mistake, it's me that's hiring you, not Edna. In fact, I could have you escorted off the premises if I chose to do so. This is officially my house now whether I want it or not. I'd sell it if not for Edna, but it's such a monstrosity that I don't think anyone else would want it."

His glare faded and confusion slid over his features. "You'd sell the mansion?"

"In a heartbeat. It's costly to maintain and much too large for just one or two people. With Adrian gone there are no more Condoloro's to inherit, so why keep it?"

"I-I thought you wanted the mansion and brought your...your *friend* to gloat and lord it over the rest of us," he confessed. "I was irked for Edna's sake."

Her hands flew to her hips. "Do I look like I'm gloating?" she snapped. "I don't even want to be here except to try to save the company, and it's sure as hell not for my sake. In fact, as soon as I figure out what to do, I won't even be living in this...this mausoleum. There's nothing here for me."

He bowed slightly. "I apologize, Mrs. Condoloro," he said awkwardly. "It appears I've misjudged you."

Poppy waved her hand in disgust. "And for Pete's sake, stop calling me that. My name is Poppy. Julian was the one who insisted in all the formal fanfare, I couldn't give two shits for all of it." She turned around and stomped back to the study with Angus following.

"It appears ye may be in need of another Angus special," Angus remarked, locking the door and coming up behind Poppy at the desk to massage her shoulders. "Ye are verra tense this mornin', lass."

Poppy groaned as his fingers found sore spots she didn't know she had. "I'm sorry, Angus, you're probably right. I've got so much to do right now though, that it's making me crazy." She glanced at her watch. "The board meeting is at 10:00 a.m. so that gives me about two hours to figure out what I'm going to say to everyone."

"Chief Flinders had a point. Ye could just fire the entire board."

"Or I could temporarily suspend them until I've completely vetted all of them." She snapped her fingers. "That's it. I need to lockdown the computer system and change the network passwords so no one can access anything except me. I need to get to the office and call IT to come in."

"Right now, I'm sure it's still a crime scene and it will be blocked off," Angus said with a frown. "Why can't ye do that from here?"

She slumped back in her chair. "You're right, we can't even have the board meeting at the office. Then she reached for the phone. "I'll just call everyone and have them meet here."

Angus put his hand over hers. "I'd no advise that, lass. Think about it. If any of them are compromised, having them in the house wouldn't be a good idea. What about a conference room at a local hotel or convention center?"

She turned around and stood up to hug him. "That's a great idea," she admitted. "I guess I should also have Vince come over and look at the security systems too and make sure the cameras and everything are working."

He leaned down and kissed her. "I'll take care of that; ye take care of yer company." He turned her around with a slap on her rear. "Get to work," he teased. "I'll find us some breakfast."

By the end of the day, Poppy was exhausted and her head was pounding—again. The board members were furious at being locked out of everything, the FBI was crawling all over the building and couldn't give her a date when she would be allowed back in, and the story of Carma Michelina was on every channel. Not exact details, but highlights which were still enough to drop Condoloro stocks to an all-time low.

Thank heavens Angus and Vince had upgraded all the security because the phone wouldn't stop ringing and someone had lobbed a bottle bomb over the front gate. She'd finally done an impromptu press release outside the mansion gates to address their basic concerns and reassure the public that she would do her best to get the company back on its feet.

No staff were leaving the mansion for a few days and Poppy had hired two guards to patrol the grounds until things calmed down. Vince had moved out to avoid the media frenzy. Chief Flinders had ordered patrols several times a day by his officers, and at night to keep extra eyes on things. The whole situation was making her extremely tense and irritable.

Angus was doing a round and making sure the house was secure while Poppy got a bath. When she came into her bedroom, he was waiting for her.

"Are ye ready for bed, lass? It's going on midnight and ye need some rest. It's been a long day."

"I'll say," Poppy replied, rubbing her temples wearily. She walked over to him, put her arms around his waist, and rested her head on his shoulder. "Thank you for being here, Angus. I'd have been overwhelmed without you today."

"That's what I'm here for, wee one, to protect and take care of ye," he growled softly. He ran his palms over her buttocks in the silky, shorty pajamas. "I'm no sure of who's going to protect ye from me though, dressed in this skimpy nightwear."

"I-I'm sorry, I wasn't trying to seduce you if that's what you mean," she replied, stiffening in his arms.

He chuckled. "It wouldn't do ye any good if ye were, I'll no compete with a dead man on his turf. I don't want memories of us together for the first time intertwined with the memories ye have of this place."

Poppy palmed the side of his face. "That's very thoughtful of you," she said, searching his face. She was relieved that he had put into words what she'd been thinking ever since they'd decided to come. "Is your special still on the table though?" she asked hopefully.

"Anytime and anywhere ye want, honey," he replied, taking her hand and leading her to the bed. "In yer bedroom, in the study, in the kitchen, anywhere ye want. Just name it."

Chapter 17

Angus glanced at his watch. It was 2:00 in the morning and he was in the study in the dark, facing the door in a comfortable leather chair and waiting for his onery lass to sneak in.

The three weeks since they'd arrived in Chicago had been grueling. The last time he'd had Poppy over his lap for stress relief had been at her request, and that was days ago. She hadn't asked again and had refused his offers.

Each night she went to bed close to midnight, only then at his insistence, and it was always with one of her pain pills to ease her headaches. She'd pass out and he'd make sure she was sleeping soundly and then retire.

Each morning, she would appear at 7:00 a.m. for coffee in the study where Molly would have it waiting for her. Coffee and toast were all she'd eat until lunch.

If she didn't skip lunch when he was busy with Vince.

She was getting sleep, so why was she so brittle and edgy?

Frankly, he was worried about her. It felt like she was losing more weight, and he didn't like that either. It wasn't until Edna had stopped him in the hall this afternoon and asked if Poppy was feeling all right that the penny had dropped. Edna had heard her up in the night when she'd gone to the kitchen for some milk. Dishonesty wasn't something Angus was prepared to tolerate.

His wee one had accomplished a lot, he had to admit. The world of corporate finance wasn't something Angus had experience with and didn't want to. Condoloro Enterprises was merging with Delanoy and the company name was changing to Colony Corporation. The CEO of Delanoy was one Poppy had sought out, not one of the many offers on the table that had come her way to help bail out Julian's sinking Enterprise. She'd gone to great lengths to erase any mob contact or influence.

After extensive interviews, she'd only kept some of the board members under the condition that they submit to a complete background check by Vince to make sure they hadn't been compromised. The rest were retired with severance packages, especially anyone who had been involved with the cashflow. The fact that they were happy to go made him very suspicious.

Of course it would take weeks, probably even months before the full extent of everything was investigated and the truths revealed. The audits hadn't implicated Abby Nesbitt, but they all knew she had choreographed the embezzlements to offshore accounts under Hanrahan's name. Ace Ducat, who she had retired to the bayou, also had suspicious investments in his name, although they couldn't be proven false. But especially suspicious were the withdrawals for Adrian's many gambling debts.

Some things they might never figure out, especially since Nesbitt seemed to have covered her bases and eliminated those she implicated. Except for Julian's secretary, Sarah

Solano. Nesbitt hadn't mentioned her and they still hadn't been able to locate her. He was afraid she was another one of Nesbitt's victims.

His thoughts were interrupted when he heard the door slowly begin to open. Poppy's slender body slipped inside and closed it before she hit the light switch. When the room lit up, he noted she was in her night clothes with a short silky robe slipped over her thin pajamas. Perfect. He wouldn't have any trouble getting to her sneaky little bottom.

When she turned and spotted him, she squealed in alarm and put her hand over her heart. "Angus! What are you doing here like a golem in the dark? You scared me half to death."

He shot her a disapproving glare. "The real question, lass, is what are ye doin' here? Ye're supposed to be in bed at this time of the night." He got up from the chair and advanced on her.

"M-Me?" she stuttered, glancing around as if she were desperate for an excuse to appear on the wall. "I... uh...forgot my reading glasses."

"Ye're reading at 2:00 in the morning?" he growled. "Ye took a pain tab, ye should be out like a light until morning." Then it hit him and his eyes narrowed. "Ye've no been takin' them, have ye?"

"I-I didn't take one last night," she confessed. "I knew I had some extra work to get out of the way and..."

"It's not just last night that ye didn't take one, is it?" he interrupted her, trying to tamp down his righteous irritation. "Don't lie to me, lass."

Finally, she lifted her chin defiantly. "What of it? I don't have to answer to you."

"If that's the way ye feel, then why be dishonest?" he bit out. He took another step towards her and she took the only backward step she could, which put her back against the door. She scrabbled for the doorknob behind her back.

"Maybe because men always seem to think they know what I need to do?" she jeered. "I have news for you, I'm a big girl. I certainly don't need anyone to tell me when to go to bed. I can figure that out on my own."

"Right now, ye're a sneaky wee lass who's earned that hidin' I warned ye about. Dishonesty and deceit are somethin' I'll no put up with." He took two steps forward and bent to scoop her over his shoulder.

"Oomph," she whined. "Put me down, Angus, this is uncomfortable."

He went to the sofa with her and stood her on her feet, then held her arms as he sat down and pulled her right across his lap. "Ye're about to get a lot more uncomfortable."

Poppy struggled and fought but Angus didn't have any trouble pinning her upper body on the couch and both of her legs under one of his.

"Let me go," she raged at him. "Don't you dare touch me or I'll have you arrested. I really will, Angus Sangster!"

Angus wasted no time in hooking a finger in her pajamas shorts and panties and dragging them down to her knees. "I don't scare easy."

He gave her two sharp spanks, one on each side of her wriggling globes. "And I don't agree with ye either. Ye *don't* know when to go to bed since ye're lookin' like death warmed over. It's really startin' to worry me. Doc has told ye to get more rest, and that ye are underweight, and he was right. Instead of getting' better, it's getting worse."

He gave her two more hard smacks to those same two globes, which were now reflecting the outline of his handprints. "Ye know these headaches are stress and lack of rest related, yet ye keep pushin' yerself beyond yer limits and tryin' to hide it from me at the same time." His hand popped twice again, very hard and very decisive.

Poppy screamed in outrage and kicked her heels up trying to loosen his leg over hers. "Doctors can only make suggestions; they can't make me do anything I don't want to. Now let me up," she demanded. She grabbed a throw pillow and slammed it back at him, hitting him on the side of his head.

He grabbed the pillow and tossed it on the floor. "Now ye really did it. Yer fiery temper needs to be doused with a good old-fashioned skelpin'."

There was nothing gentle or soothing about the spanking Angus administered to Poppy's backside. He persevered heartily until her cheeks were cherry red and she finally surrendered across his lap, unable to do anything but cry into the other pillow. He felt the fight leave her and stopped swatting her to rest his hand on her heated flesh.

"I've been givin' ye plenty of leeway and support in what yer tryin' to do, Poppy. But I won't stand by and watch ye headin' fer a nervous break-down, or destroy yer health. I care too much about ye to let that happen," he scolded.

As he rubbed her sore bottom, her sobs started to quiet down but she still hadn't said anything. She hadn't apologized either. He debated whether he should sit her up on his lap to continue his lecture, or keep her in this position in case she needed more convincing. He had to give her credit; she was a stubborn wee thing. At least she wasn't fighting him anymore.

He continued to rub her bottom with his palm enjoying the silky feel of her rounded globes. The curve of a woman's lower back where it swelled up and over her buttocks was one of the sweetest curves ever created on a woman. He could caress her body all night long.

"I intend to make sure ye listen to me and stay in bed, lass, even if I have to go buy some handcuffs to keep ye there. There'll be no more sneakin' out of bed in the middle of the night." He was expecting a vociferous complaint about the handcuffs but she didn't respond. "Are ye listenin' to me, Poppy?"

When she didn't reply, he reached down and pulled her hair behind her ear. Her face was tucked into the crook of her elbow and Angus realized she'd fallen asleep. He chuckled at himself and shook his head. This was a first. She'd fallen asleep in the middle of her spanking and talking to.

Heaving a sigh, he gently pulled her panties and shorts back into place and turned her over in his arms. She snuggled into his chest immediately. She didn't wake up; the poor mite was that exhausted. Rather than risk waking her up, he simply stretched out on the oversized sofa and took her with him.

His tadger danced even more at this new position but he ignored it. He turned over the damp side of the throw pillow and put it under his head, then pulled the Chicago Bears throw off the back of the sofa and covered Poppy. He usually slept warm anyway and didn't need a quilt. A light blanket was all he ever used, if that. Plus, he was still dressed in a sleeveless undershirt and his sweatpants.

Poppy sighed and snuggled closer into him, her head on his shoulder. That was fine by him, it felt right as rain. His lass was in his care, at least for the moment, and right where she belonged. The advantage he had over hormone-driven youth was experience and self-control which enabled him to fall asleep too. Just before the sandman grabbed him, he wondered how she'd feel in the morning?

POPPY WOKE UP SLOWLY, the smell of coffee assaulting her nostrils. Her eyes felt swollen and bleary as she pried her eyelids open. Seeing the back of a sofa in her vision she remembered Angus waiting for her in the study. He'd been sitting in the leather chair, the defined muscles of his arms clearly displayed in the wife-beater undershirt like a stern-faced buddha. She ached all over. He was right, she reflected, she was driving herself too hard, but she had so much to do, she just wanted to get it over with.

Speaking of the devil, where was he? Instinctively, she could feel he was in the room with her. Was he watching her? A small smile quirked her lips up. How she would love to have her cell phone in her hand and impudently raise it high in the air as a gesture that she was going to call the police for spanking her butt. She'd love to see those eyebrows crawl to the sky and the warning look light up his eyes. She did love teasing him. He usually responded with a friendly swat, and she'd learned to love that attention too.

Feeling the need to pee, she groaned and finally stretched her legs out to roll to her back. "Ouch," she squeaked in surprise. She promptly rolled over on her side and rubbed her bottom.

"Feelin' a mite sore?"

Angus was sitting in that same leather chair. He was dressed in his usual style, a pair of jeans and a white shirt with the sleeves rolled up. He looked fresh from the shower and held a cup of steaming coffee in his hands.

She shot him an unfriendly glare. "What did you do to me?" she complained, trying to sit up. She finally managed to get up and then stand up, her hands rubbing her butt cheeks.

"It's more about what yer doin' to me right now," he croaked in return. He eyed her up and down with a hungry look that had nothing to do with food. "Do ye have any idea how beautiful ye are with that sleepy tousled look and those long bare legs?" he growled. He sat his coffee cup on the desk and stood up.

She held her hand up to ward him off. "Don't try to butter me up after what you did. I may still call the police if my backside is black and blue, which I'm sure it is," she groaned.

He took her hand and pulled it up on his shoulder, then wrapped his long arms around her where he could massage her sore bottom. "Poor little mite," he crooned, "ye can't say I didn't warn ye. Ye knew what ye were doin' when ye chose to be sneaky and dishonest with me."

She yawned and leaned into him. "That feels really good, but I'm still not forgiving you yet."

He cupped her chin in his palm, his eyes serious. "I don't need yer forgiveness lass, I need ye to take better care of yerself. In fact, I insist on it. Ye fell asleep in the middle of my lecture last night, which means ye were completely worn out."

"Maybe it was just boring?" she giggled, unable to help herself. Then she gasped when another hard swat landed on her already sore rump. "Ouch! Angus!"

"I can pick up where we left off," he warned. "I mean it, Poppy, ye can't go on this way."

"Can we pick this up after I pee, get dressed, and have some coffee?"

Angus scowled. "I like ye just the way ye are. Once a lass is fully clothed, it's like puttin' on armor or somethin', she just gets sassier."

"I-I'm not sure why that's so funny," Poppy replied, giggling helplessly. "I can't seem to help it, but it is."

Angus rolled his eyes and led her to the half-bath next to the bookshelves. "Ye've probably lost half yer senses from exhaustion. Get in there before you let loose on my shoes," he grumped. Poppy giggled at that too.

In the bathroom she washed her hands after relieving herself and then scooped the back of her clothes down over her posterior to inspect her butt. She'd really expected to see some horrible bruises, to be honest, and was surprised to find there weren't any. Tenderly she felt some of the deeper red spots with her fingertips and grudgingly concluded she just looked well spanked. The rat had done a good job of roasting and tenderizing her jiggly globes.

She scrunched up her nose. They were jigglier than they used to be, she'd lost weight she couldn't afford to. Try as she might, she couldn't regurgitate the anger she'd felt last night. Like he'd reminded her, she'd been warned, and that warning was the very reason she'd hid her nightly excursions to the study from him. That just left her feelings to be resolved.

It wasn't politically correct to spank women these days, but her Scottish highlander was anything but politically correct. He lived under a traditional clan system that had existed for centuries and it was deeply imbedded in who he was. Dominant, protective, and all male. Bottom line—he wasn't going to change.

And neither was she.

She glanced at her watch and gasped. It was almost noon. She was supposed to have met with William Santino, the CEO of Delanoy at 8:00 a.m. at the Condoloro building. She needed her phone.

Grabbing the door handle, she turned it and shot out of the bathroom. "I need my phone; I had a meeting this morning."

Angus grabbed her hand and swung her around. "He called. I told him ye'd reschedule when ye were feelin' better."

"You should have woken me up," she protested.

"I asked him if there was anythin' urgent that couldn't wait, and he said nay. Just paperwork that needed to be signed and some decisions he didn't know if ye would approve of yet." Angus pulled her into his arms. "Ye hired him, Poppy, so ye must trust him. Let him do his job."

She bit her lip and finally nodded. "I realize you are right, Angus. I have trouble letting others handle things that are important because I want them done right."

"Are ye guilty of micromanagin'?" he teased with a sudden grin. "Employees don't grow and learn that way. They need to make mistakes and learn from them."

"I need some coffee," she replied, twisting away from him with a sigh. "Then I need a hot shower and to make some phone calls, in that order."

"Nay, ye need yer coffee, a hot shower, and then lunch with me," he told her. "I'm takin' ye out to a nice diner of yer choice and ye are going to relax and eat a good lunch. Then ye can make yer phone calls."

Seeing the set of his jaw, Poppy knew he was determined, so she gave in as gracefully as a pout could be and nodded. "Okay, fine. I am hungry. And it's been a long time since I've been to Fiorelli's. I love their Italian food."

Angus poured her a cup of the steaming brew, added a lump of sugar and a *snoot full of cream*, as he called it, then handed it to her. "Just like ye like it."

She took a sip and moaned with pleasure. "I still haven't forgiven you, just so you know. It's going to take more than a good cup of coffee and a butt rub."

He chuckled that deep rich tone that always gave her goosebumps. "Like I said, I'm no apologizin' for yer spankin' and I don't need forgiveness. I'll do it again if I have to."

She eyed him over the rim of her cup.

He eyed her right back, his arms folded across his broad chest. "Is that look a challenge, lass?" he asked smoothly. "Because if it is, we never did finish our conversation last night. The one where ye say ye're sorry for deceivin' me and ye won't do it again?"

She was instantly contrite. "I am sorry for deceiving you. I didn't like it, but I felt the urgent need to get things done and I knew you *wouldn't* want me to. So, I just didn't tell you."

"That sounds more like ye're sorry you had to deceive me, not that ye did."

She arched an eyebrow. "Is there a real difference?"

He nodded sternly. "Aye, there is. Ye didn't have to deceive me at all. Ye could have just been honest and mayhap I could have helped ye more. That excuse sounds like somethin' I've heard before in yer dealin's with yer past men. And I'll tell ye the same thing I told ye then, that tactic may have worked with them, but it won't fly with me."

She watched him warily as she finished the last swallow of her coffee and set the cup on the desk. "Look, Angus, I am sorry. Okay? And I'll try not to do it again. Now can I get a shower so we can get some food?"

His eyebrow stayed in its impossibly high stature almost in his hairline.

She managed not to roll her eyes. "Please?"

He finally conceded with a brief nod of his head as he received a notification text on his phone. Poppy made her escape and darted across the foyer, up the stairs, and into her bedroom without encountering anyone else in the house, much to her relief.

IN THE STUDY, ANGUS read the text from Vince asking him to call him when he could. Hitting the call button on the text, Vince's voice came across the line.

"Is Poppy around? I tried to text her and she didn't answer."

"She's getting' a shower," Angus replied. "What's goin' on?"

"They found Sarah Solano's body this morning. It's been made to look like a heroin overdose."

"Cripes," Angus swore softly. "Where?"

"In a dive motel down in south Chicago. Looks like she's been hiding out. The coroner places the time of death around two days ago. The hotel manager called it in when someone started complaining about a smell coming from the room. She was registered under a fake name, but she's been positively identified as Solano."

"Sounds like they are still cleanin' up," Angus observed.

"Funny you should mention that. She left a suicide note saying she was tired of hiding, and that Nesbitt was the one who forced her to implicate Adrian in the death of his father. That Adrian really hadn't been at home that day."

"Which, according to Nesbitt, it wasn't Adrian anyway. But it's one more peg in the evidence against Nesbitt," Angus murmured. "They're settin' her up for everythin', aren't they?"

"Running for cover sure enough. A dead woman can't deny or testify."

"Anythin' else?"

"I finally tracked down the mechanic who worked on Poppy's car. He said it looked to him like the brake line had

A FLOWER FOR ANGUS 261

been cut, but no one was asking about it. Since his opinion wasn't required on the bill for the car, he didn't worry about it. And he's right to a certain extent. Even if he'd reported it, the police would most likely never have investigated it, or put it down to malicious mischief given what was going on at the time."

"Understood," Angus replied. "Any news on Ace Ducat?"

"I did find a paper trail leading to Florida and the rental home he'd been living in. I was one step ahead of the FBI and they are crawling all over it now. I know they won't tell me what they find unless Morgan volunteers it. I don't want to get my digital fingerprints on their radar so I'll leave it alone from here on out. If she really did dump him in the bayou, it would be dumb luck if the body ever surfaced."

Angus chatted with Vince until Poppy came into the study. "Here's Poppy now, did ye still want to speak with her or do ye want me to pass on what ye told me?"

"Is that Vince?" Poppy asked, reaching for the phone.

"Aye." He handed her the phone and waited patiently while the conversation was obviously all on Vince's side until Poppy spoke up.

"Okay, well, thank you for checking it out, Vince. Let me know if you find out anymore."

She hung up and handed Angus his cell phone back. "Well, that's one less person missing," she commented. "Poor Sarah, she didn't deserve that. I'll have to make sure her family gets a severance package. She wasn't a junkie, no matter what anyone says. She was a mom with a nice husband and two young children who must be out of their minds with worry and grief."

"Ye knew her personally?" Angus asked.

"Yes, I'd met her family at a couple of company parties. She was a nice person. It makes me wish I could shoot Nesbitt all over again," she fumed.

Angus chuckled and hugged her. "Come on, wee one, let's see if some food will quell that ferocious temper."

Chapter 18

A week later, they were having supper at the mansion with Andrea's family when Angus got a call from Darro. He excused himself and left the table. When he came back, he looked worried, but didn't volunteer any information until after Andrea and Morgan had left with the kids.

"Is everything all right at Neamh?" Poppy asked curiously as they retired to the living room on the main floor. No one ever used it but them. Edna had her own cable and such in her living quarters and she and Ralston were very reclusive.

Angus liked the 58-inch smart TV on the wall. It wasn't something he'd ever need at Thistlewind, but it was nice to watch the Explorer's channel when he was waiting on Poppy.

"Nay, lass, it's not all right. Darro has an emergency and I'm afraid I'm goin' to have to return to Heaven's Gate."

Poppy shot him a concerned glance. "What kind of emergency?"

"Henry turned over one of the trucks and he and Dal are both in the hospital. Dal has a broken arm and Henry has a bad cut down his thigh and a crushed knee. Neither one of them are goin' to be able to work for several weeks. Sheep shearin' starts in two days. That means all hands-on deck to get the wool to market on time, and we are now four down with me over here and Bailes retired because of his arthritis last month. Darro hasna been able to replace him yet."

"Can't he hire shearers?"

Angus shook his head. "Not this late. All of the usual labor for hire is already spoken for and ye can't just hire someone with no experience. They'd be more of a hazard to the rest of us than a help." He hesitated and then ask, "How close are ye to bein' done here, Poppy? Do ye think ye can manage from Scotland now that ye have yer CEO in place and things sorted out?"

"No, I'm not ready yet, Angus," she protested. "I need to be here in person for awhile and oversee the merging and additional hiring we need to do after it's official. And...a million other things," she finished, waving her hands around in the air. "William needs me here."

Then he asked something that she wasn't prepared for.

"Do ye think ye will ever be ready? Or are ye wantin' to stay here with yer family now that ye're safe again?" His keen gaze was glued to her face.

Poppy didn't know what to say. "I...I planned on returning to Scotland."

His eyes narrowed. "Planned? Or Plan? Because there is a big difference in those two words."

"I want to be with you, Angus," she replied slowly. "I just don't know what that means for me yet."

"I understand," he replied finally, disappointed. "I'll no push ye, Poppy. Ye know how I feel about ye." He stood up abruptly. "I'll be in the study. I need to see about bookin' the first flight available."

Troubled, Poppy stood up too. "Of course, I'll drive you to the airport. Just let me know when." When Poppy's cell phone rang it was William, needing to talk to her about a new problem that had cropped up. She didn't even notice when Angus returned to the doorway of the living room while she paced back and forth gesticulating to the air as she argued with her new CEO. By the time she got off the phone it was near midnight.

Quickly, she made her way through the silent foyer to the study. The lights were off and Angus wasn't there. Then she made her way to her bedroom and opened the connecting door to his bedroom. He was lying on his side facing away from her, but he rolled over and sat up.

"I'm glad to see ye're keepin' to yer word lass. I want ye to know I'm proud of ye fer that. I can plainly see that ye're lookin' much less tired and edgy. That makes me feel a little better about returnin' to Scotland without ye. Thank ye, wee one," he said softly.

She walked over to him and stood between his knees to bend and hug him. He hugged her tightly around her middle and rested his forehead against her soft breasts. Her body ached for his touch. "Could you...do you think you..." she ventured before he looked up. For the first time, he denied what he knew she wanted.

"Nay, lass, I don't think that's a good idea tonight. I'm no sure I could control myself with the sight of yer beautiful bottom starin' up at me beggin' to be kissed and spanked. This isn't the right place or time for us. Ye are my weak spot and I have to protect ye, even from me."

Strangely hurt and suddenly shy, she backed out of his arms. "Well...goodnight then, Angus. I-I'll see you in the morning."

"Goodnight, honey."

Poppy returned to her bedroom, hurting and unsure of herself. There was no way she could just up and leave right now. After leaking a few tears into her pillow, she finally fell into a troubled sleep.

IN HIS BEDROOM, ANGUS was staring up at the ceiling, but sleep refused to come. Glancing at his watch, he realized it was going on 3:00 in the morning. His bags were already packed and Vince was picking him up soon. His flight to New York left in one hour. He got up and finished dressing, then let himself out of the bedroom and went to the study to leave Poppy a note. It was better this way. He wouldn't be able to leave her behind if she took him to the airport, and he didn't want to influence or guilt her into coming with him. It had to be her decision.

He let himself out the front door and met Vince's vehicle coming up the drive. He climbed into his car, the blue color reminding him of joking with Poppy about Vince's choices of car color.

"Thanks for pickin' me up, Vince. I really didn't want a taxi runnin' me around half of Chicago before droppin' me off at O'Hare," he joked lamely.

"I'm amazed Poppy isn't taking you to the airport," Vince replied curiously. "I was surprised to get your call. Too bad I can't go with you; I'd like to go back to Scotland one day. I can't afford it right now though. Is Poppy joining you soon?"

"Poppy has work to do here," Angus replied simply. He turned to gaze at Vince. "Anytime ye want to come back, just let us know. We can always use a good man at Neamh."

"Shearing sheep? I don't think so," Vince said with a chuckle. "I prefer the work I do, but I wouldn't mind doing it away from Chicago. Scotland really touched something in me."

"Aye, she has a way of gettin' to a man. Once ye have a taste of her, ye can't resist her. Kind of like some women," he teased, but his heart wasn't in it.

Vince didn't say anything else, as if he could somehow feel Angus's regrets. It wasn't long before he dropped him off at the airport.

"Good luck to ye, Vince," he said, shaking hands with him after they retrieved his bag from the trunk. "The offer at Neamh is always open."

"Safe travels, Angus." Vince replied.

Angus checked in and boarded his flight feeling very alone. He loved Poppy, but Scotland was a mistress that demanded he remain faithful. Born and bred in her bosom, he would forever remain loyal to her and Heaven's Gate.

As he stared down at the lights of Chicago disappearing below him when the plane was airborne, he wondered what, if anything, the future held for him and his Poppy flower? Would she change her mind about them and stay in Chicago?

He began to get an inkling of what Jamie MacNamara, Lucerne's father, had gone through. Rhonda Descant was

Louisiana born and like Jamie, she loved her American homeland as much as he loved Scotland. She and Jamie had married and stayed fiercely devoted to one another, although they had spent many months at a time apart during the course of their marriage. Rhonda had died a few years back and Jamie hadn't met anyone else who could '*hold a candle to his Rhonda*', as he had put it.

When he'd first met Jamie through Lucerne and learned his story, Angus had been positive he could never endure a long-distance relationship like that. A man would be a fool for even trying. A lass belonged in her man's bed and keeping him warm at night, not off gallivanting halfway across the world.

Now, he wasn't so sure.

At this point in his life, you'd think falling in love would be simple without the hot passion of youth clouding your judgements. Had he put Poppy in the position of having to choose between him and her family? He hadn't meant it that way, but maybe that's the way she would see it.

Brooding, he stared out at the inky blackness of the night sky. Perhaps the real root of his problem was that Poppy had never actually said she loved him. He wasn't sure she'd truly loved either of her first two husbands, and that worried him. He didn't want to fall into the category of just being needed. If his flower didn't love him the way he did her, then he didn't want to just be a convenience in her life. Someone to keep her from being lonely again now that Julian was gone.

He shifted restlessly in his seat. No, Angus wanted more than that. He wanted to love and be loved in return.

A FLOWER FOR ANGUS

The real question was, what did Poppy want?

POPPY FOUND ANGUS'S note and was furious. Why had he just left like that? She'd had so many things to say to him...like goodbye, for one. She'd been going over it all in her head while she was getting a shower this morning. She didn't know what time his flight was, but she knew he'd let her know before they had to leave for the airport.

She stared at the note in her hand. It was short and simple.

'I love you, Poppy. Let me know when or if you are coming home.'

Home? She crumpled up the note and threw it in the trash can while she paced back and forth trying to think of different ways to skewer him. She was home. Granted, she thought of Scotland and Neamh as home too, but the way she read the note, his home would never be here. Was there an ultimatum hidden in that note?

Her text notification went off and she could see it was from William. What did he want now? Honestly, she was beginning to wonder if she'd made a mistake if the man had to consult her for every decision. Ignoring it, she dropped the phone back in her pocket.

When Molly knocked at the door with her toast and coffee, she yanked it open so the girl could proceed through to the desk.

"Where is Mr. Sangster this morning?" Molly asked gaily as her plump backside jutted out in her jeans when she set the tray on the desk. When she turned back, her rosy cheeks and healthy glow faced Poppy with a beaming smile.

Poppy glowered at her. "He's returned to Scotland," she replied sourly. "He had business to attend to."

"Oh, he was such a lovely man," she gushed. "His Scottish accent was hot, even though he'd be too old for me, of course. Maybe I'll go to Scotland one day." She bustled towards the door with all the exuberance of someone twenty-five years younger than Poppy.

Poppy didn't answer as Molly sailed out the door and closed it behind her. Opening her laptop, she waited impatiently for it to boot while she poured herself a cup of the bracing brew.

After 30 minutes, she finally realized the figures on the screen hadn't changed and it was hard to concentrate. Her thoughts kept returning to Angus.

Finally pushing the chair back, she got up and wandered around the mansion feeling lost. She stepped into Julians' bedroom and shuddered. The bed was made, all the crime scene tape was gone, and it looked just as it might on any normal day, yet everything was different. Although she and Angus had technically never had sex, they were more intimate than she'd ever been with Julian. That saddened her for some reason. Like those years she'd lived had all been focused on numbers and business instead of focusing on each other. She supposed that some of it was her fault. She'd never loved Julian, she realized. He'd been a port in the storm of her lonely life. A port that she'd docked in and never left. Sighing, she closed the bedroom door.

A FLOWER FOR ANGUS 271

As she walked around the mansion, she was acutely aware that there were no pictures of her family among the many generations of Condoloro's on the walls, or around the fireplace. On the hearth in the living room there was one lone picture of her, Adrian, and Julian. Any other pictures she had of Andrea and her grandbabies were in her bedroom. The one place in the entire pompous mansion that was hers.

There was no sense of belonging here, there never had been. She'd been looking at other properties, intending to buy a little place of her own that she could make uniquely hers. She and Angus had even toured a few homes and he'd made helpful comments. He wasn't a fan of the mansion either.

Heading back downstairs, she got another notification from William. Irritable, she dialed the return number, then told him that he was the CEO and to make the hiring decision himself. He was the one going to be working with the man.

By the time dinner time had rolled around, Poppy hadn't done anything productive the entire day except mope around. Edna never showed her face, but then she rarely did. She and Edna were like ships that passed in the night in this oversized mausoleum. No sense of kinship to one another. What was she even doing here except bailing out her mother-in-law's butt?

Missing Angus terribly, she went into the bedroom he'd used and sat on the bed. Molly had already made it up with an entirely clean ensemble of bedding. The bathroom sparkled, the trash cans were empty, and air freshener from the wall socket wafted out a gentle lavender scent. No trace of him remained in the room, it was if he'd never been there.

Shivering she walked back into her own room and dug in her hamper. Finding her prize, she pulled out one of his white undershirts that he'd dropped there when he'd been teasing her. She laid it against her face and inhaled the earthy scent of his aftershave. Then she balled it up in her fist and threw it back in the hamper.

Damn him for leaving her like that!

Swiping a tear from her eye, she decided to go out to Andrea's and drop in for a visit.

Morgan looked surprised when he opened the door and she stood on the doorstep. He looked around and behind her. "Where's Angus? You two are usually connected at the hip," he teased.

"He had to return to Scotland," she snapped, pushing her way past him and going to the kitchen to find her daughter. She heard her grandbabies laughing in the playroom and could smell something cooking in the kitchen. It smelled like porkchops and rice, a dish that the family loved. Her stomach growled and she realized she'd missed lunch. Angus wouldn't like that. Oh wait! Angus wasn't here, so he couldn't complain, or scold and swat her, could he?

Stupid, overprotective man.

Squaring her shoulders, she walked into the kitchen to find Andrea taking the casserole dish out of the oven. Her daughter turned around, her smooth face pink from the oven heat. Her hazel eyes narrowed. "Why do you look like someone just kicked your dog."

"I don't have a dog," Poppy snapped. "And if I did, I'd just kill whoever kicked it." She flopped into a chair.

Morgan popped his head around the corner? "Is this girl time, or can I come in?" he asked, shooting a glance at Poppy.

Poppy shrugged. "Do as you please."

He stepped inside the doorway and took a chair. "I take it Angus going back to Scotland has you upset? The lucky dog. I'd love to get assigned to a post in Scotland."

Andrea's eyes widened. "Wait. Why did Angus go back to Scotland?"

"Neamh has some sort of emergency with the sheep and they were really shorthanded, so Darro wanted him back," Poppy grumbled. "He sneaked off like a thief in the middle of the night and didn't even say goodbye. He was gone this morning when I got up."

Andrea jerked her head towards the door as she caught Morgan's gaze to indicate he should leave. "Now it's girl time, honey."

"Are we going to have dinner anytime soon or should I take the kids to McDonalds?" Morgan asked with a sigh as he got up and shoved the chair in. His eyes glanced longingly at the casserole on the stove. Based on past experience, girl time could be a long time and he was hungry.

Andrea took off her apron. "I'll tell you what, you feed the kids and Mom and I will go to Sonic and get a drink."

Poppy almost teared up. Going to Sonic for a drink was code for when she or Poppy wanted to talk. There was something soothing about parking there and hashing out whatever was bothering them over ice cream, a cold soda, or whatever they felt like having.

"Deal," Morgan replied enthusiastically, his tall figure heading for the stove with great relish.

"Take the rolls out of the oven and turn on the pot of green beans," Andrea instructed. "By the time those are ready, the casserole should be cooled enough for the kids to eat."

Morgan eyed Poppy sympathetically. "Are you going to Scotland too?" It was the wrong thing to ask. He held up both hands and backed away as the women hit him with stony stares. "Take your time, I got this," he amended.

Morgan's question only made Poppy feel worse. She and Andrea were both silent as they walked out to her daughter's little black Ford Escape. Andrea navigated her way through traffic and finally pulled into a stall on the east side of Sonic. One they had visited many times in the past.

"Are you hungry?" Andrea asked.

"No, I don't feel like eating."

"You know Angus won't like that."

"Screw Angus," Poppy snapped. "He's not even here, so what he does or doesn't like won't matter anymore."

Sighing, Andrea pushed the red button to place an order for two sets of crispy chicken sandwich meals with fries and cherry cokes. When she was finished, she turned to Poppy.

"All right, Mom, spill it. What's going on?" she asked gently. "Why did Angus really leave? Did you two have a fight?"

Poppy's throat started to close, but she took a deep breath and sighed. "He really did have to go back, I get that."

She explained to Andrea how big Neamh was, how many men they were down, and about getting the wool to market on time. All the same stuff Angus had explained to her.

"He asked me if I was ready to go yet, but I still have a lot to do right now and I can't. I told him I'd take him to the airport," she confessed, a few tears straggling down her cheeks. "I just don't understand why he left like he did." Turning to stare out the window, she waited as Andrea rolled down her window to accept their food.

Then Andrea handed her some fries. "Eat. The hot salty flavor will make you feel better."

Poppy chuckled and wiped her face. "You've always loved Sonic fries, haven't you?" She took the bag of fries and gingerly bit into the hot goodness and then blew on it to cool it. "These really are hot."

"Just the way I like 'em," Andrea agreed, her head sinking back as she groaned in pleasure. After she wolfed down the first one, she turned to Poppy. "Are you in love with Angus, Mom?"

"Of course, but that doesn't really matter right now," she growled impatiently. "I have responsibilities to take care of, people who are counting on me to make this merger work. I love being with Angus and I miss him already, but I need to be here. I'm just so mad at him for leaving like that."

"Has he asked you to marry him?" Andrea persisted.

Poppy snorted. "He's offered himself up for marriage, a housekeeping job, an investments counselor, or just living together. Any way that I'll take him," she replied, remembering his crazy declaration. "He's such a tease."

"Has he offered the three magic words though?" Andrea persisted.

"If you mean I love you, yes. He's told me that many times."

Andrea nodded. "And you do say you love him?"

"Of course I love him," Poppy insisted, trying to remember if she'd actually told Angus that. She assumed he knew, why else would he get away with spanking her? "What are you getting at, Andrea?"

"If he loves you, and you love him, then nothing else matters. Responsibilities can fit in around love. You have to find a way to make it work. He came here because he loved you. Maybe now it's your turn? Do you love him enough to support him in his responsibilities to this huge sheep croft, or station, or farm, or whatever they call it in Scotland?"

Poppy stared at her. "I can't do anything to help Angus in Scotland, I don't know anything about sheep."

"There wasn't anything he could do to help you here either," she pointed out. "He doesn't know anything about corporate finance, but he came anyway. He handed his responsibilities over to those he left in charge and followed you to support you. At least that's the way I see it."

She took a big bite of her chicken sandwich. Then she wagged her finger at her mother after she swallowed. "And he took care of you, made sure you ate and that you rested, and almost got shot because you thought you had to meet that man in a deserted office late at night."

"But...t-the way he left," Poppy stuttered, bewildered, starting to feel guilty at what Andrea was saying. Angus had done all that and more. She was right in that respect.

Andrea had one more thing to say. "Did you ever think that he just didn't want to say goodbye like that?" she asked gently. She reached over and took her mother's hand. "Mom, I know you didn't love Julian. Dad's been gone a long time but you rarely talk about him. Your eyes light up when you look at Angus in a way I've never noticed before. You love him and you trust him. And I know that man adores you. So, what are you waiting for? Is there really anything you need to do here that's more important than your relationship with the man you love? Go get him, Mom."

Poppy stared at Andrea in wonder. She thought about the company, the merger, and all the business decisions that kept cropping up. Was there really any reason she couldn't handle them from Scotland? Was she being selfish and controlling when Angus needed her with him? In an instant, joy filled her heart as the decision she needed to make was as plain as the nose on her face. "W-Would you be upset if I happened to move to Scotland to stay?"

Andrea shrugged and grinned. "You're rich, you can jet over here anytime you like. And Morgan has applied for anything open in the UK, especially Scotland. He's always wanted to go there, it's where his ancestors are from. You can even loan me money to come over on my own, I'm not too proud to take it. Wait...do they have Sonic in Scotland?" she asked, her eyes twinkling.

Poppy burst out laughing. "Inverness has a MacDonalds, I'm not sure about Sonic, but if they don't, there's a great little pub called The Waterfront. I can find out."

"Done," Andrea declared. "Now eat your food. I'd hate to have to narc on you to Angus," she teased. "No telling what he might do."

Poppy knew what he would do but she wasn't telling her daughter. "What would I ever do without you, honey?" she finally asked, her eyes tearing up. "I don't know what I did to deserve such a smart daughter, but you are amazing."

"You can treat me to a Heath blizzard," Andrea replied eagerly.

"Done!"

They both laughed.

Chapter 19

Angus wiped the sweat from his forehead and stepped out of the noise and heat of the shearing shed for a break. Taking a metal tin from the nail on the side of the table, he put it under one of the orange thermoses and pressed the button for cold water to fill it. It was a tin that had been in his family for three generations now.

With his sweat towel hanging over his bare shoulder—he worked shirtless as did all the men when shearing because of the heat—he used one hand to shield his eyes from the waning sun as he stared up into the sky. They were starting to lose the day.

Soon, the overhead light strings would fizzle and burst into life. The nights insects would be buzzing around as the shearing continued inside the shed that stank of sheep's fear and men's sweat. Being short of hands meant they had to take turns and work around the clock to fill the orders on time. Sheep were the lifeblood of Neamh.

It was the way of the shepherd.

Since Angus didn't have a wife or children at home, he spent the majority of his time working extra shifts. He was bone tired. With his towel, he swiped the sweat off his chest and neck and filled his tin again.

As always, his thoughts turned to Poppy. What was she doing right now? Did she miss him as much as he missed her? Even Lucerne's haggis had tasted like cardboard at dinner earlier. Without Poppy, the flavor had just seemed to go out of everything.

It had been five days now and she hadn't even called. Or texted. He'd called her twice and both times it had gone to voicemail. Either she was really mad for the way he left, or she was relieved he was gone and didn't want to reconnect. Whatever the case, there was a dark hole the size of Scotland in his heart while he waited.

"Ye didn't eat much at dinner again, ye old fart."

Angus turned and glared at Darro. "What business is it of yers, lad?" he asked testily.

Darro's eyebrows shot up. "I wouldn't want ye to be slacking off because ye aren't eating enough."

"Ye just ain't happy unless ye're being a slavedriver, are ye?" Angus complained. He hadn't talked about Poppy, and no one had pressed him after he briefly told them she would be staying in the states when he returned. Darro knew him too well though, and knew he was hurting. He just wasn't ready to talk about it.

One of Lucerne's young cousins had been coming in to help them out while Poppy was gone. She'd told Darro to hold her job if they could before she left and they had agreed. Since they hadn't gotten any notice from her, technically, she was still Neamh's housekeeper. As fragile a thread as that was, Angus clung to it.

Darro clapped him on the shoulder. "Get out of here and get some sleep. Be back in the morning at 7:00 o'clock."

Angus's eyebrows crawled up. "I'm no due to leave until midnight."

"Ernie is trading shifts with ye," Darro replied. "He needs to take his wife in for an eye appointment in the morning, so I've moved some shifts around."

"She can't drive herself?"

"They will have to dilate her eyes, so she'll no be able to drive home," Darro supplied. "Come on, ye can ride back with me on the 4-wheeler to get yer truck."

Angus nodded wearily. He climbed onto the 4-wheeler with his back to Darro and his feet in the carrying rack at the back of the seat. They didn't go around behind the barn like usual though, Darro pulled right up in front of the house.

When Angus glanced towards the house, he froze in place. Was he so tired that his eyes were deceiving him? Or was he having hallucinations from wishing so hard? Whatever it was, the vision coming towards him on the flagstone path had him stealing carefully off the four-wheeler without taking his eyes off it lest it disappear. He stood up straight and took a few steps forward. "Poppy?" he asked gruffly.

She moved closer, a vision of loveliness in a pink summer dress that flared around her waist and left her arms bare. Pretty white sandals hugged her delicate feet, and he remembered when she'd painted her toenails bright pink before he'd left. She smiled at him and the sun refused to go down.

"I hear ye have need of a wife, housekeeper, or personal financial assistant, in any order or choice," she spoke in a velvety, teasing voice. "I thought I might apply."

Angus cleared his throat. "For which position?" he croaked, taking another step forward, his heart racing. Joy was beginning to fill that dark hole inside him like water flowing into a watering can and bubbling over.

"Maybe we could start with housekeeper and work up from there if an opening comes up?" she asked, batting her eyes at him.

Angus took three steps forward. "Ye're hired, lass, even if ye can't cook. Ye can fill any of the other positions any time ye're ready." He wrapped his long arms around her slender body and lifted her off the ground to hold her close.

Poppy leaned down and kissed him long and hard before Angus set her back down and took over the kiss. His tadger was dancing with the most excitement it'd seen in months. Finally, he raised his head and palmed the side of her face. "I love ye, Poppy. I've missed ye these last days."

She lifted her arms and grabbed the sweaty towel and went up on her tiptoes. "I love you too, Angus Sangster. And I *can* cook," she added.

Angus roared with laughter, his heart soaring among the stars at that moment until someone cleared their throat.

"So, ye finally managed to hire away my housekeeper, ye old coot."

Angus looked over Poppy's head to see Darro and Lucerne watching them with smiling faces. "Aye, I did. And I'll no be returning her either."

Poppy turned to Darro. "I'm afraid I'll have to give notice, Mr. MacCandish."

"It's Darro," he growled. "Ye really are family now, Poppy, so don't call me Mr. MacCandish."

"Darro," she agreed happily. Then she looked up at Angus. "Are ye ready to go to Thistlewind and show me my duties? I need to unpack."

"More than ready, wee one," Angus growled tenderly, "More than ready." He winked at Darro and put his arm around Poppy to guide her to his truck. "Where are yer bags?" he suddenly asked, stopping for a moment.

"Already in your truck," she replied with a caroling laugh.

"Ye must have been awfully sure of being hired," he teased, holding her close to his side and enjoying her laughter. He'd missed that too.

"You said I love you in the note you left," she replied simply, slipping her arm around the warm skin of his waist as they walked.

At the truck, Angus opened the door and lifted Poppy up on the step. Then he lifted her skirt and landed three pops on her rounded buttocks before he turned her around and let her sit down.

"What was that for?" she grumbled.

"For takin' so long to get here. I wasna sure ye would come…" he trailed off uncertainly, his eyes searching her face with a hunger that had nothing to do with food.

Poppy placed her hands on Angus's bare shoulders. "I'm sorry I took so long, honey. I was angry at first for the way you left, and that first day I was so lonely and miserable I was ready to do bodily damage if you dared to show your face again.

"Then I got a wakeup call from my very smart daughter. I knew I didn't want you looking for another housekeeper because I hadn't made it clear how very much I love you," she whispered. "Whatever it takes, we can make this work, can't we? Because I already know I want to be where you are, even if it can't be all the time."

"Ye're the only housekeeper fer me," he assured her, "and aye, we will make it work. I don't want to be away from ye for a single minute that I don't have too. We may be complicated, but we will figure it out together."

Poppy ran her palm over his bare stomach with her tongue between her lips and a longing in her eyes. "I hear there's a fairy glade and waterfall near here with flowers that only bloom at night. It sounds like a perfect place for a couple in love to exchange rings. Have you heard of such a place?"

Angus's eyes widened. "Aye, I have, would ye like to see it?"

"I would love to see it."

"How soon?"

"Now?"

His heart pounding and uncertain of what she meant, he replied, "Ye'll have to walk in a little way."

"I'm good with that."

Fifteen minutes later, Angus had the bag over his back from the last time they'd gone on their picnic. He'd left it in the back of the truck from their excursion to Loch Ness. They were headed into the trees, listening to the sound of the waterfall as they followed the path with a flashlight.

"It's no that far, are ye good?" he asked. He didn't want her to sprain an ankle at this point. It was a good thing the moon was full; it made the path easier to find.

A FLOWER FOR ANGUS 285

At last, they came into a small clearing where a lazy stream meandered through the heavy grasses on its downward journey. Ahead of them was a lovely waterfall making its way over outcroppings of rocks and between boulders to finally splash into a glistening pool at the bottom.

Poppy stopped and gasped in wonder. "This is so beautiful," she whispered, as she looked around. "I-It's magical." She reached out to touch one of the delicate blooming Jasmin flowers seeming to glow in the moonlight.

"I need to go for a quick swim and get some of this sweat off of me," Angus whispered throatily. "Would ye care to join me? It's a hot night." His eyes gleamed as he stared down at her.

"I'd love too," she replied.

Angus began taking his boots off, watching her the entire time. Was she really wanting to do this? All the fatigue and worry slipped away as he watched her eyes turn slumberous while he undressed. Finally standing naked in the moonlight, his tadger was full, proud, and waving slightly at her as if to beckon her. She licked her lips as her eyes went up and down his full length.

"Now it's yer turn," he croaked, his heart beating rapidly.

Poppy began to undress as if she was born to be a tease. First, her sandals dropped into the grass. Then she reached beneath her full skirt and slowly slid her pink panties down. Angus's pulse began to hammer in anticipation.

"Can you unzip me?"

She turned her back to him and his big fingers fumbled with the delicate zipper until he finally got it started on its downward path. Once down, she stepped back around and began to ease it off her shoulders, one shoulder at a time as if she were born to dance that age old siren call of a female luring her mate.

When the top half of her dress slipped fully to her waist, his breath caught in his throat. He found himself staring at one of the prettiest little pair of breasts he'd ever seen. Plump red nipples surrounded by deeper reddish-brown aureoles were perked cheekily on a pair of full, ripe globes that gleamed like satin in the moonlight. He literally ached to touch, fondle and taste them.

Then suddenly, the dress was pooled around her feet, leaving her completely naked to his hungry gaze as his eyes traveled on down to another one of the sweetest curves ever created; the curve of thighs clinging together to hide the treasure awaiting within.

Angus could barely speak; his mouth was so dry. "Ye are standin' there like a beautiful, delicate flower in the moonlight, lass. I'm afraid to touch ye."

"I'm not afraid to touch you," she murmured boldly, stepping forward and running the tip of her finger along his manhood in admiration. "Is this all for me?" she teased gently. "I'm not a young girl anymore, I've got motherhood scars and I hang a little lower than I used to."

"I've got a few trophies from life myself, wee one," he said tenderly. "We wear them with pride." He cupped her breasts gently in his large hands. "And aye, I'm all yers if ye want me," he assured her fervently. "Now, and forever, Poppy."

"Is cooking a requirement?" she teased suddenly, her eyes lighting with mischief.

"It's no a requirement, but I'm glad that ye can," he teased back.

She stepped into his arms then, and pulled his head down for a kiss. "Now, and forever," she whispered against his mouth as his arms slid around her slender body. "This is where I want to be married, Angus."

Angus's heart thundered. "Are ye sure ye're ready for that, wee one? Cause I can wait until ye are."

"I've never been surer of anything in my life, Angus Sangster," she whispered. "I can't wait to belong to you."

Then Angus picked her up and took her into the pool, their bodies glistening as the water streamed off their heated skin. When they were through playing in the sparkling moonlight, he took out the blankets from his bag in the back of the truck and spread them on the soft grass.

As the night breezes gently caressed their damp skin, he laid Poppy down to worship and adore her with all he had to give. And she gave right back, all he could have asked for and more.

Angus already had Poppy's ring; she just didn't know it yet. His fear that he might never be able to put it on her finger was gone. After tonight, she would totally belong to him. His flower was in his arms at last, and he didn't intend to ever let her go.

The End

Epilogue

"*Oh! What a tangled web we weave when first we practice to deceive.*"
Sir Walter Scott

Julian Condoloro denied his own flesh and blood. It was an act that spun the first weave of an evil spiderweb of betrayal, lies, and deceit so intricate that it would never be totally unraveled.

As Poppy worked hard to create a new company from the ashes of the Condoloro empire, she began to understand how truly brilliant Carma Michelina had been. With the girl's genius IQ, she could have built a lasting empire for the Condoloro's that would still be standing.

By throwing away his daughter, Julian lost his own life, and subsequently, everything he'd wanted to leave in legacy. In her pain and fury, Carma truly had dismantled his perfect life, piece by piece, just as she'd vowed she would.

Even more tragic were the other innocent lives that were destroyed in the process of achieving her evil revenge. Adrian Condoloro, Nevil Hanrahan, Sarah Solano, Ace Ducat, and others along the way. Not to mention the lives of the families left behind.

Those who survived didn't want to talk about it.

As Angus had predicted, once the news was out about Carma, her mob contacts scarpered for their holes, eliminated witnesses, and lawyered up. No one was talking. The FBI finally declared the investigation closed against Carma Michelina after two long years of digging into seedy backgrounds where truth and justice was all relative depending on your reasons for being involved.

Poppy was finally off the press's radar, which made Angus happy. Like predatory wolves falling upon roadkill, they went after Julian's reputation and Carma Michelina's heinous acts of revenge against her father. And of course, Julian's mother, Edna, whose life was suddenly in the public eye in a way she'd never experienced before.

The auditors hadn't been able to prove embezzlement from Condoloro Enterprises because the books were all in order and every expenditure accounted for, no matter how far they dug into them. Carma had covered her tracks completely.

Because of the press's voracious appetite for scandal, Edna finally married Ralston and left her beloved mansion behind. They settled into obscurity near some of Ralston's family, hoping to finally find some peace in their remaining years.

Poppy sold the mansion and it then became a historic home and museum. The Condoloro legacy would be a line in history stating that the family had once owned a mansion from Chicago's enlightening gilded age of 19th century architecture. And that legacy actually belonged to the building itself.

Angus married his Poppy by the waterfall on a beautiful summer's evening surrounded by close family and friends. Look deep into your imagination and picture them there amid the backdrop of Scotland's starry night sky, surrounded by glowing jasmine flowers in the moonlight. Can you smell the heather drifting in off the moors? Hear the gentle gurgle of the moving stream, the rushing sound of the water tripping over rocks on its way down the mountainside, and their simple declarations of love and devotion to one another?

I know you, my readers, may find this story a bit different. In Angus and Poppy's story, I wanted to get a feel for today's modern societies. Express how the world is an open book that can be embraced. And get a glimpse into how hard it can be to trust new love and second chances after life has chewed on us for a while.

It doesn't happen overnight. And it's different from that first young love where forever lies in front of us, and we envision walking together through it all.

Gone are the days when a young lass or lad, might leave their homeland and follow their love across seas, or to another land where they most likely would never see their immediate family members again. In today's societies homelands are just stepping stones to the world.

Relationships can also be very complicated with both men and women having careers and dreams that are unique to the individual. Neither one is more important than the other, and finding a balance where both can grow is challenging.

But one thing that doesn't change is love. It is the constant thread that binds us to each other, and has done so since the beginning of time. Embracing that thread and holding on tight despite what the world throws at us is the real challenge.

Poppy and Angus are now tied to that golden thread and creating their own story on Heaven's Gate and in Angus's beloved Scottish home, Thistlewind.

The End

I HOPE YOU ENJOYED their story. Thank you for reading. If you have time and loved Poppy and Angus, consider leaving a review on a retailer of your choice. Authors really depend on reader reviews.

WHAT'S NEXT FOR OUR Heaven's Gate families?

SEEING HIS FRIENDS around him falling in love, Jamie feels the loss of his Rhonda even deeper than before. Is it possible there is someone out there who could *'hold a candle'* to his lost love? Stay tuned and find out!

If you would like to be a member of my newsletter and get a free copy of Dusty's Ghost Town, join me here![1]

---

1. https://sendfox.com/storiestolove

> When Dusty switched places with her identical twin, she didn't expect to fall in love. Now her sister wants him back.

[2]

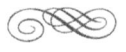

Hang out with me on Facebook in my fun group, The Storytellers. Myself and three others run this fun group and have takeovers, prizes, and other fun stuff.

---

2. https://sendfox.com/storiestolove

[If you would like to be a member of my ARC club and get a free book in advance to review, join me here.](https://www.facebook.com/groups/2789758034671101)

---

3. https://www.facebook.com/groups/1032804233848992

4. https://www.facebook.com/groups/2789758034671101

Don't miss out!

Visit the website below and you can sign up to receive emails whenever Brandy Golden publishes a new book. There's no charge and no obligation.

https://books2read.com/r/B-A-ZXWM-AXJIC

BOOKS 2 READ

Connecting independent readers to independent writers.

Did you love *A Flower for Angus*? Then you should read *Christmas Housekeeper Wanted* by Brandy Golden!

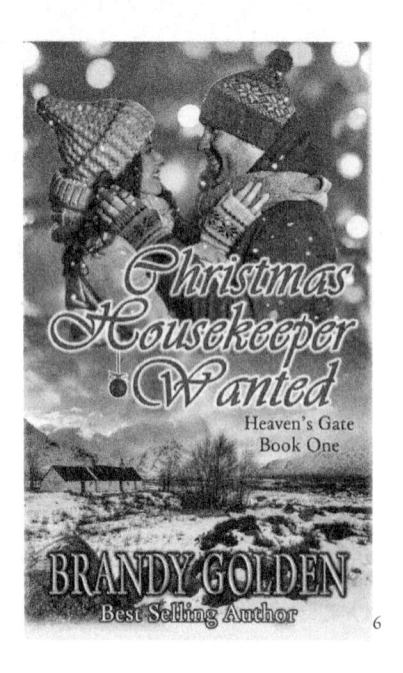

Christmas Undercover: A spirited housekeeper, a brooding highlander, and a holiday wrapped in mystery.

Lucerne MacNamara has a problem only a Christmas miracle can solve. Her agency's housekeepers are fleeing from Darro MacCandish's remote Heaven's Gate estate, leaving her business teetering on the edge. Facing a damning lawsuit, her last resort is to disguise herself as just another employee to face the surly highlander head-on.

In the depths of the Scottish Highlands, Darro MacCandish is a man with little patience for incompetence, demanding a housekeeper who can handle his home's chaos and his children's needs. If Lucerne MacNamara can't deliver on her contract and provide him with a competent employee for the holidays, then he'll have her in court on Christmas day if that's what it takes!

As Lucerne braves the winter chill and Darro's icy demeanor, she delves deeper into the tangled web of deceit and frayed relations and turn up way more than she bargained for. Amid the stark beauty of the highlands and the warmth of holiday cheer, will she discover the truth behind her employees' discontent and mend a heart as forbidding as the landscape? Or will the secrets she uncovers ignite a yuletide showdown that will change their lives forever?

Read more at https://brandygolden.com/.

Also by Brandy Golden

Brocton Chronicles
The Maddie Stories
A Shotgun Wedding

East Coast Spitfires
Taming His Irish Spitfire
Taming His Feisty Kitten
Taming His Whirlwind
Taming His Honeydoll

Heaven's Gate
Christmas Housekeeper Wanted
A Flower for Angus

Standalone
Marlie's Christmas Keeper

Catching His Snow Bunny
Hot Little Firecrackers
Protecting Vidalia
Back Off, Love
A Lass Worth Fighting For

Watch for more at https://brandygolden.com/.

About the Author

I'm a writer of compelling romantic stories in all settings. I love the American west cowboys, the Highlanders of Scotland, and the spitfires of contemporary romance.

My stories will always have strong males who don't mind turning a feisty young woman over their knee if the occasion warrants it. Sweet heat and passion, combined with some discipline make these stories of any genre captivating and enjoyable.

I live in the midwestern United States with a loving husband, five children, and five grandchildren, plus 3 furbabies. I also enjoy gardening scrapbooking, and of course, reading. Especially romance!

What you won't find in my stories is excessive foul language, overly descriptive and detailed sex, or BDSM. Well, mostly no BDSM. I do have a hint of it here and there, but I have talented friends who write that very well.

No, I'm more a fun-loving, John Wayne-style romance writer with just enough spanky spice to sizzle and keep you glued to the pages.

Enjoy the glow of romance, my friends, it's all around us..
Brandy
Read more at https://brandygolden.com/.

About the Publisher

In 2020, I finally got my opportunity to go independent in publishing my books. This is a journey I'm enjoying so far, and I hope you are enjoying my creations. Thank you for purchasing from Brandy Golden Books

Printed in Great Britain
by Amazon